THE FORTUNATE
BROTHER

ALSO BY DONNA MORRISSEY

DONNA
MORRISSEY

THE FORTUNATE
BROTHER

VIKING

VIKING

an imprint of Penguin Canada Books Inc.,
a division of Penguin Random House Canada Limited

Published by the Penguin Group
Penguin Canada Books Inc., 320 Front Street West, Suite 1400, Toronto, Ontario M5V 3B6, Canada

Penguin Group (USA) LLC, 375 Hudson Street, New York, New York 10014, U.S.A.
Penguin Books Ltd, 80 Strand, London WC2R 0RL, England
Penguin Ireland, 25 St Stephen's Green, Dublin 2, Ireland (a division of Penguin Books Ltd)
Penguin Group (Australia), 707 Collins Street, Melbourne, Victoria 3008, Australia
Penguin Books India Pvt Ltd, 11 Community Centre, Panchsheel Park, New Delhi – 110 017, India
Penguin Group (NZ), 67 Apollo Drive, Rosedale, Auckland 0632, New Zealand
Penguin Books (South Africa) (Pty) Ltd, 24 Sturdee Avenue, Rosebank, Johannesburg 2196,
South Africa
Penguin Books Ltd, Registered Offices: 80 Strand, London WC2R 0RL, England

First published 2016

1 2 3 4 5 6 7 8 9 10

Cover design: Lisa Jager
Cover image: (man and dog) Ibai Acevedo/Getty Images;
(clouds) GYN9037/Shutterstock.com

Manufactured in the U.S.A.

LIBRARY AND ARCHIVES CANADA CATALOGUING IN PUBLICATION

Morrissey, Donna, 1956-, author
The fortunate brother / Donna Morrissey.

ISBN 978-0-670-06606-3 (paperback)

I. Title.

PS8576.O74164F67 2016   C813'.54   C2015-908753-8
eBook ISBN 978-0-14-319621-1

www.penguinrandomhouse.ca

FOR MY BROTHERS, TOM & GLENN,
AND OUR BELOVED FORD

*There is no despair so absolute as that which comes with
the first moments of our first great sorrow, when we have not yet
known what it is to have suffered and be healed,
to have despaired and to have recovered hope.*
—GEORGE ELIOT

ONE

T he river's pulse was sluggish, wearied with winter's run. He
laid aside his fishing rod and dropped beside it, equally
wearied with too much thought from rambling through his
father's house. *Gawd-damnit, Kyle, stop chewin' them fingers,* Sylvanus
was always grumbling. He shook off his wool mitt and chewed
now at a hangnail that was sending slivers of pain through his
thumb. *There's people who cut themselves to escape the pain in their
heads,* his friend Kate had said the other night, strumming her
guitar beside the bonfire. *That why you chewin' your fingers, Kyle, to
escape a pain in your head?*

Gawd-damn. Least it was his fingers he chewed. If Kate was
right and his mouth was big enough, he'd have his head gnawed
down to a stump. He looked upriver to where his father was likely
staggering to catch up. Too many swallows of whisky too late in
the day. He was usually drunk and sobered up by now.

His own mouth was dry from drink. He'd broken his own rule
back there, drinking before dark. He scooped river water into his
mouth, sloshed it around, and then spat it out and sat back. Across
the river, massive wooded hills of the northern peninsula sighed

through the fog. A long flagging reach downriver and the water buckled against the northern cliff wall, pooling itself into dead black depths before elbowing out of sight through a thicket of still leafless alders and drowning itself into the sea just beyond.

He glanced upriver again, listening for his father, Sylvanus Now. They'd heard a few hours before from some of the boys angling for trout that Trapp was back for another of his infrequent night visits when he visited nobody and spoke to nobody and then vanished again before sun-up. Trapp. Weird, feral Trapp. Prowling through the darkened places where he'd once lived. Then vanishing with the light of dawn, leaving nothing in his wake but raised brows and the hackles of folks from the Hampden outport. Trapp. Aptly nicknamed, for he carried the dark, disagreeable, secretive ways of all the Trapps. *Bad blood,* outport people said of the two Trapp brothers who'd relocated there during the government's resettlement program. And thank God the rest of the Trapp clan had gone forty miles farther down the shore in Jackson's Arm. They—the two Trapp brothers—had kept to themselves on the wooded hillside above Kyle's home. They'd started up a sawmill and bad-mouthed anyone who set foot over their property line. Everyone had applauded the mysterious burning of the screaming sawmill just two years ago and the Trapps' subsequent packing up and moving with no forwarding address. Except for this younger Trapp. The prowler. He was from the Jackson's Arm side of the clan. Never did live in Hampden, simply visited his uncles regularly and buddied around with Ben, the nicest fellow in Hampden, who always let Trapp hang out no matter his sly looks and his creeping and skittering about like something untamed. He'd gone to university with Ben until they both mysteriously dropped out mid-semester and vanished into the oilfields of Alberta.

Trapp. One of the last to see Chris alive. He'd been working the rig alongside Chris when the accident happened. And each time Sylvanus heard that Trapp had been seen squirrelling about he'd lean greedily into the news, into the concreteness of something that linked him to the last minutes of his son's life. Like a lost Christmas package found, mouldy and dank with age. Holding something that might soothe him, bring him peace.

Kyle felt nothing. He remembered a yarn about a monkey's paw that granted an old woman her wish that her son, dead for a number of years, would be returned to her. He was. The stench through the wooden door saturated the house and the old woman fainted, knowing he'd been returned as he was—ten years dead. Skin dried, shredding from husked bone. Nope. Kyle Now was done with wishing. He was settled into the hollowed ache of his brother's death, and if this ache was the closest he could feel to Chris, he'd suffer it through till his own demise. At least it was something. Without it there would be nothing.

His father had said nothing back there with the anglers. Hadn't said Chris's name once in the three years since they buried him. Wouldn't let anyone else say it either. Dropped his fork at the supper table once and bolted out the door when Kyle, naming the bowls as he laid them on the table for dessert, named one for Chris out of habit. If not for the desolate look on his mother's face, Kyle would've run from his words too. Ducked into his room and buried his head so deep into his pillow he would've smothered all thought.

His mother knew that. She had touched his hand to stay him. And then sipped her tea in quiet and he wanted to touch her hand, too, but couldn't. Oh, he wished he could. He wished he could drag his father back to the table and they'd all say a prayer to Chris as his mother wanted. And act as though he was present in spirit like the good folks and ministers preached. But easier to envision celestial worlds floating through the firmament than Chris sitting in that empty chair at the table. And so Chris remained, foremost amongst them but hidden beneath their shirt collars like a great festering boil begging to be lanced.

A horned owl swooshed out of the trees above Kyle's head with a loud *ho-ho-hoo hoo* and he ducked, cursing the bird. The snapping of sticks sounded behind him and his father broke through the brush, head down, shoulders down, walking heavy. Rowing against a poisonous river of grief for three years now, going nowhere. Time wearing past him. Threading grey through his glut of dark hair and thickening his belly and rutting that once strong face and throat. He caught sight of Kyle and grinned, the corners of his dark eyes tight. He'd been bawling back there.

"Thought you fell in and drowned," said Kyle.

Sylvanus grunted. "That's it now." Laying aside his rod, he dropped his rucksack and sat on it with his back resting against a stump and pulled a flask of whisky from his inside coat pocket.

"Leave off, old man, for fuck's sake," said Kyle. "Mother's going to kill you."

"Think now, I'm scared of your mother?"

"Might help if you were. Another heart attack waiting for you."

Sylvanus tipped the bottle to his mouth, his hand trembling. Hiking his shoulders, Kyle stood. "Not waiting." He started downstream, ignoring his father calling after him, coaxing him to wait, to have a nip. Gawd, he hated that coaxing in his father's voice, the greed in his eyes as he sucked back the liquor. As if it was going to fix the pain gnawing his innards.

Kyle kept to the path, his boots squelching through mud. He ducked through a tunnel of alders whose leafless limbs scratched his face and whipped cold past his ears. A few minutes later and he broke through onto a fetid muddied bank. The river ran swollen beside it, its surface flat and silent and white beneath its caul of fog. He trod past chip bags and wrappers partly submerged in mud and broken beer bottles and charred fire pits from night parties. He stopped, scuffed some of the glass into the river, picked up a couple of chip bags and stuffed them in his pockets, cursing the irresponsible young ones. He stood up, then leaped back with a yelp from a pale, pointed face sifting through the fog before him. Tawny hair and ruffs of sideburns, reddish like a fox. Fine green eyes, the dazed look of someone lost inside himself, and yet furtive, sharp with tension as though readying to spring.

"Ha ha." Trapp's silly, nasal laugh.

"Ha ha your fucking self," said Kyle. He forced his shocked limbs to move and walked rapidly along the riverbank, coming to a footbridge beyond which his father's truck was parked, a black smudge through the mist. Three crumbling concrete pillars from an old logging operation rose to the side of it like ancient ruins.

He got in the truck and started it and blasted the heat and pulled the stick into drive—and then pushed it back into park and slumped in his seat, cursing. Cursing at his fright and stirred up feelings from seeing Trapp, and cursing that he couldn't go home without his father. She'd be there making supper. She'd be watching. She was always watching when they came through the door, noting Sylvanus's bleary eyes and whisky breath. Kyle hated it. Hated her disappointment each time, her knowing that her husband was no longer finding his comfort in her. And then the bickering.

Three beer, Addie, three beer, I only had three beer.

And the whisky you washed them down with.

Now Addie, now Addie . . .

Don't now Addie me . . .

The same. Always the same. Least the river kept on flowing, no matter how much crap it carried. Always shifting bedrock and cutting through ice and changing its song. Felt like he'd been circling the same eddy for so long now that he was outside the passing of time. Sometimes he was surprised to look up into a summer's sky and see instead the trees shaking their yellowed leaves or snowflakes falling all too soon and soaking his lashes. Felt like the one long day for three years now. The one long dull day, caught on a cloud of grief hovering over his house.

Water dripped from his hair and trickled cold down his neck. He reached under the seat, found another of his father's whisky bottles, and took a quick nip to warm himself. He watched the fog through the windshield sculpting itself into Trapp's pale pointy face, shifting into the fierce blue of his mother's eyes and then into the dark of his father's, and then widening onto the dark blue hood of the truck. The cursed truck Chris had left home to pay for. That and the boat. The good lord had taken a hand in sinking the boat a week after Chris's passing. Crushed it against the side of the wharf with a ton of drifting ice from the spring thaw.

He wished the ice had crunched up over the road and crushed the truck, too. Rammed it against the cliffs and crunched it down to a heap of metal. Kept him from driving it through the outport like a hearse the first couple of years after Chris's accident, his father drunk and slumped against him, whimpering like a cut dog. Circled the outport so many times old men in their windows started keeping count. Thirteen times one Saturday. Seventeen times another. Each circle ending with Kyle parking near the graveyard down on the Rooms and looking past the crumbling granite headstones to the newest one lodged over the hole where Chris lay. *Christopher Now. 1957–1980. Taken Too Soon.* He'd stare for hours at that headstone, his father whimpering and suckling the whisky bottle beside him. Stared till his eyes turned to stone and his tears dried up like an old riverbed.

Shame, drinking over his passing and getting maudlin with your own sorry self.

Drinking! Now Addie . . .

And having Kyle driving you around like that, not fit.

Now Addie . . .

Don't now Addie me, drinking before you leaves the doorplace in the mornings.

Three beers, I haves three beers . . .

And the whisky you washes them down with . . .

Don't talk, don't talk, for fuck's sake don't talk, he'd plead silently with his father each time he drove him home drunk before noon and she'd be standing there, waiting. But Sylvanus had the staying power of a sapling beneath an easterly wind when she took a swipe at him. Not that he'd ever learned from it. No, by jeezes, he'd never learn to keep his mouth shut, as though he could argue himself out of shame.

One beer, Addie, I had one beer.

Too drunk to see past your boots.

I can see far enough to the Rooms. That's as far as I'm going—the graveyard on the Rooms.

Drinking yourself dead.

Now, Addie, the pope serves more in church than what I drinks.

You knows a lot about the pope, you do.

If what they're preaching on TV is right, we'd all be better off not going. Sickos.

That what you says to the reverend when he's burying our dead?

Now Addie . . .

You dare hide your drinking behind him.

I wants him back, Addie, I wants him back . . .

Times Kyle sank into the couch with his hands over his ears, shutting them out. His older sister, Sylvie, sitting across from him in Gran's old rocker by the stove, her face hidden inside a book. Those first years neither Kyle nor his sister left the house for long. There were fist holes in the walls reminding them of those times. A smattering of them led down the hallway and one was smack in the middle of their parents' bedroom door. Not that their father would ever lay a hand on his Addie. But times her tongue would lacerate his drunken mind to the point where he'd hit a wall just to feel the smack of his fist splintering wood. Kyle understood that. No different from him chewing his fingers. Except Kyle's was a peaceful brooding. He'd done nothing to aid Chris's leaving for the oil rigs in Alberta with Sylvie that morning. But his father had been sick—heart attack from working himself to death fishing for cod that were too scarce to pay the bills and so he doubled his work-load with cutting and hauling logs for the sawmills too. Heart just up and called it quits. New boat and new truck parked out by the door like hungry dogs, growling for their bank payments. And Sylvie. Good good Sylvie stepping up to the fates. Came flying from her high-paying job in the oil-soaked fields of Alberta like Persephone, wife of Hades, Lord of Underground Wealth. Took Chris back with her to the oil fields to help wrestle those snarling dogs and six weeks later Chris was dead. Poor sister. And now she was gone. Off backpacking in Africa somewhere, bewildered by how it all turned out, that her feet continue to walk above the sod whilst Chris's reside in the shadowed depths of the underworld.

At times Kyle cursed Sylvie and Chris both. For leaving him torn between two grieving parents whose desired end could never be found in him. For his feeling lame because there wasn't enough of him to fill their hearts. Times he wished for a sword to cleave himself in half: one traipsing behind his father, keeping him from the loneliness of his pain, the other shadowing his mother, help-ing her cleanse her house of grief.

He stirred in his seat, a sliver of pain darting through the quick of his thumbnail. He'd been chewing his nails again. He reamed his hand into his pocket. Foul! There was something foul about Trapp showing up all the time and never talking to anyone. There was something foul about the whole thing. Sylvie coming home alone with the body. Then Ben coming with Trapp in tow. All three had been tight when they worked the rig. All three had taken a hand in looking out for Chris when he joined them. And yet only Sylvie came home on that flight bearing Chris's coffin. Sylvie and their mother. Addie. Flying the skies for the first time to help Sylvie bring Chris home. Else Sylvie would still be out there, cowering in the closet where Addie found her. Too dis-traught to stand. And Ben off searching for Trapp who'd run from the accident and couldn't be found. They returned three months later, Trapp and Ben. Shame-cast eyes. All three of them—Sylvie, Ben, and Trapp—with shame-cast eyes and a broodiness accom-panying their grief. He'd never understood that. Never under-stood what stalked their sleep at night and eventually sent Ben and Sylvie prowling through savannahs and jungles, leaving Trapp behind to roam in darkness.

His father's dark shape sifted through the thinning fog. Kyle sat up and started the motor, stomping down on the gas pedal to quiet its revving. Sylvanus kicked the muck of his boots against the truck tire and near fell over.

"Cripes, Mother's going to shoot you," said Kyle as his father climbed aboard. "You all right?"

Sylvanus darted a crooked finger towards the windshield. "Drive."

"Smell the booze a mile away."

"That's it now."

"*That's it now*. Right." Kyle eased the truck over a rough track of tire-flattened beach rocks and turned right from where the river fanned out over the beach before flowing into its shallow mud flat at the mouth of the bay. He drove them across a gravel flat that served as a soccer field during the dustier days of summer. A nice clapboard cabin stood on the inner side of the flat, its back pushing against the encroaching alder bed. Kate's place. Her door was closed, white smoke clouding from her chimney. Wood must be green. Perhaps he should check whether she had enough wood splits to keep her fire hot.

At the end of the gravel flat he turned left onto Wharf Road, a rutted thoroughfare leading between the rocky edge of the sea and the steep hillside to its right. A few hundred yards down and the road T-boned onto a long sagging wharf. To the right was their one-storey house with its front step resting on the wharf and heavily treed hills rising straight up behind it. He parked in front of the weathered woodshed and jarred his father awake with a punch to the shoulder.

"Mother's going to kill you. Get in the shed till you sobers up." He got out of the truck and Sylvanus kept sitting there. "Go on, get out. Get in the shed. I'll tell her you're fixing your rod."

"Come with me."

"Fucking go by yourself." *Jaysus!*

He went into the porch and hung up his coat and kicked off his boots, his damp wool socks smelling like overcooked mutton. The inside door was ajar and he stepped in through to the front room. She wasn't moving around the kitchen fixing supper as she usually was at this time, but sitting quiet in Gran's rocker. She was leaning towards the woodstove, her head bowed before its hot orange flames licking at the glass door. Thinking about Gran, he figured, and stepped softly towards her. He often sat there himself, thinking about Gran who'd drifted from them as quiet as a puff of smoke up the chimney a year following Chris's passing. It was nice, after the horror of Chris's stark white face, to see Gran's all sweet and peaceful on a lacy pillow.

"How's she going, Mom."

Addie startled onto her feet like a snuck-upon lynx and scampered into the kitchen.

"Where's your father?" she asked, hauling down the plates for supper.

"The shed. Fixing his rod. What's wrong?"

"Supper's soon ready." She took down the cups, chinking them in their saucers, her back to him.

"Mom?"

She stopped and looked at him and his heart jolted. Her eyes, always frightfully blue, were darkened and wide with—with what?

She raised a hand to touch him and he stepped back, then bolted to the washroom. He skimmed off his clothes and stepped into the shower, turning on the faucet and holding up his face to a spray of hot water. The last time he'd seen her face shrouded with such sorrow was when she stepped off the plane from helping Sylvie bring Chris home. From straight across the tarmac as he stood inside the airport watching her through the thick panes of glass he had seen her sorrow. Seen it in the way she kept her chin erect. In the way her eyes had determinedly sought his through the crowd gathering around and watching alongside of him. And he'd been surprised by such sorrow, for he'd expected to see in her eyes the keener suffering of grief instead. Three babies buried from the womb: she knew grief. Knew its dark and twisted path all fraught with madness and hate and fear and its narrowed arteries choking with self-blame. And perhaps she hadn't the strength to walk through it again. Or, as he'd seen when she reached back through the doorway of the plane that day and helped Sylvie's shocked-bent body through the narrow cylinder, perhaps her knowing disallowed another indulgent walk. Perhaps she'd learned how hope eventually creeps through darkness, making inroads through to an easier tomorrow. And that was her task then, to bear her grief with a hope that might shelter him and Sylvie through the coming days. And she had. Cradled and carried them as much as they would allow her. Oftentimes this past year, despite Sylvanus's drinking, hope continued to grow in her eyes and he'd been turning to it more and more, hoping to offset the grey clouding his.

Water sluiced down his back, scrubbing the day's dirt off his skin. It caressed the smooth humps of his buttocks and streamed down the backs of his legs and plashed around his feet before suckling itself down the drain. He kept his face to the jettisoning spray of the nozzle and felt its heat flush open his pores and he flattened his hands against the shower stall as though keeping his insides from being flushed out and sucked down the drain along with the water. He had bolted from her that day at the airport, too. Bolted out onto the highway and thumbed a ride with a trucker who left him sitting in silence, staring out the side window. At Hampden Junction he climbed out of the truck with a grateful nod and started running the ten miles home, jumping into the ditch and cowering whenever he heard a car coming because he didn't want anyone seeing him, didn't want to talk, didn't know what to say or do since that one ring of the phone had altered his being and it felt like somebody else was running in his shoes. When he got home, the house was swarming with aunts and uncles and cousins and friends who'd been coming and going since the news swept through the outport like a squall of wind.

Young Chris was killed. Killed on the oil rigs in Alberta. An accident, a bad accident.

Cut through him, too. Had loosened his bowels and sunk a hole in his stomach that all else sank into. He would've liked to cry. But the good folk kept shouldering him, kept finding him as he tried to hide. Kept bringing him back amongst them, rubbing his back and laughing and nudging him to laugh when they did. He did. Shame creeping up his face once, when he laughed too hard and imagined his mother and father hearing him from their torn pillows. And perhaps dear old Gran had heard him too as she lay in her room with her own host of women keeping vigil and wiping her teary eyes with tissues pulled from their too full bosoms.

He wished they could have soothed him. He wished they could have filled that hole cratering his stomach and helped him straighten his legs from their cramped fetus curl and make him feel whole again. He had gnawed his nails and held back his cries till his throat ached and his fingers bled and Chris was buried and they'd all left and then he cried. He cried all the time. Crawled behind the woodpile and cried. Crawled beneath Chris's old workshirt in the woodshed and cried. Cried walking home from the bar in Hampden and from the beach fires at night, leaning into the space where Chris had always walked beside him, grunting like a bear sometimes to scare him.

His mother kept looking to him, willing him to share his grief with her, to let her share hers with him, but he couldn't. Frightened that the weight of her pain would fuse with his own, toppling him. He couldn't bear being with Sylvie, either. Couldn't bear it. Afraid of the shame or guilt or grief that was robbing her eyes of light. Afraid she might talk, might tell him what really happened that day on the rigs and what she had or hadn't done that might've prevented it, and he wanted nothing of it. It was an accident.

An accident—cold, clean words that evoked no image. They evoked no thoughts, no questions that might send him raging towards her or someone else with the finger of blame and hate and condemnation. Please God. Tell me no more.

She'd tried to tell him one drunken night outside the bar. Tried holding on to him, her wet face pressed against his, and he'd pushed her away and ran and was still running. Running from everything.

He shut off the faucet and took as long as he could to dry himself and put on clean clothes. He wanted to slink into his room and bar the door, but she'd heard him.

"Go call your father, Kyle." She was hovering over the table, holding a cast-iron frying pan, her wrist bending beneath its weight as she scooped fried potatoes onto their plates alongside pork chops and onions. He opened the door and roared out to his father and took his seat back at the table. She lay the frying pan back on the stove and came up behind him, scruffing the back of his head with her fingers, the cool tips of her nails grazing his scalp.

Jaysus! He ducked away. "Still groping for head lice," he said, feeling sheepish as he always did when she showed him affection.

She went back to the sink and he listened to her kitchen sounds. It was his favourite thing when Chris had first left for Alberta, sitting at the table and munching toast and reading a comic and half listening as she swept and tidied, passing along bits of gossip. It was always Chris she'd talked to before. It was Chris his father had talked to. And then, with Chris flying off with Sylvie, they both started sitting with him and chatting him up and cripes it was nice and he was often feeling like the sun between a pair of sundogs.

Then the call. The chatting stopped. And he became one of those things she helped tidy before putting away.

She came back to the table and sat light as a pigeon, her dark hair pinned back, face small like a girl's. Pale. She looked at him and smiled reassuringly and his fear deepened.

"What did you say your father was doing?"

"Fixing his rod."

"Get any trout?"

"Water's too high."

"All that rain. Sure, you knew that before you left."

"He likes going."

"Wish he was still the warden. Only thing he liked more than fishing cod was guarding that river." Her hands were steadied as she sugared her tea and poured in a drop of milk.

"Might get the salmon back yet," he said. "Open the river agin. Get his job back."

"I hope he finds something soon. Keep his mind occupied." She lapsed into silence and his stomach rolled. "Eat your supper," she said.

He picked up his fork.

"Did you hear about Clar Gillard?" she asked. "Tied Bonnie to a chair at the fish plant and sprayed her with oven cleaner."

"What!"

"That's what he did, then. The cook hove a pan of cold water over her soon as he started, but she still got burns on her skin."

"Didn't she leave him months ago?"

"Still treats her like he owns her. Barbarous devil. I'm after telling her a couple of times now to phone the police on him. I phoned her agin awhile ago. Told her if she didn't, I was going to."

Kyle was looking at his mother in surprise. "Since when did you start talking to Bonnie Gillard?"

"Why wouldn't I?"

"That's just it now, you never talks to nobody any time, and now you're *phoning* Bonnie Gillard?"

"Perhaps it's time I got out more."

"And you picks Bonnie Gillard to hang with? Next thing Clar'll be coming after you."

"Let him come."

"Right. Just what we needs. Crazy like his father, everybody quivering like rabbits around him."

"He'll not find me quivering like a rabbit, then."

"I seen rabbits bite. I seen him skinning rabbits, too. Size of his hands, he'd snap her like a wishbone. Seen him carry a dead moose through the woods once—antlers and all. Slung across his shoulders like it was a dog's carcass. Why don't she just move away?"

"She's been living with her sister down Hampden the past month."

"I mean Toronto, someplace."

"I'm sure he knows his way to Toronto."

"How come she don't call the cops herself?"

"Because he punishes her all the harder, after. My, Kyle, you think she haven't thought of them things? You're like everybody else—believing the woman haven't got a brain because she's Jack Verge's daughter."

"How come she keeps going back with him, then? Don't make much sense to me."

"You knows what makes sense to her? You walks in her shoes? All you know is talk."

"Nothing wrong with talk. Might keep her from going back this time, everybody talking."

"Suppose they gets it wrong—do talk help then? Might help if everybody cleaned out their own closets."

"Jaysus, Mother, he's been knocking her around for years."

"I'm not talking about Bonnie or Clar, I'm talking about you."

"Me!"

"Yes, you. Got lots to say about things not your concern. You needs to be like everybody else, tending to your own concerns." The sharpness of her eyes as she stared at him, her consternation, as though she were seeing something on his face known only to her. He fought not to look away.

She went back to picking at her food, but he could tell her thoughts were still on him.

She looked up as the front door opened. Sylvanus entered quieter than a draft of wind and took his seat at the table. He fixed his eyes on his plate and guardedly lifted his fork.

"Get your rod fixed?" asked Addie.

His brows shot upwards. "Who broke my rod?"

Jaysus. Kyle gave him a warning look but Addie appeared too taken by her thoughts to notice. She buttered a slice of bread and laid it by Sylvanus's plate, and as if she didn't know what else to do with her hands, she rested them on the table, small and pale as clam shells.

Kyle stared into the rusted brown of his cup of tea. Spoons chinked against china. Forks clicked. A hiccup from Sylvanus. Kyle coughed to cover it and asked his mother to pass the bread.

"Perhaps you should call the police," said Kyle. "Sounds like he's on the warpath agin."

"Who?" asked Sylvanus.

"Clar Gillard."

"I almost called them yesterday, then," said Addie. "He was throwing sticks into the cemetery and then getting his dog trampling over the graves to fetch it. Chris's grave."

Kyle's hand froze midway to spearing a bit of spud. He tried to speak but couldn't. He looked at his father whose face stiffened like a mask, his eyes hard as rocks. He looked at his mother—that's why she was off. Watching Chris's grave being desecrated. That bastard. That pretty smiling face bastard Gillard.

"If I thought I was dying, I'd take him with me," said Addie, her voice filled with such loathing that Kyle forgot his own rage and both he and his father looked at her. She picked up her fork, forcing a smile. "He drove off fast enough when I stood up. Eat your supper, Syllie. There's other things to talk about. I was talking to Elsie on the phone this morning."

Jaysus. Kyle sat back. As if there wasn't enough on the table.

"She said Jake and her boys quit building their house with Newfoundland and Labrador Housing and that the two of ye were taking over the building of it."

"We were waiting to tell you after supper," said Kyle. "Yeah. They couldn't handle it. So, we thought we'd take it on."

"*We*. What do you know about building a house, Kyle?"

"Helped Dad build Uncle Manny's house in Jackson's Arm last summer."

"And that makes you a carpenter?"

"I liked it. That's how you find out what you like, by doing it. Imagine, if Uncle Manny never moved back from Toronto, I might be signing on for philosophy like Sis. That got her the big job, didn't it?" He tried to soften the edge in his tone but she caught it and rapped his knuckles.

"You worry about yourself. Else, straightening used nails with a rock is all you'll be good for."

He grinned, knowing she'd like that—him taking a trade at the nearby vocational school in Corner Brook the coming fall instead of driving across the island to university in St. John's. There was a time when she would have balked at his mentioning trades. Her girlhood prayer was to be educated and live in cities and become a missionary and travel to foreign places and she was forever resentful of being taken out of school when she was just starting grade nine to work the fish flakes. But now—since Chris, and since Sylvie flew to Africa weeks ago—she'd had the shine rubbed off her prayer beads.

"Whatever you choose, you'll have to start making plans soon enough," she said. "What's wrong with you, Syllie? You haven't said a word."

"He got his mind bogged down with blueprints," said Kyle. "Hey!" He touched his mother's hand with his fork. "Somebody got to take it over. They near froze last winter in that shack."

"They'll always live in shacks. They don't take care of nothing."

"They never had nothing to keep clean before, did they?"

"Their father had as good as we, he just let it all rot down around him. You must be addled, Syllie, to work with Jake agin. He didn't mind leaving you in the lurch back in Cooney Arm when all the fish was gone."

"He was just chasing the fish, Addie." Sylvanus had laid down his fork and was staring at his food. "Why'd he do that?"

"Who, Clar? Because he heard I was urging Bonnie to call the police on him, that's why. Thought he'd have a little fun with me. Get past that now, Syllie, that's all he'll ever get out of me. Tell me about Jake—"

"Why? What's going on you wants to call the police?"

"They had another fight. What about Jake's boys? They're home, why can't they finish building the house? Didn't that younger one do carpentry in trades school?"

"Wade," said Kyle. "And Uncle Jake's going to be working on a fishing boat for the summer. Wade needs help."

"They needs help cleaning up the mess they've already made."

"We needs five thousand up front to buy the supplies," said Kyle. "Perhaps not that much. I think they got the footing laid for the basement. We'll see when we goes down—we haven't been down there yet."

"You took it on without even seeing it? Well, sir. And suppose now I needs that money?"

She didn't speak further. Kyle laid down his fork. It was coming. She lifted her chin in that defiant manner of hers and he was struck once more by her fortitude. That whatever this new thing thickening her cloud of sorrow, hope was already ignited in her heart and offering itself as a shelter for him and his father.

"I have to go to Corner Brook tomorrow. See the doctor. I— There's a little lump in my breast. They did some tests already."

Sylvanus blanched. Kyle closed his eyes, cringing as his mother spoke the word, that dirty little word, that ugly little word, cancer. Breast cancer. He'd known three women with breast cancer and they were all dead. He was on his feet and heading for the door and outside before his mother could reach him. He bolted up the road and started running through the night made darker by the damp shroud of fog, his feet picking his path from memory. To his right he could make out the dark ridge of shoreline and hear the water sloshing around rocks like some ancient demon slithering in and out of sight beside him. He took the turnoff onto the gravel flat and kept running, closer to the alder bed and away from the orange dome of Kate's bonfire down by the water. He heard the strains of her guitar, her voice trilling through the fog like a distant psalm guiding his feet through the dark. He came to the river and found the footbridge and crossed it and veered upriver over wet mounds of dead grass that slipped eel-like around his ankles. No longer did it feel as though someone else ran in his shoes. For three years now he'd been mapping this artery of grief. He kept winding his way upriver. When he could no longer hear Kate, when his ears filled with the river water rustling through the grass and slapping against the rocks, he lowered himself to his knees and opened his mouth and his voice rose from his belly and carried over the water like the cry of a loon.

TWO

———

He'd been sitting for some time. A bottle smashed against a rock to the other side of the river and he rose, legs cramped. Another bottle smashed, the yelps of boys sounding like young wolves tearing up the night. He walked, wiping at his eyes. The night, the fog, smothered him. Couldn't see a thing, not a damn thing. He kept his step high so's not to get snagged by the clumps of wet grass and alder roots. He inched back across the foot-bridge, cringing as more bottles shattered against rock and the young boys hooted. He'd like to grab them by the neck. Smell of smoke came to him and he veered left, away from the boys, his feet crunching through coarse rocks as he made his way towards the sound of the river spilling into the sea. The rocks became muddied, silt-covered, and soon he was padding silent as a muskrat on the soft sediment fanning out from the mouth of the river and spreading along the shoreline. The snapping orange of Kate's fire melted through the dark.

She was bent over, holding on to her guitar and feeding the fire with bits of sticks and driftwood. Her greyish white hair fluffed out from beneath a toque and braided down her back. There were always half a dozen bodies lodged about, drinking beer, having a smoke, but only Kate yet this evening. Kyle sat on a white-boned log. He started jiggling his foot. To keep himself from standing back up and running off again, he clamped his attention onto Kate more tightly than the capo clamping the neck of her guitar.

"Skyless night, Kyle." She pushed back her toque and the greyish fringes of her hair faded into the fire-softened fog crowding around her and she looked to be sitting in the maw of some white god. She reached behind her for a six-pack and shoved it towards him.

He popped a can of beer and guzzled it near dry. She lowered the capo onto a different fret and tested the higher pitch of the strings and he leaned forward, elbows resting on his knees, foot jiggling so hard his body shook.

"Got me a new song."

He belched and spat into the fire and watched it sizzle into nothing and turned back to Kate, watching as she put a pick between her lips, twisted the keys, *plinged* on a string, twist twist, *pling pling*. She looked to be fifty with her shroud of hair, or perhaps forty when the sun shone through her wire-framed glasses and into her kelp-green eyes. She was from away and came one day about a year ago with a trailer hitched to a truck and bought Seymour Ford's old cabin just to the other side of the gravel flat. She was from Corner Brook, she said, an hour's drive west, and she said her name was Kate Mackenzie and that she wanted to live by the sea. She said no more and bore with a smile the gossip shadowing her step to the store or the post office or the beach. And she didn't go anywhere else. Except for out-of-town excursions that sometimes lasted for days. Visiting family, he supposed. Didn't matter. That's what he liked about Kate—that he could just be himself sitting with her, for she wasn't connected to nothing or nobody he knew and was never moaning or groaning and wore only the song she was figuring on her face. And she was always figuring a song. Had boxes of half-written songs. *Turning days into words, Kyle.*

"*Cover me,*" she now sang, fire dancing on her glasses. "*Cover me, I feel so cold.* You feeling cold, Kyle?"

He shook his head, leaning over his knees and staring at the fire, foot jiggling.

"*A blanket of stars in the midnight sky, Shimmering love streams from dark tear-stained eyes, Cover me.*"

He closed his eyes, her voice crooning around him like a lullaby, and he wanted to curl beneath the tuck of the log and sleep.

"*Cover me, I feel so cold, Cover me, am so alone . . .*"

He finished the beer in three long swallows and popped another, the fizz from the trapped air a comfort sound to his ears. Kate faded from her song, looked at him. An expectancy tensing her face. She often did that and always turned away whenever he queried the look. She turned away now. She tightened a string and loosened another one and then looked up as muffled footsteps sounded on silted rock. Clar Gillard's hulking shoulders appeared through the fog, his rounded features softening into a smile. His black Lab trotted from behind, tail wagging and nose to the ground, sniffing the rocks, sniffing at Kyle's feet, sniffing at Kate's, his eyes glowing like sparks in the firelight.

Kyle stared at Clar in silence.

"Evening," said Kate. She took a silver flask from the folds of her coat as Clar sat at the far end of the log. She unscrewed the cap and passed it to him. He grasped it with hands big as mitts and took a nip. Then he passed it back, his face squeezing up.

"You ever put mix in that?" he asked in a slow drawl.

"Breakfast time I puts a little juice in there."

Clar took a beer from a weight-sagged pocket and looked through the quivering heat of the fire at Kyle. "Want one?" He offered the beer with an uncertain smile.

Kyle shook his head, wondering at that uncertain smile. Like a youngster's after toddling too far from the doorplace and wondering if he should go farther. It was a nice smile. And nice crinkling eyes. Hard to think someone with nice smiling eyes would trample graves and spray his wife with oven cleaner.

Kate strummed into the silence and the dog trotted over to Clar, staring up at him, ears pricked. He barked, tail wagging. Nipping his beer between his knees, Clar leaned forward and cupped the dog's smooth, shiny head with both hands and ruffled its ears with his thumbs. The dog wagged its tail faster and Clar blew a short puff of air into its black leathery nostrils. The dog snuffled and licked its chops. Clar blew another puff into the shiny black snout and the dog whined. It tried to twist away. Clar gripped its jaws, holding it closer. "What's you going to do now eh, what's you going to do," he crooned and blew long and easy into the dog's nostrils, gripping tighter to its struggling head. The dog's haunches went rigid, its nails grappled onto rocks. Clar kept blowing. Kyle got to his feet.

"Let the fucker go, asshole!"

Clar grinned up at him, the dog's head still cupped between his hands, his thumbs caressing its jaws.

"Need to get yourself a set of bagpipes, Clar," said Kate.

"Or a fucking balloon," said Kyle. He sat back down.

Clar rubbed down the Lab's quivering haunches. "Go. Get," he said, smacking the dog's rump. The dog skittered through the fog, tail folded between its hind legs. Clar stood up and drained his beer, weaving a bit—first sign to Kyle that he was drunk— then hove the bottle towards the sea. He dramatically lifted a finger for silence, then smiled when he heard the plash. "G'nite," he said and sifted into the fog after his dog.

"Somebody should shoot that sonofabitch."

"Just another poor boy, Ky."

"He's a prick."

"Flouting his poverty."

"How the fuck's that, Kate. He's got everything."

"But his father's heart."

Jaysus. "You makes everything sound like a song."

"That's what we are. Love songs gone wrong."

"Yeah. Well. Someone should capo the crap outta that one. Arse." He got to his feet, dropped a buddy pat on Kate's shoulder, and headed off.

Their room door was ajar when he went inside the house. A dim light peered through the crack from a night lamp his mother read under before sleeping. Most nights he crept past their door and dove beneath his blankets to muffle their voices as they often-times bickered with each other. In the mornings he was always astonished to find them tucked into each other like a skein of wool. This evening he peered through their half-opened doorway and his father's head was on his mother's bosom as though he were already asleep and she was cradling him, one of her hands holding on to his as though she were frightened of wandering lost through her dreams. She was gazing at a framed picture of Sylvie and Chris and himself on her wall and he knew it was Chris she was gazing at. His eyes, so earthy brown and eager. His smile wide and open. His cropped blond hair. The golden boy, long before death took him. Framed and hanging beside the picture was a pencilled drawing Chris had done of their father sitting in a boat on moon-rippled water. Or, and Kyle could never tell, perhaps it was Chris himself, looking expectantly towards the stars.

Did you know you'd soon be amongst them?

"Did you close the door, Kyle?" his mother asked in a half-whisper.

He nodded, knowing she'd heard and was just wanting something to say.

"Now, don't go worrying," she said.

"I won't." He bumbled to his room and into his bed and across his pillow and the silence without their arguing resounded through his head and he stared like a hawk into the dark.

He'd scarcely fallen asleep when dawn trickled an ashy grey light around the edges of his blinds. In the kitchen his mother poured him tea and smeared partridgeberry jam on his toast.

"Your father's out in the shed," she told him. "Nursing himself, no doubt."

He stood by the sink and watched her, feeling within himself that hushed quiet of a mourner already at the wake. She leaned past him for the dishcloth and he smelled her scent of lavender and remembered Sylvie once saying how she thought as a youngster that lavender was a flower that smelled like their mother.

He followed her to the table as she carried his tea and toast, sitting in the chair she hauled out for him.

"Eat it for me too, I suppose," he said and flinched as she pinched his ear.

"Now, I don't want no foolishness," she said to him.

He swallowed lumps of toast and gulped them down with the tea.

"And try keeping your father sober."

"What about Sylvie?"

"She called day before yesterday. We won't be hearing from her for another week."

"So—she don't know?"

"I didn't know for sure when she called. It's fine she don't know, let her have her holiday."

He felt a stab of resentment, a *strong* stab of resentment.

"She should be here."

"There's nothing she can do, only worry."

"We can call the embassy there, they'll find her."

"*Call the embassy.* Yes now, we're doing that. Foolish. The doctors haven't made any decisions yet, and there's nothing she can do anyway. Let her have her trip." She put her purse on the table, rooting through it. "Take this." She took out a packet of bills and laid them on the table. "Nine hundred. I'll get the rest from the bank this morning."

"We won't go ahead with that."

"Yes, go on. I spoke too quick last evening. He likes building. The pride he took building this house—you'd have thought he was building a castle. I'll keep five hundred in the bank."

"Would—will that be enough?"

"I'll know more when I talks to the oncologist today."

"I'll go with you."

"No, stay with him. Bonnie's taking me."

"Who?"

"How many Bonnies do we know, Kyle. That's her outside, now. Go get her some coffee. Use that mug on the table there, it's clean. I'll finish getting ready."

"Christ, Mother, you don't need Bonnie Gillard driving you to Corner Brook."

"Rather have her now than anybody else. She knows how to keep her mouth shut, that's for sure. Now, go get that coffee." She vanished into her room and he tried not to stare at the bold form of Bonnie Gillard as she came in through the door—her too white pants and too white jacket and blood-red blouse and shoes and red handbag and lipstick and white plastic discs pinned to her ears. And a big dark scarf curled loosely around her neck.

Addie came rushing out, apologizing for being late, and faltered for a second upon seeing Bonnie, then quickly smiled.

"My, don't you look nice. Perhaps I should have pressed something. Kyle, did you get Bonnie a coffee? I'll just be another minute."

"Take your time, I got lots of it," said Bonnie. Her voice was loud, like her colours. Kyle noticed her eyeing his mother's trim dark sweater and pants as she hurried into the washroom, and he noted her quick glance at her own red and white checkered self. She crossed the room and sat down, a cloud of cheap scent trailing behind her. She was about forty, first signs of age etching the corners of her eyes. Her jacket strained across her wide back as she folded her arms onto the table, her wrists stretching a mite too long for the cut of her sleeves.

He reached past her for the mug resting on the table and she drew back and he saw for the first time a little rash of blisters, glistening amidst a swath of salve, on the right side of her face near her hairline. The right side of her neck, partly hidden behind the scarf, was equally burned and blistering and swathed with salve. She looked up at him, her eyes big and brown and bold. Their black orbs pulsated softly and he turned from her, shamed for having looked so deep. Taking the cup to the sink, he poured her coffee.

She stood up as Addie came out of the bathroom, toilet flushing behind her. "All ready?"

"I suppose I am, can't think properly this morning." Addie

crossed the room and lightly pulled Bonnie's scarf away from her neck. "Looks awfully painful, dear. You sure you want to do this?"

"I could sit home and suffer it out," said Bonnie, and she smiled. "A bit like you now, likes keeping to myself. Hates everyone gawking and talking at me."

"We're a pair, then," said Addie, knotting a silk scarf around her neck. "I'll be back sometime in the afternoon, Kyle. There's baked beans from yesterday in the fridge for dinner. My!" She shivered as though struck by a sudden draft and pulled the flimsy scarf from around her neck. "I can't find my wool scarf," she complained, looking around the sofa and hummock. "Have you seen it, Kyle?"

"Take mine, it's a woman's anyway."

"Don't you be foolish. If your father can wear his now."

"Under his shirt collar."

"Because he likes the feel of it. And so do you."

"Too short."

"They're stylish. It was their Christmas presents—cashmere," she said to Bonnie, catching the soft woollen scarf Kyle was tossing her from the depths of his coat pocket. She folded it around her neck and smiled. "I was hoping for one to get cast aside. Small chance," she added ruefully. "They haven't took them from their necks since they unwrapped them."

"Making her feel good is all," said Kyle. He caught his mother's smile and smiled back reassuringly. "Drive safe, then," he said to Bonnie, and with a last reassuring look at his mother, he plunged his arms into his coat sleeves and went outside. The air was dampish to his face, the fog rising from the land and hanging in wisps above the hills and fading into dove-grey skies. He stepped around Bonnie's shiny red Cavalier, thinking things must be good in the fish plant these days. His father was hunched down at the end of the wharf and looking across the bay whence he'd floated them all those years ago. Kyle barely remembered Cooney Arm. Could no longer distinguish between memory and stories told and retold by Chris and Sylvie and his dear old gran and his mother sometimes about the man Sylvanus was back there. Prancing about his stage-head and boats, fishing from five in the morning to sometimes ten at night, netting and gutting and curing fish and drinking one beer a week and sometimes not that. Kyle did remember one moment from back during his father's hand-fishing days: his father taking him in the boat one windy fall morning, hauling his nets. Christ, but didn't he look big standing up in that boat with his oilskins and sou'wester black against the sky. And not a fear as he stood in that wind-rocked boat, knees bending to roll with the swells. And he, Kyle, white-knuckled to the gunnels.

Everybody and their dog had moved on from those days of hand-fishing and hauling nets but his father mourned them as he would a fresh dead mother. *There's them who can't change with the times and those who won't,* his mother told him. *And your father's both kinds.*

Kyle was kinda proud. He liked his father's story. Liked how he was the last one out after the seas were overfished by greed and governments were paying everyone to leave. The story was still told how Sylvanus thumbed his nose at the relocation money and stayed till the last fish was caught, stayed till they nearly starved, and then sawed his house in half with a chainsaw and floated both halves up the bay and landed them atop this wharf and declared to his astonished Addie—*This is as far as she goes. By Christ if I can't work on the sea, I'll sleep on it. No gawd-damned mortal telling me where I sleeps.*

Kyle stepped quietly up to his father as he crouched at the end of the wharf. No doubt he'd been proud back there in Cooney Arm, building that house. His castle. For sure it was he then, doing the sheltering. Building a good house for his family, providing. And was then driven out. Not just by governments but by death. The death of three babies, death of the codfish, death of the fishing culture he'd woven himself around from the inside out. He'd brought them here to this wharf where the death of his eldest son awaited him. And now this. A life shaped by death.

Sylvanus looked up and Kyle drew back with a start. The dark of his father's eyes broiled with hatred. It was as though all the deaths and dying had been gathered in the one grave and laid at his feet and it was his weakening as a man that had caused them. He hove his shoulders forward and rose, starting towards the truck, his body jerking with anger. Addie's face appeared in the window and Sylvanus faltered and then resumed his hard-hitting steps to the truck. Guilt, cursed Kyle. Guilt that he was failing them. Guilt rotting him like an old shack built on wet ground, leaving no shores strong enough to shelter himself or his family through those coming days.

Starting the truck, Kyle drove them down the heavily potholed Wharf Road, ignoring the whiff of whisky as his father took a swallow from the flask beneath the seat. The sea was flat calm, gulls like black pods resting on its sky-whitened waters. He drove past the gravel flat to his right, smoke still trickling from last night's bonfire, Kate's curtain drawn. Wharf Road yielded onto Bottom Hill Road a few hundred yards farther along and Kyle hung a sharp left onto the paved stretch, doubling back the way they'd just come except it was leading uphill from the valley and cradled by tall, knotted spruce trees.

As they crested Bottom Hill he looked at the same sunless sky vaulting over the mile-wide corridor of ocean, walled on both sides by wooded hills, its horizon fading to nothing forty or fifty miles out. Beneath him and spreading out from the foot of Bottom Hill were the felted rooftops and smokeless chimneys and sleeping doorways of Hampden. The community sloped down another hill to the shore and the quiet lapping of the sea. Quiet. Everything so quiet. As though no sin had yet been committed on this day.

A whimper from his father, a soft mewl. Kyle covered it with a cough and eased them down Bottom Hill and along the main road, passing a store to the right with its weekly specials in blue marker taped to the window. He passed the Anglican church and a sunken-roofed bungalow with unpainted add-ons where Bonnie Gillard now lived with her sister. He passed a poppy-red house, a sunny ochre one, and the violet two-storey—and took a longer look at its windows yellowed with breakfast light. Julia's house. Julia. Chris's girlfriend.

He passed a clump of newly vinyl-sided houses, the rage these days, and turned left, heading downhill. The flag hung limp from its pole near the post office and muddied water streamed like a brook down the guttered sides of the road.

A short, rotund man with wire-framed glasses and suspenders hiking his flannels up past his belly doddled along the roadside just as he'd been doing the past sixty years, watching the morning light breaking through shadows around him. Dobey Randall. He'd be here this evening, walking the opposite way, watching the same sun go down and the light fading back to shadow. The old-timer turned a gummy smile onto Kyle and Kyle tooted his horn and the road turned sharply to the right at the bottom of the hill where the government wharf extended into the sea.

They drove for a mile along the shoreline and slowed, passing the tidy settlement of the Rooms and the whiffs of smoked salmon floating from Stan Mugford's smokehouse. The graveyard lay beyond the last doorstep. Kyle sped up Fox Point Hill, away from the headstones and the bouquets of plastic flowers on Chris's grave, flattened sideways and faded by the snow-wet winds of winter.

Another two miles of shore road and they rounded a black cliff. Kyle slowed down coming into the Beaches—twelve houses sitting with their backs to the wooded hills behind them, their doorways opening onto the strip of road and rocky beach separating them from the shifting waters of the Atlantic. A knot of youngsters hovered in the middle of the road, taunting him till they saw he wasn't going to break speed, and then broke apart to blasts of his horn.

"Ye'll get your arses trimmed!" he roared, rolling down his window, and then rolling it back up to a chorus of laughs. The eldest of them pinged a couple of rocks off the tires and Kyle grinned. "That young Keats. He'll be strung up yet." He looked back at the youngsters shooting fake bullets at the truck. "Little bastards." He looked at his father who had scarcely noticed. The road ended a few hundred feet past the last house and before them lay the gouged black earth, readied for building.

Switching off the motor, Kyle kicked down the gas pedal to stifle its dieselling. "Might as well get going, hey. See the mess they got made. What—just going to sit there?"

Sylvanus was slumped in his seat like a spineless effigy.

"Come on, b'y, let's get out."

"No courage."

"C'mon, dad." He touched his father's shoulder gently. "C'mon, now." He opened his door and got out. He walked to the edge of the site and glanced back, seeing his father slowly unfold himself from the truck. He waited and then they walked about the excavation, their boots squishing through mud. They both shook their heads. Looked like a tornado had pitched itself through a hardware store and emptied its wares onto the site before blowing off. An upturned wheelbarrow half mired in mud. Couple of hammers and boxes of nails soaked open. Picks, shovels, and an axe lay in a murky pool. Six or seven gallons of paint stood haphazardly beside a pile of two-by-twelves that were half-lodged on a mound of gravel being washed out by rills of rainwater.

"Well, sir," said Sylvanus.

"Not a clue," said Kyle.

"What a mess, what a mess."

"And what's they doing with the paint? Footings not laid and they're buying paint?"

"Not a clue."

Kyle stepped around fifteen or twenty bags of cement that were uncovered and wet from the rain. He kicked at a bag and it broke open, the powder too wet to spill.

"Ruined, all ruined." He kicked at the other bags. "Every one of them." He bent, picked up a hand-carved wooden gun out of the muck. He glimpsed a couple of red eight-shot ring caps half submerged in mud beneath the cement bags. "Them youngsters," he said to his father. "Using the cement bags for blockades. How much stuff now, did they muck off with?"

Sylvanus stepped over muddied puddles and followed along the trench dug for the footings. He bent for a closer look.

"Sure, look at that. They only got them dug three feet down. No more than three feet, should be four. Show, get the tape and measure that."

Kyle hunted for a yellow measuring tape from amongst a debris of tools and stood by his father, looking for a place where the footings weren't flooded. Extending the tape across the width of the trench, he leaned over, reading the measure. "Fourteen by eighteen inches."

"Well sir."

"What's it supposed to be?" asked Kyle.

"Sixteen by twenty-four. Turned down. They would've had it all turned down by the inspectors." He looked skyward. The white was starting to darken. "Gonna rain. Bad time of year to be building." He stood up, scratched his head through his cap, looking about.

"Here they comes then."

The roar of a V-8 engine without a stick of pipe in her sounded a full minute before the four-door Dodge came into sight and halted by the truck. Two young fellows got out—the youngest stout and pretty-faced and fair, the other dark and skinny and already sunken into his chest cavity like his father, Jake.

"Uncle Syl. How's she going?" asked the pretty one, Wade.

"How's she *goooin*," asked the other, Lyman, in his slow, deep drawl that tired Kyle on his most patient of days.

"She's not *gooin* nowhere no time soon," snarked Sylvanus. "Which one of you is the carpenter?"

"He," said Lyman, pointing to Wade.

"Me," said Wade.

"And they didn't tell you to keep cement out of the rain?"

"We went to buy tarps but it rained 'fore we got back."

"Well, sir, well, sir." Sylvanus shook his head. "If you buys cement in April, you buys tarps along with it. Unless you got a garage or woodhouse. You got a garage or woodhouse?"

"Told father we needed tarps," said Wade.

"Where's your rebar? You going to pour cement without rebar?"

"Oh, come on, Uncle Syl. I was getting it but Dad was there arguing we didn't need doubling up on the rebar. And he had it all measured wrong so I left it for the next trip."

"We got the trenches dug before the rain started," said Lyman. "We thought we'd have the cement poured, too. Right, Wade?"

"Right."

Sylvanus went back to the site, muttering, "Well sir, well sir."

"We heard about Aunt Addie," Wade said quietly to Kyle.

"Feels awful bad about that," said Lyman.

Kyle nodded. "Say nothing to Father. Come on. Let's start cleaning up." He pointed the boys to the wheelbarrow and shovel and the bags of cement. "Break it all open, them bags. Start shovelling it around. It's all ruined." He buddy-punched Wade's shoulder and went over to where his father was eyeing the sky.

"She going to hold?"

"Might. Be slow going, pouring cement in this weather. Cheaper buying a small cement mixer than renting one. Be days working around the rain." He looked around the site again, the trenches to be deepened, the rebar to be laid, the wasted cement, the wasted sand. He rubbed tiredly at his neck and started a slow walk to the truck. Kyle went after him.

"We'll just do it," said Kyle. "We'll just take her step by step and day by day. We'll just do it."

"Courage is gone."

"She don't want you giving in."

"Sin. Sin. Everything she been through."

"She might be fine. You lives ten, twenty years with what she got."

They came to the truck and Sylvanus rested his head against the door.

"Shit! Come on, Dad. We'll drive to Deer Lake and get what supplies we needs and keep 'er going."

Sylvanus opened the door and got inside, reaching beneath the seat for his flask of whisky. Kyle stood for a moment, then went back across the site and had a word with his cousins. He walked back to the truck and climbed inside and began the ten-mile run to the highway. The rain started as they headed west towards Deer Lake, a light drizzle against the windshield. Sylvanus kept tipping back the whisky. Kyle said nothing, no matter his mother's words. He was talked out trying to keep his father from the booze. As long as he was sober again by the time they got home.

In Deer Lake they bought more cement and rebar and corners and wire mesh and tarps and other things Sylvanus named off from a mental list. After the truck was loaded, Kyle picked up a bucket of chicken and a couple of beers and they sat in silence by the Humber River and he drank a beer, watching the river pass and watching his father nipping at his whisky, the chicken growing cold between them as the river kept passing. Passing and passing. A slow wear as subtle as time on each pebble it touched and a new song beginning without the other ever ending. And he, Kyle, just sitting there watching. Watching and watching from some gawd-damned eddy that kept on circling.

What the fuck. What the fuck was time anyway. A clock that ticks. Revered like a god. What if we just threw it away. Threw it into the river. And he heard himself like a song, *Then you lie silent, Kyle. You lie silent till the ticking takes up in your head. It's called hunger. It becomes your tick-tick-tick and you either move with it or lie in sleep with the dead.* He looked at his father who'd drifted into sleep, his jaw lodged into his shoulder and his cheek creasing up like an old road map too weathered to read.

Kyle drove them towards home, elbowing his father awake when he geared down onto Wharf Road. The rain had drizzled out, a shaft of sun warming the muddied gravel flat coming up on his left.

"What—back already?"

"Already? Cripes, time for bed. Wake up, old man."

"What's we doing—we going to unload?"

"Thought we'd go straight home. She'll be back from Corner Brook by now. What's this, now?" Kyle had just taken a sharp corner, and sitting before them and blocking the road was Clar Gillard's green Chevy truck. Clar was standing on the rocks beside the road wearing a T-shirt and jeans, indifferent to the damp coming off the sea. His Lab was out in the water and swimming laboriously towards him, black skull bobbing, a log as big as a fence post clamped in its jaws.

Kyle tooted the horn.

Clar glanced back at them and then bent, grasped the log from the dog's mouth, and with forearms rippling hove the log back out in the water. He linked his thumbs in his belt loops, watching the dog paddling back out.

"What the fuck's he doing." Kyle tooted louder. Clar never looked back. Sylvanus grabbed the door handle and Kyle snatched for his father's shoulder. "Hold on, old man."

Too late. Sylvanus was tearing out of the truck with curses and Kyle groaned, feeling his father's eagerness for anything that might extricate him, no matter how temporarily, from his misery right now.

"You move it, buddy, or I'll drown it and you in it," Sylvanus yelled at Clar from the roadside. Without waiting, he hauled open Clar's truck door and reached inside, yanking the stick out of park. Digging in his heels, he jammed both hands against the steering wheel and started pushing the truck towards the edge of the road.

"Christ sakes, Christ sakes, old man," and Kyle was out of the truck, seeing his father dead from another heart attack. Clar Gillard was leaping from the rocks and back onto the road.

"Hold on there, you. Hold on!" Clar shouted at Sylvanus.

Sylvanus stopped pushing and turned to Clar. His breathing

was harsh, wormlike cords thickening up the side of his neck as
he spoke. "You keep the fuck away from me and mine, buddy, if
you wants to keep walking. Else I'll cut you down the size of the
last headstone you trampled over."

And he would, thought Kyle. Holy Jesus, the fury distorting
his father's face was the stuff of books. Clar Gillard's face relaxed
into that nice smile of his. He whistled for his dog and, breezing
past Sylvanus, slipped inside his truck. The Lab dredged itself
ashore and dropped the log, his sides sucking in and out from
exertion. He shook himself dry and leaped into the back of the
truck, tongue lolling as Clar eased off down the road towards the
wharf, the road too narrow to turn around where they were.

"Come on." Kyle nudged his father. "Before he starts back."
He got in the truck, his father beside him, chest heaving. "Wants
another heart attack, do you?"

"The likes of that."

Kyle grinned and thumped his father's shoulder. "Like the
dog," he said and started driving. Clar was pulling a U-turn in
front of the wharf as they rounded the bend. Bonnie was standing by her red Cavalier parked near the woodshed. She leaned
back against the car as Clar braked and poked his head out the
window, saying something to her. She said something back and
Clar's fist shot towards her face. She swerved sideways, escaping
his fist, and Clar hit the gas, his truck jolting forward, gravel
spitting behind his tires.

"Lunatic! Watch him," shouted Sylvanus and Kyle squeezed
his truck against the cliff as Clar swiped past, his outside tires
scarcely gripping the crumbling shoulder of the road. Kyle
watched in his side mirror as the green Chevy burned down the
road. He pulled up beside Bonnie and swung out the truck door,
his father beside him.

"Did he get you?" Sylvanus asked Bonnie.

She shook her head, lightly touching the tip of her nose. "Just a graze."

"Not fit. He's not fit," said Sylvanus, and headed towards his woodshed. He turned, wagging a finger. "Watch out he don't come back."

"Give a whistle if he does," said Kyle. "Might be better if you're not here," he said to Bonnie. "Stirring up trouble for the old man."

"You don't have to worry about Clar. He'll not touch your father."

"Makes you say that?"

She glanced up at the wooded slopes, beyond which the roar of Clar's truck could be heard gunning up Bottom Hill. "Your father's proud. Clar's not proud. He got nothing to be proud over. He's scared of men like your father." She gave a satisfied smile. "That's what I told him. That's why he swung at me—I hit a mark."

"Don't sound like you're much scared of him."

A hurt look flickered across her face. He was struck by that— that she felt hurt, not fear.

"Your mother," she said, her voice quieting. "You need to go in. And your father, too. She has something to tell you." Touching his arm, she got in her car and slowly drove away. He stood there watching her. Fear pumped through his heart. It suffocated his brain and tasted like sulphur in his mouth. He went to the house and could see Addie's shape through the window. He heard his father call from the shed and then call again but he couldn't move, couldn't tear himself from the window, couldn't leave her.

He went inside. She was sitting at the kitchen table, her coat still on. She beckoned for him to sit, her eyes so fiercely blue they held him to her. She said the cancer was in both breasts. She said they wanted to remove them and launch an aggressive attack with chemo and radiation. *It may extend my life by five, ten years and who can think beyond that,* she said. He tried to twist away from her but the strength in her eyes held him in place. *Hope, Kyle. They're offering much hope. Others have done well with the same cancer and treatments.*

But he was done with hope. It took her babies and Chris and he had no more courage for hope. Hope had failed her too many times. Rather that she had never hoped. Rather that it was just those babies she grieved and not the pain of lost hope as well.

She bore his choked sobs with a bowed head. When he was done she leaned across the table and gripped his hands and spoke softly but firmly. *I don't fear death, it's taken too much from me. I owe it nothing. But I'll learn to hate like your father if it takes you from me too. This isn't the worst thing to happen. Losing him was the worst thing. And knowing it'll be hard for you is the second worst. The biggest thing you can help me with is taking care of you. I already lost your father; the bottle got him. But you must tend to him while I'm sick. Keep him from me when he's drunk. There's nothing sacred about a drunk and I'll not have my coming days defiled more by his drinking.* She rose and held his forehead against her belly that bore him. She stroked the back of his neck and then kissed his nape and removed herself and gathered the cloth off the table. *Go get your father now. It's time for supper.*

He wiped his eyes and nose, made his way outside, and stood gazing down the darkening hull of the bay. He walked to the side of the house and sat down, his head thrown back, gazing at the ashy sky, wishing it was dark and there were stars. Chris loved the stars, loved sitting right here and gazing up at them. *Proud evening star in thy glory afar*—he was always quoting from some poem. Once when Kyle was small and playing outside in drifting snow, Chris came home with a box of Cracker Jacks and led him to this very sheltered spot and they sat with their backs to the house and

Chris packed the snow snug around them like a blanket and fed him half the Cracker Jacks. One for Kyle and one for himself. One for Kyle and one for himself. Except for the glazed peanuts. Those he kept and popped into his own mouth. He always remembered that. How good he felt, banked in with snow and his mouth opening like a baby bird's and Chris feeding him the Cracker Jacks. First time he had knowingly felt love. Before that it had been fed to him daily like bread and he hadn't noticed. He always loved Cracker Jacks after that; they were his favourite sweet. Oh, Chris. That something like this can be happening with Mother and you not know. He thought of Sylvie and his heart closed in anger. *You should be here.*

He sat there for another long minute, the hazy light beginning to wane. The light went on in the kitchen, throwing a pale shimmer on the seawater gurgling around the pilings beneath him. He got to his feet and went to the shed for his father.

THREE

———

He opened the shed door to a smell of damp sawdust. It was darkish inside, his father a phantom-grey sitting hunched on his chopping block. He was filing the steel-toothed chain from his saw laid across his knees. It was always his way to do something while he drank. Justified his time. And he was always sitting in the near dark. Times Kyle got up in the middle of the night for a drink of water and his father would be sitting at the kitchen table with no lights on, staring out the window at the water shifting restlessly around the pilings. Sadness tugging his face. As though the sea had lost its wonder and he was struggling to get it back.

"You have to go in," said Kyle. "You have to," he repeated as his father kept his head down, kept his eyes riveted to the slow gentle chafing of steel against steel. Kyle approached him and put his hand over his father's misshapen knuckle. "You have to go in. She's waiting." He stood back as his father heaved up a shoulder, deflecting his words. "You have to go in!" he pleaded from the doorway. "I'm going down Hampden, down to the bar. Tell her, so she don't make supper for me. You hear me, Dad? You'll go in now?"

His father nodded and he started up the road. He walked past the gravel flat; Kate's car wasn't there, her blinds closed. He turned up Bottom Hill and looked back and thought he glimpsed Kate's blind move in her window. He paused. He stepped nearer the edge of the road, staring harder, and something else caught his eye. Angled left of Kate's eave and farther in through the high-grown alder bed nearer the river he saw a smidgen of red, the colour of Bonnie Gillard's car. He couldn't figure it—the old park road cut through the alder bed, but not that far. Too mucky to drive a car. And it was where the river roiled the hardest and was the most swollen.

He continued up Bottom Hill, but his feet dragged. He looked back again, couldn't see the car. Backtracked a few steps—there it was. Just a glimmer. It was getting dark and he turned towards the bar but couldn't make himself go forward and cursed. Women. Never knew what they'd do. He turned back, walked quickly down onto the gravel flat and cut an immediate left onto a narrow, rutted road, grassed down the centre and long since left to grow over. He peered at the ground—too much water flooding the tracks to see tire prints. He kept going, tramping near the edging of brush to keep his feet dry, stick branches scratching at his clothes. He came to a clearing that used to be a park, out of the wind, and with swings and picnic tables. The picnic tables that hadn't been dragged off were rotted now, the swings just broken chains dangling from skewed posts. The wind had proven a better mate than mosquitoes.

He looked about the thickly sodded clearing and saw bits of tire tracks on the drier clumps of nettle and quickweed heading towards the river. He followed them, his boots sinking through muck, and cursed again, feeling the damp seep through to his socks. Gulls squawked irritably above him. Swampy patches of land gave up their rotting smells. The car must have been driven fast to gut through this muck without bogging down. Another thirty feet ahead and to the right was the clump of brush where he thought he'd spotted it. Ruptured mud holes in the soaked sod testified that the car had suddenly been revved up and reamed through the brush. His heart began thumping and he broke into a run. The alders thinned, the wind broke through, cold on his face, and a red slash bled through the thicket. There was the car, back tires bogged down in mud. The back door on the passenger's side was open, no one inside. He roared out *Hello!* The river roared back. He hauled and slipped his way up the small embankment in front of the car and looked onto the bloated, fast-flowing water of the river. He couldn't see farther than a few feet downstream. He tried cutting through the brush. Too thick. He went back to the car, saw the keys dangling from the ignition. He walked away, thought about the young boys and their nighttime drinking parties just over the way, and backstepped, taking the keys and pocketing them. Couldn't trust them little bastards. He headed back across the clearing and onto the swamped, grassy road, coming out beside Kate's. Her car was still gone. He started towards Bottom Hill, paused—her blind was partly open. He could have sworn it was closed earlier. He yelled out her name.

Silence. A flock of gulls rose with a cacophony of squawks above the river. He took the scuffed path from Kate's door, went up to the riverbank, and stood looking upstream. The gulls were spooling, squawking. Seized with a sense of urgency, he ran towards the old ruins and climbed on top of a concrete ledge. Holding on to a twisted length of rusted rebar, he leaned as far as he could over the ledge, seeing farther upriver. As if to an unseen call, the gulls floated back down to where they'd been resting a minute before. The river flowed deep, darkened by the evening light. He shivered in the sudden damp and leaped off the concrete block, starting back to the road. Kate's blind was still half opened and he swore to Christ he was being watched. *What the hell, not my business,* he told himself and started up Bottom Hill, walking fast. Cresting the top, he looked down upon Hampden. A thick fog was creeping over the darkening sea. It crept over the wharf and through the backyards and, lifting a grey tentacle, wrapped itself around a yellow light flaring through a window in Bonnie Gillard's sister's house. The light twinkled and then blackened like a dying star.

He cut away from Bottom Hill onto a twisted dirt road flanked by brush. It was getting dark now. The one streetlight had been rock-smashed years ago by mischief makers and he kept himself tethered to the road by the faint glow of the barroom lights creeping through the brush. A low rumble of voices floated towards him as he neared. Loud whispers. Giggles. The ones not yet old enough to get inside the bar. They plied him for smokes, booze, or whatever and he shucked one of them a dollar bill. Inside the smoky cavern of the bar a crowd was growing, shoving tables together and arguing good-naturedly with razzing neighbours. A bunch of old-timers hunched around their regular table nearest the door, playing spades through the thick haze of their home-rolled smokes. On the bandstand at the back of the bar, a scrawny kid with an electric guitar was testing his mike while the other band member—his uncle—balanced a bass on his knee and fiddled with the dials on an amp. An old sod hyped with drink was waltzing himself around the dance floor to Waylon Jennings pining "Why Baby Why" from the jukebox. Nearest the dance floor was a table of Verges, Bonnie's clan. Big hair, big dark eyes. Pick out a Verge anywhere. He was about to approach them when the eldest sister, Marlene, came through the door from the women's can, scrunching her hair behind her ears and laughing at the old sod waltzing his way towards her.

"Hey!" Kyle slid along the bar towards her, pulling Bonnie's keys from his pocket.

"Hay's for horses, Sweetie." She took the old timer's hand and swirled away with him across the dance floor and Kyle let the keys slide back in his pocket.

"Here you go, bud." The bartender slid a whisky and ginger his way. He drank it back and held out his glass for a refill. His buddy Hooker, hair razored to his skull, had spotted him from the back of the bar and was coming towards him. Looked like he was going to church in his white collar and black jacket. He slowed to a saunter as he passed the table where his girlfriend, Rose—saucy bangs and saucy tight sweater—was sitting, absorbed in a chat with her friends. Coming up to the bar, he slapped Kyle's back and gave him a heartening grin.

"What's she at, buddy! Your mother all right? Heard she was sick." He called to the bartender for a Black Horse and slapped Kyle's back again. "What's up, buddy—see fucking Roses back there?"

"Roses?"

"Eh, yeah, she likes me calling her Roses."

"Ye getting married or something? What's with the duds?"

"She ditched me agin."

"Right. New clothes gonna get her back."

"Man, I must be dumber than a fucking trout. Always letting her reel me in and dump me back out."

"Find yourself a different pond, bud. Listen, can we go outside for a minute?"

"Have a drink, first. Hey buddy," he yelled to the bartender. "Cancel that Black Horse, pour us a couple whiskies. How's Syl? Heard Trapp was sneaking about agin."

"Yeah, what's that about? Where's he living these days?"

"In Corner Brook, somewhere."

"What's he always fucking around here for? Nobody here belong to him no more."

"Yes, b'y. And not like he ever lived here, hey, b'y. Hung around with Ben one summer. Don't think he ever stayed much with them uncles of his."

"Best thing ever happened, that sawmill burning down. Crazy fuckers, the Trapps."

Hooker nodded. "Weird. Weird the way Trapp keeps sneaking back. Not like Ben's still here—whatever the fuck Ben seen in him."

"Ben. He's got a soft spot for all the underdogs."

"What about your sister?"

"Sylvie's no fan of Trapp. Only tolerated him because he's Ben's friend."

"When they getting back?"

"Don't know. Few weeks."

"I allows they'll be married soon. Married." He sniffed. "That'll take the fun outta *ro-mance*." He tossed Rose a snide look and turned to the flat-faced bartender. "Where's the drinks, old man—oops, sorry, bud. Here, pour one for your honey." He threw a few bills on the bar and handed Kyle a drink, taking the other for himself. "Cheers. What's up? What's on your mind? Listen." He gulped his drink and, leaning in, patted his jacket pocket. "Got a few spliffs here. Afghani, man. Black as spades. We'll go for a smoke in a bit. Got a few uppers, home. Get them later, if you want, all right, buddy? Your mother's going to be fine, guaranteed."

"I'm all right, b'y." Kyle toasted Hooker, the whisky burning good in his belly.

"And Syl, how's he doing? Always gets stirred up when Trapp's about."

"He had a few."

"Figures. Got a shot of shine for him out in the car. Nice shine. Fucking premium. Snuck it from the old man's larder."

"Thanks, bud. Old man will like that."

"Here's to Syl. And to your mother. Got some nice dried red clover back at Grandmother's. Good stuff—makes good tea for what ails you. Bring some up to your mother, if you like."

"Jaysus, like the old country doctor," said Kyle, clapping Hooker's shoulder. He pushed aside thoughts of Bonnie's car and threw back his whisky and ordered another for him and Hooker. One thing about the outports. You never suffered alone. Everybody was your brother or aunt or cousin or neighbour and they knew your dead like they knew their own.

"Look at her back there, look at her," said Hooker, sneaking a glance at Rose. "She been stonewalling me all night and which ain't working because I'm stonewalling her. She'll have leg cramps from sitting in that chair before I gives her a look this evening. I always smells like pot, she says. That's her thing, right? She hates that I smokes pot."

"Buy her some flowers, b'y."

"Hey. Love don't care if it's flowers or pot. Love is blind."

"So's hate."

"You saying she hates me?"

"I'm saying it sucks to be blind."

"It's here, bud," said Hooker, patting his heart. "You loves through here, not your head. Too cerebral, my friend. Hey, who's that there—how's she going, b'ys?"

Skeemo and Sup were coming through the door. "W'sup? W'sup?" asked Sup. "Hey, Kyle, man, w'sup?"

"How's she going, brother," said Skeemo. "Heard you're going to university in the fall. Got your courses picked? Get at it, buddy. All the good stuff be gone. Fucking studying ant's tracks across the Himalayas all last year. Here they comes, then." Two dead-alike brothers were pushing into the bar, dressed in bush jackets and padded vests and scuffing mud off their open-throated Ski-Doo boots.

"Cripes, what's she, Halloween out there?" asked Hooker. "Going dancing or hauling wood, my sons?"

"Hauling you in a minute, proddy dog," said the taller one, Todd. "Slide over, help a man get a drink. Hey, bud, couple of Blackhorse!"

"What's that smell?" Skeemo made a face towards the brothers. "Gawd-damn, ye still smearing motor oil behind your ears? Women likes cars, ya effing baywops, not timber jacks."

"Shaddup!" said Todd. "Last woman you had was greyer than her roots down south. Here, Snout." He passed a beer to the shorter brother with the wide flaring nostrils. "How's she going, Kyle, man. Heard your mother was sick?"

"She's fine, b'y."

"What do you mean, grey down south?" asked Hooker.

Jaysus. Kyle grunted. The brothers snickered through mouthfuls of beer, one of them bent over, spraying his boots.

"What's so funny? They goes grey down there?"

Jaysus.

"Never seen your poppy pissing?" asked Snout.

"Heard Syl went after Clar Gillard," said Skeemo.

"Naw, just his truck."

"Fuckin' arsehole."

"Sick fuck."

"Cruisin' for a bruisin'," said Snout. "Here, have a smoke."

"Naw, quit." Kyle drained his whisky and rapped his emptied glass on the bar for another.

"Where's Syllie this evening?" asked Hooker.

"He's home, b'y."

"What happened anyway—Clar blocked the road or some-thing?"

"Yeah, he was pissin' around with his dog."

"Heard your mother told Bonnie to call the cops on him," said Todd. "That's enough to get him going."

"Suppose, b'y."

"Keep your eye on that sick fucker."

"Hey, Kyle, man, heard your mother's not well?"

Kyle drank deep from his whisky and felt the heat spreading through his chest and ordered a double. Todd pulled a flask from his inside pocket and Kyle took a mouthful of tequila that burned his tongue and distorted his face and singed tears from his eyes. He nearly blew it across the room but managed it down his gullet and shoved the flask back at Todd.

"What's, you gone pussy?"

"Give it here," said Snout.

"Take it to the can, wanna get us kicked out?"

"Hey, Kyle, man, they're saying it might be bad."

"I'm sorry man. Gawd-damn!"

Julia walked past. Julia. Chris's girl. Straight blond hair sliding across a willowy, slender back, a sideways glance at him. Hooker hung his arm around his neck.

"She's home early from university. Starting work with Roses at the truck stop in on the highway."

"Should brighten the place."

"Ask her to dance, b'y, when the band starts."

"Shove off."

"She never went out with him, you know. Just graduation."

"Piss off, Hooker."

"Hey, just saying. What's she at, Snout, b'y?"

"Nothing, now. Crab plant's closing for a week. Listen, Ky, your old man need help with Jake's house? Me and Father can give a few days."

"I'll come," said Todd.

"Can't tell a screw from a nail," said Snout.

"Screw you, arse!"

"I'll give a hand," said Hooker.

"Thanks, b'ys. I'll tell the old man."

"Come on, let's grab a table," said Sup. "Whoa, who're those girls over there?"

"Whoa, look at that tall one, butt like two clenched fists."

"From Springdale—stay the fuck clear. Their men are on the highway by now with ball bats."

"*Ball* bats! What the fuck's a *ball* bat?"

"They bats balls with 'em, don't they?"

"You talking about a baseball bat?"

Jaysus.

"Do bats got balls?"

"Sure, b'y. Big ones. That's why they calls your old man batty—he got big balls."

"Is a bat a bird?"

"Yes, b'ye, like you. That's why we calls you Big Bird."

"Always wanted a big bird."

"Go sit with Alf Pittman's wife. She likes a big bird, twat on her."

"How'd you know about her twat?"

"Borned Edgar, didn't she—fuckin' head on him."

"Ever hear of stitches, low-life? I had a tumour in my belly twice the size of Edgar's head. Nothing there now but a pretty seam."

"Shoulda left out a stitch, you'd have your own twat."

"For you, arse, you gets any closer."

They scraped back chairs, settling noisily around the table. The boys kept putting drinks in front of him, and Kyle kept drinking them. The band started up with their bass and guitar and electronic drummer and its beat pounded through his head. He got up for a piss and staggered. Passed Julia going to the can and looked away. Kept walking.

Found his way back to his chair. Pushed aside somebody trying to haul him onto the dance floor. Rose called his name and he faked not hearing. He watched the horde of dancers shaking and twisting and Rose stood before him, too-tight sweater and a saucy grin. She grabbed his hand, yanked him to his feet and onto the dance floor. He caught a scowl from Hooker and winked and pushed away from Rose and staggered into Julia and her arms folded around his neck and his body folded around hers, soft, sweet . . . *put a candle in the window* . . . and he swayed with her and Creedence and his dick started swelling against the tautness of her belly . . . *I feel I've gotta move* . . . and then he pushed her away, Chris's girl, she was Chris's girl, and he was starting to sweat and he took long swaggering strides across the bar and made it outside and stood in the cone of yellow from the overhead light above the door. Fresh air caroused through his head. Fast. Too fast. He staggered off the steps and onto the road. Someone whispered near his ear and he startled sideways and was met with a meaty fist cracking against the side of his jaw and pain splitting through his head. Last thing he saw before hitting the ground was Clar Gillard's nice rounded face smiling at him.

He woke up to a pounding head and Creedence's final guitar lick. He saw the cone of light through a scraggly screen of dead timothy wheat. He was lying in a ditch across from the bar. His back was sore and his shirt hauled up, bared skin against rough, cold ground. He sat up—jaw aching, head splitting. He tried to clench his teeth but couldn't from the pain. Mouth tasting like rust. Jaysus. It was bleeding in there.

He spat and got to his feet, reeling towards the bar. The young ones had gone off; there was no one about. He thought of going back inside and getting the boys and tracking down that fucker Gillard. But his feet were already embarked upon the road, weaving towards Bottom Hill, and it was easier to keep going. The road T-boned Bottom Hill near the top and he looked down Hampden way for Clar's truck—scarcely a light visible through the fog.

He was starting down the back side of Bottom Hill when he heard a creaking sound coming through the woods. There was a pathway coming up to his right, a shortcut down through the brush, passing the scorched remains of the Trapps' sawmill and ending at the bottom of the hillside, directly behind his house. His father had cut the trail to shorten their walking distance to Hampden. Faster route getting to school in the mornings than walking the length of Wharf Road and then cutting back up Bottom Hill. Kyle hurried past the shortcut. Rather a longer walk than passing that creaking, stinking ruin in the dark.

Another creaking started to his left and he picked up his step. Jaysus. He hated this gawd-damn stretch of road; there was always someone seeing a bear prowling around here. Chris wouldn't be scared. One night like this they were both walking down Bottom Hill and heard something coming up the road towards them—*click-clap, click-clap, click-clap.* And then a reddish pinprick of light appeared in the distance, weaving through the dark in their direction. Kyle almost had a fit thinking it was a fucking bear, and he drew back, readying to throw himself off the road and thrash insanely through the woods. But Chris reached back and took his hand and it was warm and strong and he, Kyle, was a big boy of thirteen or fourteen but he let his older brother lead him towards that *click-clap, click-clap* and the reddish pinprick eye burning closer. Chris's step never faltered while Kyle's heart was kicking with fright. And then the thing was in front of them. A young fellow running with two Pepsi cans stuck onto the bottom of his boots, smacking his hands to his sides, a cigarette stuck in his mouth. Chris released his hand and they kept walking. Kyle looked back.

"What's that fucking idiot doing?"

"Scaring off bears," said Chris.

Kyle thought for a minute. "Good thinking. But he's still a fucking idiot!"

Chris busted out laughing. It felt good, his making Chris laugh like that. Felt more like a friend than a kid brother. It was the first time he had ever felt a sense of his *self*.

He wished Chris was here now; he wished his big warm hand was holding his. "Where you at, old buddy?" he called to the heavens. He felt himself choking on unleashed tears and bent over to get a grip on himself. He bent too far and staggered off balance. He was closer than he thought to the edge of the road, and with a yelp, he fell over. Rolled down a rough slope, his shirt scraping up his back and his ribs striking against the cold rough bark of a black spruce. He tried to get back up, tried to pull his shirt back down, but the pain in his ribs cut off his breath. Jaysus. He heard something or someone cry out—a faint cry—more like a scream, a weird scream.

He lay still, listening, and heard nothing, only the wind rifling through the trees. The fog crept through the woods and drifted over his face like melting snow, and he smiled. Julia . . .

A knife-cutting pain through his ribs. He opened his eyes to darkness and wet ground pressing against his face. He tried to move—oh Christ, his ribs. He held on to them and crawled back up the bank to the road, wondering how the hell he'd ended up down there. He smelled smoke. Someone had a fire lit. Kate.

He started down Bottom Hill, legs straddling the quavering road like a fisherman negotiating a heaving boat on choppy seas. He turned onto Wharf Road and then onto the gravel flat, his stomach roiling. He bent over and vomited so hard he emptied his stomach with one heave. His stomach kept heaving and he fell to his knees now, gagging on bile and gasping for breath. Water leaked through his eyes and nose and his head spun and he held it in his hands. Jaysus.

Dragging his coat sleeve across his mouth, he stood. He waited a moment, his stomach settling. He weaved cautiously towards the glow of the fire. It was just Kate sitting there, picking at her guitar strings.

"Hey." He lowered himself onto a log opposite her and missed, his butt hitting the beach rocks hard. "Hey, Kate. Sing us a shong—*song!*"

Kate tightened a key on the neck of her guitar. She didn't look up, didn't speak, didn't smile in greeting. Her fingers weren't calm and fondling and patient with her tuning, but fidgety and stiff. She tightened and plinked and tightened. Her hair wasn't braided tonight, but fluffed out in soft, rippled curls that floated around her shoulders. Hardly ever saw her hair loose. Going to church, sometimes. She always went to church Sunday mornings.

"What's up?" he asked. A dog barked from up the road and he shivered. "Arse. Near broke my jaw." He wriggled his lower jaw.

"Who, the dog?"

"Close enough. Gillard. He sucker-punched me."

Kate bent her head over the neck of her guitar.

"Down by the bar. Just out of nowhere. Punched me."

"He's been prowling about of late. Something getting him stirred again."

Kyle wriggled his jaw some more. "Don't think it could wriggle if it was broke?"

"No."

"Yeah. Good, then. What's up, Kate?"

"The moon's up, Kyle. Somewhere." She gave him a wan smile. She popped him a can of beer and he sucked back a mouthful, sloshing it around and spitting it back out, staring after it for blood—couldn't rightly see. He reached for a stick and gave the fire a good stoking. Flankers popped like orange stars. He laid the stick down and sat back, feeling nauseated again. He watched Kate's fingers plinking at her strings in a non-rhythmic manner.

"Hey, got a new song?"

"Not a night for singing."

"Got a new song, though? You always got a new song."

"Yeah, I got a new song."

"Let's hear it."

"Don't got the words yet."

"What's it called?"

"Papa's Quilt."

"Kinda quilt?"

"Made from my grandpoppy's PJs."

"His PJs? Is he dead?"

"He is. My mama made me the quilt."

"Sorry, Kate."

"He's not. Be over a hundred if he was still alive."

"Right, then. I like old men. Old men piddling about. Was it all right then, when he died—or passed? My sister Sylvie. She don't like saying dead. She says passed. Like they've passed on by and are still passing."

"It was a nice passing. I'm sorry, Kyle. We don't all get the gentle goodbye."

He lowered his head, then got the spins and sat up rapidly. He heard a series of low coughs coming from over by the river, some-where.

"Someone back there?"

Kate strummed her guitar.

"I think I heard someone. Over there. You hear anything, Kate?"

"A boat, I think. Someone in a boat."

"In this fog? Fools."

"Lots of fools around, Kyle." She kept strumming, her face turned from him.

"Seriously. They can drown in this."

"Death bothers you, don't it?"

"Thought it bothered everybody."

"Been walking to greet us since the minute we were born."

"Cheery thought."

"Nothing's perfect, Kyle. What would we sing about?"

"Pissin' in the rain?"

"Pissing's good."

"Let's hear a song, then."

She shook her head. "Not tonight. Go on home now. Might want to check on your father—drinking and driving. Saw the cops out earlier."

"Father? You seen Father tonight?"

She stopped strumming and gripped the neck of her guitar as though it were an irksome pet, laying it aside.

"Kate, you seen Father tonight?"

"Yes. Earlier."

"He was here? He was here, Kate? *Sonofabitch!*" He stumbled to his feet. *Sonofabitch, sonofabitch, he left her alone. When she was so needing someone with her.* Holding on to his ribs, he staggered across the gravel flat and turned down the black stretch of Wharf Road, cursing. Water suckled over the beach rocks to his left and suckled down the black cliff wall to his right. It suckled from his eyes and through his nose and his mouth and he felt like he was being corroded by water and he wiped at his eyes and his face, trying to make it all stop before he dribbled into bits by the roadside.

He got to the wharf and softened his step. No need to wake her. He crept to the door and stumbled. Christ! Felt like he was getting drunker. He reached for the doorknob, but then noted a sliver of light coming through the drawn curtains and peered in. Bonnie Gillard. Sitting at the table with his mother. Their heads were bent towards each other like two crooks in a crowd exchanging secrets. He couldn't see his mother's face, but he could see Bonnie's. She was bawling. He pressed closer to the window. His mother took Bonnie by the shoulders and gently shook her.

He looked around but there was no sight of Bonnie's car. Then he remembered. His hand instinctively went to her keys in his jeans pocket. She'd tried to off herself, that's what. And was now bawling to his mother about it.

He staggered sideways, near fell. Clutched onto the windowsill to hold himself steady. Good. Good then, his mother wasn't alone.

He stumbled to the side of the house and slumped down against it. Good. He didn't have to go sit with her. He couldn't bear it. He couldn't bear another thing. His mouth was parched; he wanted water. He turned his head and pressed his throbbing jaw against the cool of the clapboard. Fucking Clar Gillard. He slid sideways and was half sitting, half lying, keeping his ribs from touching the wharf. To hell with it. He let himself fall to the wooden planks and near cried from the pain and then stared up at the fogged-in night, wishing for stars.

He shifted for comfort. He groaned, his ribs aching. He was shivering. What the fuck. He opened his eyes. Had he slept?

He tried to sit up. A dog was barking and snarling, its nails scrunching through beach rocks. He leaned sideways to see through the dark and felt himself falling, falling over the wharf, and as he clung onto the grump he stared in astonishment at a dolphin's head flickering white out of the water. The dog—Clar's dog—danced on the water's edge, snapping and snarling, and then plunged into the water towards the dolphin. *Get back, get back,* Kyle yelled and the dolphin threw back its head and made its *tic-tic-tic*-ing laugh. It sank back into the sea and now Kate was looking down at him, *tic-tic-ticing* with a steel slide on her guitar, and she was crying, her tears dripping thick and bloodied onto his hands. He cried out, scrubbing his hands clean on the rough, splintered planks of the wharf, but her tears kept bleeding down her face and the night behind her morphed into a blacker shadow of itself, threatening to engulf her. He tried to say her name but it warbled in his throat and the dog's barking grew mad, frenzied, its nails cold, hard, gritted with sand as it scampered over his hands. *Ee-asy boy, ee-asy . . .*

———

A cold ashy dawn shouldered him awake. His body hurt and he was shivering uncontrollably. His bloodied hand rested beneath his cheek. He raised his head and pain cut a sickening streak through his skull. He lifted a hand to his jaw, flicked his tongue around his teeth—they were all there. He ran his tongue over lips that were crusted with dried blood and tasted like stale water in a rusted rain barrel. Clar must've busted his mouth.

He tried to sit up and moaned. His ribs! Like shards of bone jabbing through flesh. He fought his way from beneath the bulky weight of a tarp. What the fuck—where did that come from? He pushed himself onto his arse and was jolted fully awake by his father's hulking frame leaning against the side of the house, staring down at him.

"What, you tucking me in, now?"

"Your mother's up. Time to go in."

Time to go in. Right, you old fucker, why didn't you stay with her last night, he wanted to yell, but couldn't. His father's stubbled face needed shaving and his scruffy hair told he hadn't been to bed yet, either. And the legs of his jeans: stiff, wrinkled, and damp-looking. Pissed himself agin.

He looked away. Never could bear the shame in his father's eyes after a night's boozing. Those times his father did catch him looking only added to his shame.

He tried to stand, his legs too palsied. He grasped onto the side of the house and rose and got the spins so bad he near fell over the wharf. The dog. Clar's dog. On the beach and staring up at him and whinnying like a sick horse. *Fuck's wrong with you.*

Addie rose from her chair by the table as they entered. "What happened to your face? And your hand?" she asked Kyle.

"Fell down." He gestured to the back of the house. "Coming down the path. Tree roots everywhere. Think I drove a tooth through my jaw. We should clean up that path—break a leg some night, coming down there."

She listened as he rambled. Sylvanus pulled off his boots, the smell of damp wool rising from them. He took off his coat and Kyle removed his, and they stood before her like naughty boys caught sneaking home after a night's shenanigans. Her face was pale, her hands, the skin on her throat—all pale, whitish, ethereal in the greyish light, as though she were already leaving them, fading beneath the folds of her clothes.

"I'm telling you this, Sylvanus Now," she said, her voice low yet fervent, "and you hear me good. If not for you drinking yourself to death and taking Kyle with you, I'd take no treatments. Rather live out my days with hair on my head and my eyes open than traipse about like the living dead on drugs. That's the only reason I'll take this treatment—to keep another of my boys from an early grave. But I won't fight it alone. If you takes another drink, I'll stop the treatment."

"Now, Addie."

"Don't now Addie me. I'm doing this for you and Kyle and I wants something in return, I wants you off the booze, the both of ye. Do you promise me that?"

She was speaking to them both but it was Sylvanus she was staring at. Waiting. For him to lift his eyes, show himself. His shame.

Kyle tore past them and locked himself in the washroom. He twisted on the shower and stripped off his clothes. He stood in the hot steam and scrubbed his skin, scrubbing it clean, scrubbing it hard, trying to scrub out that knotted lump of upset inside his belly that couldn't be touched, couldn't be assuaged no matter how hard he scrubbed. Water. It could forge trenches through stone. It could wear skin to bone. But it couldn't so much as fray that knot of nothing in his stomach.

FOUR

———

His father was sitting at the table by the window, drinking coffee, when he came out of the shower. Addie was laying a plate of beans and runny egg yolks before him and Kyle's stomach curdled and he lunged for the door. Holding on to the grump, he spewed into the water, his ribs spearing through his side like knives. He looked up, seeing two men in a boat paddling offshore from the outcropping of rock and cliff that blocked his view of Hampden. Hooker's father, Bill, and his grandfather. They were standing now, tensed, looking ashore towards the rock face. Their voices grew louder, alarmed. Bill grabbed the oars and, still standing, rowed furiously towards the cliff, vanishing behind the outcropping.

Kyle heard his mother coming to the door, calling him, but he eased himself down over the wharf onto the beach and trekked across the shoreline towards the outcropping. As much to escape her attentions as to satisfy his curiosity.

During high tide the only way around the outcropping was by boat. This morning the tide was out. He climbed across wet rock made more slippery by tide-abandoned kelp. He'd been climbing around here since he was a kid, shortcutting it to Hampden. The front of the outcropping spanned a few hundred feet of rugged rock face, a small inlet forged into its centre. Hooker's grandfather was holding the boat steady near a clutch of rocks before the inlet. Bill was out of the boat and hunched over, looking down at something amongst the rocks, his face scrunched up as though tasting something nasty. Straddling the rocks opposite Bill was Clar's dog, whining and pawing at the head of a large pool of water left over by the tide. Something greenish was floating in it.

"What's going on?" called Kyle. No one looked at him. He came closer and then went down on one knee, his breath sticking in his throat. Clar Gillard. Half submerged. Flat on his back, arms and legs strewn out as though he were basking in sun-warmed waters. Blue jeans suctioned like skin to his legs. Greeny brown seaweed shifting with the water over his chest and bobbing around a face that was grey and frozen like clay on a winter's morning. His mouth was stretched open, his eyes wide and emptied. Clar Gillard did not look pretty in death.

"Teeth marks on his shoulder," said Bill. "Looks like the dog dragged him ashore."

"His truck's over on the wharf," said the old man. "Was there all night."

"He must've fallen overboard," said Bill. "Drunk, I suppose."

"Don't think he could swim," said the old man. They both looked to Kyle as if he might know.

"He ain't never gonna learn now," said Kyle. A wavelet lapped at Clar's face and trickled into his opened mouth. The dog whined and Kyle closed his eyes, dizzy. He held on to the cliff and got up.

"You'll call the cops?" he said without looking at Bill. He stumbled back around the outcropping and lurched across the beach, cursing the fucking tequila and whisky from the night before. Bad mix, fucking bad mix. He climbed gingerly onto the wharf and crouched by the grump, legs trembling. Sylvanus came out of the house, buttoning his coat and hauling on a toque. Addie behind him.

"Clar Gillard's drowned. Caught on the rocks around shore."

"Caught where?" asked Sylvanus.

"Around the cliff face."

They both looked towards the cliff. Their faces were blank. As if he'd just told them about a piece of driftwood he'd found over there.

"He's dead," Kyle repeated. "His truck is parked on Hampden Wharf."

"Fell over?" asked Sylvanus.

"Don't know."

"Probably drunk," said Addie. "Hope they buries him outside the fence. Kyle, you'll have to drive me to the hospital tomorrow morning; Bonnie's car is in the garage. And—from what you just said—I expect she'll be wanting her privacy."

The garage. He remembered the car keys in his pants pocket. The car sunk to its rims in mud. "When did she tell you that now, her car's in the garage?"

"Yesterday afternoon. When I last talked to her."

"When you *last* talked to her?"

"Yes. Yesterday afternoon."

Her words, uttered with such conviction, silenced him. She turned and went inside and he went after her, but she hurried into the washroom, closing the door, as though she knew he had questions. He got Bonnie's keys out of the dirty jeans he'd left lying on his bedroom floor and then stood outside the bathroom door.

"Mom?"

She didn't answer. His father tooted the horn, anxious to get to the site, thought Kyle, to get away from everything. From her. He looked at the closed bathroom door again and went outside. Climbing in beside his father, he clicked his tongue disagreeably as Sylvanus rummaged around beneath the seat, pulling out a flask of whisky.

"She got through to you, hey," said Kyle. "I'll not bloody cover for you and she'll keep her word. You can bet on that one."

"Drive," said Sylvanus, pointing a gnarled finger towards the windshield.

Kyle turned the ignition key and gunned the motor, seeing in the rearview his mother peering from the doorway. She was looking towards the cliff beyond which Clar Gillard lay drowned. The key to Bonnie's car dug into his leg from inside his pocket. His mother looked to the truck, near wringing her hands. He saw the worry on her face. Felt his father's growing impatience sitting there beside him, gripping that flask of whisky. He pulled the keys from his pocket and saw his mother's hand go to her heart, his father's finger jabbing at the windshield, ordering him to drive, and he felt the desperation of a landlubber on a sinking ship, trying to figure which of them was his captain.

He swore, let go of the keys, and stomped on the gas, speeding down the road.

"Well, what the hell happened to Clar, do you think?" he demanded of his father. "Fell over the wharf, drunk? What're you doing?"

Sylvanus was raising the whisky bottle with both hands like a priest wielding a cross to ward off evil. The bottle was still capped, the seal unbroken. Kyle braked. "What're you doing?" His father's shaggy dark eyes blistered with tears. Winding down his side window, Sylvanus flung the bottle into the sea with the same vigour Clar Gillard had hove the log for his dog to fetch just the day before. He screwed the window back up and jabbed his finger towards the windshield again.

Jaysus.

Kyle drove them up the road. His father's face was closed, too closed to speak, too closed to be spoken to. Kyle looked towards Kate's, and saw that her car wasn't there. He looked past it and down to the end of the gravel flat and the bed of alders beyond which Bonnie Gillard's car was sunk to her arse in mud. He swerved off Wharf Road onto Bottom Hill and then, partway up, he braked. That weird scream. The one he'd heard last night after rolling into the ditch. Bejesus if that wouldn't be Clar Gillard . . .

"Fucking nerves are shot," he said to his father's startled look. Releasing the brake, he drove on.

In Hampden they passed by Bonnie Gillard's weather-wearied hutch where she lived with her sister. No lights on in there. Nor were curtains drawn. Perhaps they'd never had any—too strapped buying bingo cards, thought Kyle.

"Watch it!" Sylvanus grabbed the dash as Kyle swerved the truck, scarcely missing old Dobey Randall with the hitched-up pants and light-glazed glasses.

"Trying to give me a heart attack?"

"Shouldn't be on the road," Kyle muttered, catching the old-timer's bewildered look in his side mirror.

"Perhaps you shouldn't be," said Sylvanus.

"Fucking thorny this morning or what?"

"That's it now."

"That's it now, what? Going to be an arse the coming days? Just what she needs."

"Drive."

"Right."

He hauled a right at the bottom of Hampden Hill, glancing at Clar's truck parked on the wharf. Lyman and Wade appeared ahead of them on the road just before the Rooms, walking hard into a growing breeze, their windbreakers billowing off from their backs.

Kyle rolled down the window. "Where's your car?" he hollered.

"Broke down!" Lyman hollered back. They climbed into the dump, the truck still moving. "You hear about Clar?"

Kyle nodded and looked to the sky, wondering how the hell bad news travelled on the wind and good news waited for its turn at the supper table. The clouds were clearing, ponds of blue pouring light onto the greyish face of the sea and the dark stubble on his father's chin. He rubbed his own chin, hands too shaky to shave that morning. Chris's face, smooth as their mother's, passed before him. It was the one thing he had over Chris—whiskers. Might've started looking older than Chris had there been time. Soon he *would* be older than Chris ever was. He gunned past the cemetery where Chris lay beneath his sodden blanket and wished to Christ he could gun as easily through his own rutted thoughts of gloom and lament.

At the job site Sylvanus was out of the truck and heading across the lot, Wade and Lyman behind him, yammering about their father coming home drunk the night before and their mother driving him down to the basement to sleep with the horse.

"The horse? He got his horse in his basement?" asked Kyle.

"Kept it there all winter," said Lyman. "Mother didn't like that either—he cuttin' a hole through the porch floor to throw food down to him, hey, Wade?"

Kyle stared at the young fellow as though waiting for the last line of a bad joke.

"He got him took out now," said Wade. "Put to pasture on the road."

"Ye going to stand there all day?" Sylvanus called, and Kyle tossed Wade the keys to the truck.

"Go up to Fox Point. Get more beach sand." He went over to where his father was kneeling beside the corner footing. "Did you hear what they just said—about Uncle Jake having a horse in his basement?"

"Had a crow in his bed last year—ask your Aunt Elsie. Get the spades. We digs her down another foot."

Kyle got the spades and started trenching away from his father at the southwest corner. The good stiff ground was easy to shovel and solid for building. The sun crept through cloud, filtering warmth on the back of his neck. He eased out rocks with the tip of his spade and smoothed over the holes and bent and measured the trenches, keeping them the same height. The wind brushed at his face and the sea washed over the shore and washed over his thoughts and the only time he felt content was when he was measuring, sawing, and hammering. He glanced at his father, who was kneeling by the trench and examining its depths and needing no ruler or marker to show him the dimensions. He was proud of his father's precision and irritated by the rumble of the truck returning and their work interrupted.

"Clar Gillard got knifed," Wade was blathering before the truck door was shut behind him. "In the guts."

Kyle let go of his shovel and Sylvanus rose as the brothers hurried towards them across the site.

"Murdered," said Lyman.

"Right in his guts," said Wade.

"Yup, murdered."

"Bled out, not a stain in him."

Sylvanus went back to his digging.

"Is the cops out?" asked Kyle.

"All over the place," said Lyman. "And they're coming down now to talk to you, Kyle. Right, Wade?"

"Right. They heard about your fight last night. With Clar."

Sylvanus stood back up.

"Is that what they're calling it. Fucker sucker-punched me," said Kyle.

"Fred Snow seen it. He was in the can. By the time he got his belt done up, you were gone," said Wade.

"Must've took time to fix his hair, did he?" said Kyle. "Never seen nothing till Clar's fist crunched my jaw," he said to Sylvanus. "Woke up in the ditch across from the club."

"Fred told a couple fellows," said Lyman.

"But you was nowhere to be seen when they went out looking," said Wade.

"And the cops were down to Bonnie Gillard's place this morning."

"But she was home all night," said Wade.

"That's what her sister Karen told the cops, right, Wade? That Bonnie was home all night."

"Right. But nobody seen her car."

"Nobody seen her, either. Floyd Murphy's sitting by his window with a sprained foot since yesterday and he never seen her coming or going. Or her car. But it was too foggy last night to see much."

"But *Mrs.* Murphy seen her this morning looking through her room window."

"So she's home but nobody sees her car."

"Perhaps she lent it to somebody," said Kyle.

"We'd know it if she did. Right?"

"Ye fellows going to trim that plastic?"

"Right, Uncle Syl," said Wade. "Three-quarter-foot strips."

"Don't take your eyes off them clouds. If she starts raining when we starts pouring, you gets it covered fast."

"Else it's like fish on a flake, hey, Uncle Syl? A drop of rain and the whole thing's dun. Get it? Dun? Done?"

"*Dun?*" asked Kyle.

"Dun. Dun, b'y. Mould on a fish. If they gets wet drying on the flakes," he said to Kyle's blank look. "Jaysus, b'y, where you been?" Wade winked at Kyle as Sylvanus started back to his shovel, muttering something about them all being too smart for him. "Some mood, ain't he, Kyle, man?"

Kyle gave a commiserative nod and picked up the ends of a couple of two-by-twelves. He dragged them over to the corner his father was working on. Murdered. Clar Gillard was murdered.

He threw down the wood and picked up his spade and started digging.

"How come you never spoke about the fight?" asked Sylvanus.

"Wasn't a fight."

"It was something."

"Fucker clocked me one."

"How come you never spoke about it?"

"Would've. Had time."

"You could've got that in."

"That's it now, was nothing to it. I come out of the club and he cracked my jaw. Woke up in the ditch." He looked to the road as the whine of a faulty alternator preceded Kate's old Volvo. Throwing down his shovel, he started across the site, rubbing his hands on the sides of his jeans.

Kate was getting out of her car, her grey braid trailing beneath a wool toque and her fingerless gloves a grey arc as she waved in greeting. She closed her car door and he felt again that patient, expectant air around her as she watched him approach. Her grey-green eyes appeared to be twinkling behind the lenses of her wire-framed glasses, but up close he saw they weren't twinkling at all, just light dancing on glass. He didn't see Kate much outside her nightly fire. How many times, he now wondered, was he tricked into thinking she was smiling when she wasn't?

His jeans were creeping down his hipbone like he was losing weight and he hooked his finger through a belt loop, jerking them back up. "Looking for the inspector's job, Kate?"

She waved towards the cousins fumbling with the roll of plastic they were spreading out. "Expect you got all the help you need." She pulled a pack of smokes from her back pocket and lifted one to her mouth and offered him one.

"Still quit."

She struck a match to her cigarette and pushed back tendrils of hair flickering about her face from the wind. "Clar Gillard got a hole in him," she said, tossing the match aside.

"They know who done it yet?"

"Nope. The cops are out from Corner Brook, questioning everyone they sees on the road. Thought I'd tell you what I told them. That I picked you up in my car around eleven-thirty last night, walking home from the club. And we built a fire and talked till past midnight when your father showed up with Hooker. And that you went home shortly after. Your father followed around a half hour later. Oh, and I happened into your mother earlier—she was taking a walk. She says she don't' remember when either of you got home, she was sleeping."

Kyle was staring at her in surprise. "That's nice of you, Kate. But why the hell would you tell lies to the cops? And would Mother bother telling you—"

"The cops talked to her before me. It's fine," she said to his sudden look of consternation, "they're talking to everybody. That's how they learned about your fight with Clar. They spoke with Hooker first and he come to me and we fixed up the details, smooth it all over."

"Smooth what all over? Jesus Christ, you thinking I need an alibi?"

"No, b'y, calm down. I'm just following along with Hooker. He told the cops your father was passed out in the truck behind the club all night . . . picked it up from there."

"So—why wouldn't I have drove the old man home in his truck? Why would I have walked?"

"You weren't thinking straight. Took a punch to the jaw and a blow to the head when you fell. Hooker went looking for you in your father's truck. Look, this is Hooker's blabbering and that's what we're stuck with. Go with it—beats having your old man drinking and driving." She got back in her car, tossing the better part of her cigarette into the ditch. Kyle went after her.

"What's all this to you? Lying to the cops, that's a bigger rap than the old man's driving record."

"Perhaps I'm just thinking about your mother, Kyle. Looks like she got enough on her mind these days. Go tell your dad where he was last night."

Kyle stood himself before her car door, keeping her from closing it. "You thinking I put the hole in Gillard?"

"Not thinking nothing. Word is you left the bar between eleven and eleven-fifteen. Then had a fight with Clar and nobody seen you after. So happens I seen you. Around eleven-thirty." She started backing up. He let go of her door and she drove off, pulling it shut.

"Eleven-thirty-five," he yelled after her. "More convincing when it's specific!" Least, that's what he'd learned from watching cop shows.

Sylvanus was bent over, digging. His cousins were hunched over the sheet of plastic they'd stretched onto the ground, readying to cut. They looked at him curiously as he strolled past. "What did you do last night?" he asked, bending down beside his father.

"You going to work today?"

"Asking what you done last night."

"I done nothing. I done what you done."

What I done. Kyle rose. Rocked back on his heels. *What I done. Right. Drunk and bawling in a ditch. That's just the size of it,*

now, isn't it? Me drunk and bawling in a ditch and you drunk and bawl-
ing in the truck. Some loopholes ought to be drawn tight. God bless Kate.

"The cops are coming," he said to his father. "Hooker said you were passed out in your truck all night. Behind the club."

Sylvanus placed the tip of his spade against the curved side of a rock embedded in the footing and levered it out, his face wincing as though he'd levered it from his ankle bone.

"Is that where you were?" asked Kyle.

"Must have. I woke up there."

"And Hooker drove you to the gravel flat around midnight. I was already there having a beer with Kate. I left and went home and you came home after you finished a beer with Hooker— around a half hour later. We better stick to the story else Hooker will be nabbed for lying. Making you look good—drinking and driving. You got all that?"

Sylvanus looked at him hard. "What's there to get? Truth, isn't it?"

"Sure, b'y. By the way, the cops after talking to Mom. She told them she don't' know what time we got home, she was sleeping."

Sylvanus went back to digging.

"She's thinking like Hooker, I suppose. Don't want you hauled in for drinking and driving."

"Bit late for that."

"Whatever. That's what they're after saying. Better go along with it." Kyle looked up the road. A blue and white police cruiser hummed into sight. "Yup. Dogs getting run over around here this morning. Not used to this kinda traffic. We better go talk to them."

"They wants me now, they can come here. Get their shoes dirty."

"Suppose, b'y. Wouldn't want to seem too eager, hey." Kyle picked up his spade and jabbed its pointed tip into the soil, half watching the police car pull up alongside the truck and park. Two cops got out and started across the muddied floor of the site towards his cousins. They were square shouldered and sober faced, walking the bow-legged walk of just about every cop he'd ever seen on the tube—like they had a billy bat reamed up their arses. His cousins let go of the plastic and stood big-eyed and nosy as the cops came up to them. Kyle couldn't make out what they were saying, a garble of sounds. Wade's voice tense with excitement, Lyman giggling too loud over something Wade was saying.

The cops took their leave of the cousins, and Kyle bent himself around his shovel as they approached. One was portly around the belly and with heavy jowls and a wattle starting to droop over his tightly buttoned shirt collar. His pants sagged at the knees as though he'd been called away from a comfy desk job. The other was younger, leaner, with small raisin eyes and a crooked nose that had been broken once, maybe twice. Probably why he's a cop, get the bastards who squished his snout.

"How you doing, *bays*," said the elder, taking on the outport talk. Jaysus. Kyle forced himself to stand at attention. His father kept on digging and the cop spoke louder.

"Sylvanus Now?"

"Yes, sir."

"Sergeant MacDuff here, sir. Few questions for you. Might I have your attention, sir?"

"I'm listening." Sylvanus kept on shovelling.

"Your *full* attention, sir?"

Sylvanus straightened, raising dark eyes onto MacDuff and pointing his spade at the cloud starting to fill in.

"I got fifty bags of cement to pour before *she* starts pouring. You do your job, *b'y*, as I does mine."

MacDuff turned to Kyle.

"You're Kyle Now? Would you go with Constable Canning, sir?"

Kyle laid aside his shovel and followed Constable Canning across the site, trying to think of a cop show where a sergeant rode in a cop car with a constable. His cousins were staring openly and he motioned for them to keep working. Coming to the police car, he faced the constable who was already scribbling in a notebook, eyes shaded by the brim of his cap. He looked back at his father who was still shovelling as MacDuff stood beside him, scribbling in his own notebook.

"I understand you were in a fight with Clar Gillard last evening?" asked Constable Canning.

"No, sir."

Constable Canning looked up from beneath the brim of his cap.

"He sucker-punched me."

"Why did he do that?"

"You'll have to ask him."

Constable Canning raised his cap with the butt of his pen and spoke in a bored tone. "We would, son. But he's dead. Why did Clar Gillard hit you?"

Son? Jaysus, the fucker had but ten years on him. "I don't know."

"Somebody smashes his fist to your jaw and you don't have any indication why?"

"Not when it's Clar Gillard. Too much pressure on the limbic system, they says. But looks like it's cured now." Kyle smiled.

"Murder's not something to be grinning about, son."

"Call me Kyle."

"Had you seen Clar Gillard earlier that day, Kyle?"

"Yes, sir. He was blocking a public road with his truck while he played with his dog. So, I waited till he was done and then drove home."

"It's been reported that you had words before you drove off."

"No sir, I did not."

"Your father?"

"You can ask him that."

"Kyle, you and me can drive to Deer Lake and we can talk about it some more if you like."

"My father started pushing Clar's truck off the road to clear it. Clar got the message. He stopped playing with his dog and got in his truck and drove off."

"Were there words exchanged?"

You move it, buddy, or I'll drown it and you in it.

"I don't remember none."

"When did you see Clar Gillard after that?"

"Outside the club around eleven. He was standing in the shadows and fisted me in the face. I woke up in the ditch."

"What did you do then?"

"Started walking home."

"How long were you knocked out?"

"A minute. Boys were still singing Creedence. Clearwater," he added at a blank look from the constable. Jaysus. "It's a band. They were singing the same song when I woke up."

"And then what did you do?"

"What I just said. I went home."

"Why didn't you go tell somebody in the club what happened?"

"Don't need nobody fighting my battles."

"So you went after Clar Gillard yourself?"

"They calls that putting words in your mouth in cop shows."

Constable Canning looked up as though pained by an abscessed tooth.

"This is a murder investigation, Kyle. Not a fool's game. Just answer the question."

"What is the question?"

"What did you do after you woke up?"

"I started walking home."

"Did you go after Clar Gillard?"

"No. I did not go after Clar Gillard. I started walking home."

"You went straight home after the altercation?"

"There weren't no altercation. I was sucker-punched."

"You went straight home after Mr. Gillard hit you?"

"No. I started walking home and Kate picked me up."

"Kate—?"

"Kate Mackenzie. You spoke with her earlier."

"She told you that?"

"There's not a soul in this outport don't know it."

"Does anyone know who knifed Clar Gillard?"

"I imagine the person who done it."

"Do you know who that might be?"

"No. I do not."

"At what time did Kate Mackenzie pick you up last night?"

"Around eleven-thirty. Eleven-thirty-five, actually. Her dashboard clock was lit up. First thing I seen when I got in the car."

"Where were you when Kate Mackenzie picked you up?"

"The other side of Bottom Hill. Walking home."

"She drove you home?"

"She drove me to her place and we had a fire on the beach."

"How long were you there?"

"Bit past midnight."

"Was there anyone else there besides you and Kate Mackenzie?"

"Father and a buddy of mine showed up. Hooker." He looked over to where his father was no longer shovelling, but standing straight backed, face to face with the sergeant.

"Would that be Harold Ford?"

Kyle nodded.

"When did Harold Ford leave?"

"I don't know."

"Why don't you know?"

"I left before he did. And went home."

"What time was that?"

"Around midnight. I couldn't sleep. Jaw hurt. And so I was sitting on the wharf when Father showed up. We both went inside together. I remember the clock on the stove—it was twelve-thirty or twelve-forty."

"Who was home when you went into your house?"

"No one. Mother. She was in bed."

They both looked up as MacDuff approached. He was scanning the shoreline, and then looked at Kyle questioningly.

"When's the squid rolling?" he asked.

"Squid don't roll," said Kyle.

MacDuff looked puzzled.

"Squid strike. Capelin roll. We done here?" he asked Canning.

"For now." Canning snapped his notebook shut.

"When do squid *strike* then?"

"Early June."

"Perhaps I could buy a few. Anybody selling a few dried ones?"

"Nobody sells dried squid."

"That's a shame. Anybody I can pay to jig me a few?"

"Sure. Working for minimum wage—cost about hundred and fifty dollars to jig, gut, split, salt, and dry a pound of squid. Still interested, talk to Hector Gale. He might cure you a pound. Yellow house up the road, green facings."

MacDuff stared at him suspiciously and then went to his car. Canning was ahead of him, door opened and scuffing the muck off his boots before getting in. The old fellow sank into his seat and took off his hat, scratching his grey scraggy comb-over and squinting along the shoreline. He gave Kyle another suspicious look and then turned to Canning, who was peeling back the pages of his notebook and holding out something for MacDuff to read. Yet another suspicious glance at Kyle—from both of them this time. Or perhaps the look wasn't for Kyle. His father was approaching from behind—step soft, wary. As if he was hunting.

"What did you tell them?" Sylvanus asked as the cops drove off up the road.

"What I told you."

"Is that the truth?"

Kyle looked into his father's eyes. They were hot with tension, frightening and vague. He felt his own tension rise, the same sense of vagueness overtaking him.

"Back to work," said Sylvanus.

Kyle followed him across the site. His hand kept going to his pocket where Bonnie Gillard's car keys lay. He should've told. But gawd-damnit, it wasn't his to tell.

"I told them to go on home, ain't no one here bawling over Clar Gillard," his cousin Wade called out to him.

"Ye gonna cut that fucking plastic?" Kyle went over to where his father was now on his knees, hammering in a peg. He touched his hand to the keys. His father glanced up at him and jabbed a finger at his spade lying on the ground.

"Pick it up, pick the gawd-damn thing up," he ordered.

He let his hand fall to his side. Jaysus.

FIVE

———

The long trumpeted cry of a gull awakened him. The heels of his mother's good shoes tapped the floor as she hurried down the hallway and then back again, pausing by his door.

"You up? We leave in a half hour." Her voice strained with forced lightness.

"Right." The hospital in Corner Brook. Her operation.

"Your father already left for the site. He walked."

"Walked?" Hell. Aside from hunting and logging, his father hadn't walked farther than his nose his whole life. "I would've drove him down."

"There was no talking to him." Her voice faded off and he heard the washroom door open and close. He dredged himself from his bed, the floor cold beneath his feet as he dressed. His tea was poured and stirred and waiting by a plate of toast and eggs. His father'd walked. Well, sir. He sat at the table and looked through the window at the sea, rippling greyish away from him. A southerly wind. Least it was warmish outside. Likely somebody driving along had picked him up by now.

He grasped his mug of tea and blew tepidly onto its scalding rim. His mother hurried from the washroom and across the hallway into her room. She hadn't mentioned anything about police being there the day before, asking questions. He never brought it up, nor did his father. Neither of them wanting reminders of both their shame that night. A dresser drawer scraped open. Another. She emerged with an armload of folded blankets, bustled into Gran and Sylvie's room, and within a minute was coming down the hallway again and into his room. He heard the dull thud of his pillow and blankets hitting the floor as she stripped his bed. All her activity took him back to the summers they'd spend in the old Cooney Arm outport where they'd once lived, helping Gran tend the vegetable garden she planted every spring. There was a cliff near their house and he'd watch his mother, those times she became dispirited, climb a steep path to the top. Couple of times he followed her. It was vicious up there, everything swept bald by the winds and the cliff face dropping several hundred feet straight down into the swirling mass of ocean. He could see his mother now, hunched like an old woman, gripping onto tree roots and brambles and dragging herself up that steep path. Scarcely enough energy to stand. *Low-minded* they called it back then. She's *got down*. She'd be gone for hours up on those cliffs some days. But when she got back she'd be upright, shoulders squared, a steadiness to her hands as she took up her cooking and scrubbing in the house and then weeded in the garden till the flies or the rain or the dark drove her in. He felt the same energy consuming her now as she scraped open one of his own drawers and shut it and then her shoes *tap tap tapping* to the washer in the back room.

He noted her small suitcase by the door. Her good raglan was folded across it and in one of its pockets he saw a glimmer of red. Her little book of prayer. She read it all the time after Chris was buried. *It's what keeps me going when I get scared,* she said to him once. Scared. His mother scared. She was scared now. He pushed aside his breakfast plate and went to the door, hauling on his boots.

"Kyle," she said, coming into the kitchen, "you haven't eaten a bite. Kyle!"

He held himself erect by the door frame as she came up behind him.

"As well to take your father with me if you're going to act like that," she said sharply.

He picked up her suitcase, took it to the truck, and started the engine, warming it for her. He rubbed his bruised ribs, rubbed them hard just to feel the pain of it over the angst in his guts. The morning chill leached through his clothes and he shivered thinking about Clar Gillard splayed out in the icy seawater. His mother climbed inside the cab beside him and was quiet as he drove and he wanted to puncture that growing solitude between them, wanted to ask her about the cliffs of Cooney Arm, but the words stuck like sawdust in his throat.

"You talking with Bonnie?" he asked, thinking he might mention his seeing her sitting at their table the night of the killing and that he knew about her car. Get her mind off this thing waiting ahead. She gave a dismissive shrug. But she was choking with words, he could tell. Just like Sylvie. Choking with words. Wanting to talk about *things*. *Things* about Chris and the accident. *Things* about him, Kyle. *Things* about themselves. And he never knew what *things* they wanted to tell him or have him tell them and he bloody didn't care about them things. Just leave it alone, leave it the bloody hell alone. Christ, he was working on getting *things* out of his head, not shoving more in.

He flicked on the radio. "See what the weather is," he said, and half listened to some broadcaster sounding hollowly through the truck as he felt her choked-back silence and that he was abandoning her on a sinking boat. He turned off the radio and leaned over the wheel, looking skyward. "Guess we can see the weather," he said, scrutinizing the patchworked whites and greys and scattered pieces of blue. "If you can read that. Warm enough?"

She made some agreeable sound and he looked at her and her pallid cheeks. There was a hard light in her eyes. She was wearing her summer scarf around her neck, a thin silky thing patterned with ripe red roses that he swore he could smell.

"Why aren't you wearing a warm scarf? Thought you liked my *stylish* scarf."

"I left it in Bonnie's car the other day. This will do."

"She could have brought it back, I suppose."

"Perhaps she didn't see it."

"Not a hard thing to miss, a scarf sitting on the seat."

"My, Kyle, I got more to think about than a scarf this morning."

"I don't like you being mixed up with her."

"Why, what's wrong with her? You got more to worry about than *her*. Sucking back on the bottle like your father. How would you like it if I'd done that? I could have. After Chrissy died. I wanted to."

Jaysus.

"Don't you be taking after him, numbing everything with drinking. I'm glad I didn't give into it. There's good to be found in everything, even grief. I've learned that." Her voice trembled with feeling yet her words were hard, without gratitude. They echoed through the cab like a confession wrung from her heart and he felt the unworthy priest. He tried to speak, but couldn't.

She flicked the radio back on with impatience and he hated himself. When they drove into the winter-worn town he was relieved to see her attention taken by patches of lawns starting to green and burlapped shrubs sitting like cloaked gnomes hedging the driveways. She liked cities. The sun flickered and he was glad for the sudden shaft tunnelling through the truck and settling warm around her face. And for brightening the canopied storefronts they were now passing, the white-collared shopkeepers sweeping clots of rotted leaves from their stoops and flooding gutters.

"Father says you always wanted to live in a city."

"That's what your father knows, now."

"Heard you say it myself."

"Perhaps I would've liked it one time."

"Sylvie wasn't long taking off after she finished school. Wouldn't know she was half raised on a fish flake."

She gave him a sharp look. "Sylvie done what she was supposed to do—finish school and go to university. What's wrong with that?"

"Nothing. Think I got the old man in me. Likes the woods."

"Never hears you talking nice about your sister."

He opened his mouth to protest but closed it. They crested a hill, below which the red-bricked hospital sprawled like a crusted sore. Grey smoke belched through smoke stacks and row upon row of frameless windows mirrored the ashen sky, black stains tearing from their corners and dribbling down the brick face. At the entrance to the parking lot he slowed to take the turn and his mother gripped his arm.

"It's a bit early," she said, her voice a thin whisper he didn't know.

He shivered and lurched them onwards down the street and yielded onto a main drag that took them past Pizza Huts and takeouts and smartly dressed mannequins in shop windows. He cut through a ribbon-bannered car lot and passed a school, its yard strewn with hollering kids, and a quiet neighbourhood behind it that flowed up, up, up a steep hill. The houses thinned, the hill plateauing onto a bit of a parking lot deeply cratered from winter's frost. He parked near the edge of the dropoff and they looked down over the city. Sulphuric smells rose from a smoking pulp mill that headed the harbour while nice shingled homes and shops and oak trees encircled the mill's land side as ribs might encircle the life-giving heart.

To the northeast and beneath the white dome of sky was the indigo ridge of a mountain range, the range that became the hills of Cooney Arm.

"Almost see home," said Kyle.

She nodded.

"Almost see the cliffs of Cooney Arm. I followed you up there once," he heard himself say to her silence. "Wind near ripped my hair out."

She put her fist to her mouth and he could see that her lips were trembling and he needed a drink, sweet Jesus he needed a drink.

"You looked calm as anything on that cliff top. All squished in amongst the tuckamores. Like they was an armchair. Come to think of it, I followed you up there a couple of times. Always made sure I kept outta your sights. You threatened to beat the crap outta me if I ever went up there."

"Like your sister. Always sneaking around."

"Still wouldn't be landed if that wind got a good snatch. Freaked the crap outta me, that wind."

"Timid."

"Timid. Jaysus. Everything was moving up there—clouds skittering, trees rocking. And below, water skittering with white-caps. Got dizzy. Had to crawl back down."

Her hands were in her lap, fingers laced.

"Fired you up some, being up there. Had the go of ten people when you come back down. Always wondered why you went. Why? Why did you go up there all them times?"

She shook her head.

"Must be some reason."

"Made me feel good, sometimes. All that grandness around me. Your father said the same thing about sitting in his boat on the water."

"I suppose."

"It's fine to be nervous."

"I knows that."

"Everybody feels nervous about some things."

"I'm nervous about every fucking thing."

"Still got to move ahead. We're blessed like Job then, when we feels the fear of something and does it anyway."

"Getting your head around something, that's what's the hardest."

"Think of something bigger than you."

"Right. Bears. That helps."

"I thinks of my babies I never rocked. That's what I'm doing now, rocking them. Nothing else matters then."

His mouth was dry. He'd seen her enough times, sitting by those three little white crosses in Cooney Arm. Three babies that never survived infancy. "Done something to you, losing those babies."

"That's it, now, like your father says. Some people have illness, everybody has something. It's how you carries it—that's what you take into the other world with you. That's the only thing we takes. Now, then." She looked at her watch. "We'd better go."

Kyle started them back down the mountain road. He parked beneath the overhang of a new addition to the eastern side of the hospital. Taking her suitcase from behind the seat, he walked too fast, slowing for her to catch up each time the *clip-clip* of her shoes on the concrete started fading. He held the door open and they entered into a spacious foyer where people swirled and shifted around and he stood amongst them like a leaf in an unsure wind.

The fan-driven air dried the wet that kept dampening his eyes and his throat felt dry. She touched his hand and guided him towards the elevators and up to the third floor. He followed her down a long corridor littered with medical carts and past workers with impatient eyes and bewildered patients in green jackets pushing their IVs before their slippered feet. The smell of bleach and alcohol brought more water to his eyes. At the nurses' station his mother was met with a flurry of smiles and charts.

"You're a bit late, Mrs. Now. We thought you'd stood us up. We have to hurry. Perhaps you can wait in the family room just down the hall," Kyle was told. "We'll come for you when she's ready. Just a few minutes."

His mother gave him an encouraging smile and he walked down the ward. Gaunt faces stared at him from doorways, nervous eyes. Inside the waiting room he sat at a round table with a puzzle half pieced together and stared along with a few others at some talk-show host on the TV flashing a white smile as she chatted to them.

He got up and paced the ward, his workboots big and clumsy on the polished floors. He went back to the talk show and listened to words he couldn't hear and tried not to fidget. The host waved goodbye and the news came on, then another talk show, and he wondered if they'd forgotten him.

"Mr. Now?"

He jerked to his feet and went out into the ward. She was lying on a gurney being wheeled towards the elevators by a couple of aides in blue jackets, a nurse at her side. She looked tiny and exposed in a pale green hospital gown, her hair combed back, her eyes biggish and bright as they flitted about like a frightened bird's. She raised her hand for his when she saw him. He clutched onto it. Awkwardly walked alongside the gurney as they wheeled her in through the elevator doors.

She tugged his hand, half whispering, "I have to put this on" as she looked down at a puffy plastic cap sitting on her chest.

"She's vain, your mother is," said the nurse. "Doesn't want to be seen wearing her granny cap." Addie smiled and Kyle was glad for the nurse's stream of banter as they descended to the second floor and down a short corridor. They stopped before a double set of doors, a little window in one of them—the pre-operative room, the nurse called it. "And this is where you best leave us, Mr. Now. We'll have her back to you in three or four hours."

His mother's hand was cold in his. He forced himself to look at her and was relieved. Her eyes were veiled. She had already left him, had left them all. She was tucked inside herself like a babe within a womb and swear to jeezes he could hear her rocker creaking. She gripped his hand and forced her dry lips to smile.

"Go," she said, surprisingly loud. "Go out for a walk. To a nice restaurant. You best make him leave, else he'll follow me inside," she said to the small group gathering around her. They laughed and she gave them a cautioning look. "He'll be fainting before the doors are closed," she said. They laughed again and he was proud of her, talking to them all so brave like that, making them laugh.

He squeezed her hand, wanting to tuck it inside his armpit to warm it. He bent over and kissed her brow. She clutched onto his arm, drawing him nearer.

"Be here when I comes out," she whispered harshly. "And take that cap off my head soon as they wheels me through those doors."

"I will, I will," he promised, trying to grin.

"And find a nice place and have your lunch. Will you? A nice place."

He nodded and she smiled as though he'd just given her something nice and then they were wheeling her through the door and her silky soft palm was still clutching onto his hand and it tore his heart out to pull his hand away. The doors closed and he cupped his hand to the little window, catching one last glimpse of her small face and fading eyes and one last smile as she spotted him at the window. Then she was gone. And his heart shrank as it must have that first moment he was gripped by unseen hands and pulled from the warmth of her belly. Oh, Jesus, sweet Jesus, don't take her, don't take her, you greedy bastard, you've taken enough.

He hastened down the corridor, head down, wiping his face. Through the hospital doors and across the parking lot to the truck. Inside, he started the motor and gunned it down and drove through a maze of streets. Near sideswiping a city bus, he slowed and parked before a fancy storefront and got out. Farther down the street he saw a Holiday Inn. He went inside and found the lounge and sat at a table before a wall-sized window that looked out onto the cars snarling past. The chair he sat on was pinkish and padded and swivelled. She would like it. He ordered a beer and soup but was told it was a buffet lunch. He got up and went into the dining room across the way and took a shiny white plate from a stack on an island and walked around an array of food, passing the plainly cooked dishes of chicken and beef and spuds. Instead he scooped onto his plate the fancy lentil salads, the broccoli and cauliflower soaking in cream sauce, the stir-fries and different foods he knew she'd like. Taking his plate back to his table, he sat, folded his napkin on his knees, and forked the mess into his mouth and tasted nothing of it. City life. What she was cut out for. He'd heard his father moan those words often enough over his fifth or sixth or tenth swallow of whisky in the mornings. City life. Nice clothes. Sin. Sin she was took out of school, working them flakes. And he helped keep her in the outports by marrying her and having babies and he was too damn stubborn to move and her first three babies died because there was no hospital close by.

The third one died in a hospital, Kyle was always quick to remind him, but his father never heard. Too intent on mortifying himself with his hair shirt. And suppose she had never married you, Kyle now thought, wiping his mouth with the white linen napkin, what the hell then? There wouldn't have been a Sylvie and a Chris and three dead babies. There wouldn't be a me. And she'd be living down the street somewhere in a fancy house with shrubs and with no cancer. Jaysus. As well to say that Adelaide Now defied her fate to marry a fisherman and was now victim of her own ills. Not to mention all her youngsters were bastards. Perhaps that's what was in store for him—to discover at the pearly gates that he was little more than fate's bastard.

He folded the napkin into a perfect square on his knee. He saw in its perfection his mother's determined shoulders as she pulled herself up that cliff path in Cooney Arm. He saw her bony hands gripping the roots of trees, dragging herself up, inch by inch, her chin defiant against the awful wind snatching at her. Finding shelter for herself amidst the clumps of wind-stripped tuckamores at the top, she'd crawl inside herself for hours, and when she rebirthed herself again she was a force no wind could topple. Adelaide Now was no come-by-chance. She took fate by the throat like an unruly dog and bade it do her bidding. She was her fate. And they stood to learn from her, he and his father. Two arseholes walking like stiffs, scared of farting for fear of crapping their pants.

He paid his bill and went back to the truck and drove around the town till he found a park area and there he stopped. And waited.

SIX

Outside the hospital Kyle stood patiently behind a scrawny old man shuffling in through the door, a parka over his hospital gown, dragging his IV pole with brown-splotched hands and reeking of pipe tobacco. Finally he pushed past the old geezer, near hooking his coat on the pole. Jaysus. Inside, he caught sight of a purple toque and a long grey braid vanishing inside the elevator doors.

"Kate!"

She turned, the light glancing off her glasses, and the door shut. She'd seen him, he was sure. He reached the doors but the elevator was already rising. It went straight up to the sixth floor and stopped. He jabbed the down button and it came directly back down and he stepped inside and stared hard at the sixth-floor button. He hit third.

At the nurses' station they told him his mother was still in recovery. Perhaps another half hour. He went back to the elevator and took it to the sixth floor. It opened onto a small square foyer bared of everything but a barred window and time-dulled walls. Before him was a double-wide door with a small, wire-meshed window. He gripped the handle; the door was locked. He peered through the window and down a long corridor. An orderly dragging a trolley banked with linen. A couple of old-timers tottering about in pyjamas. One of them reached for the arms of a nurse who was hustling past with a stethoscope swinging from her neck. She spoke to him, smiling kindly. Kyle heard nothing because of the soundproofed doors. It was the psych ward.

He drew back. Some things weren't his business. Just as quickly he leaned forward again—Kate was coming from one of the rooms. She simply stood there. Her toque was off and her jacket too. Her knees buckled and she slumped against the wall as though needing its strength to hold her up.

What the hell? He raised his hand to rap on the window but his view was suddenly blocked by a young man about his own age with a wide nose and wider smile.

"Get away, move!" Kyle yelled, but the fellow kept staring at him, his voice sounding like a low moan through the glass. *Ooopen the doooor ooopen the doooor.*

"Gawd-damnit, get outta the way!" The face vanished and Kate had vanished and Kyle jiggled the door handle, again to no avail. He blew out a deep breath and walked about the foyer, his arms stretched over his head to open his lungs. What did he know? He knew nothing. Her name was Kate. She played guitar beside a fire at night. He knew nothing. It wasn't his to know. Else she'd have told him by now.

He jabbed the elevator button, suddenly anxious to get away before she saw him. On the third floor he dawdled, wanting to go back up to the sixth, but felt he shouldn't. His mother would be back by now.

The orderlies are still with her, they told him at the nurses' station. He caught his breath and moved towards her room,

dragging his feet, heart kicking. They were moving her from the
gurney onto her bed. Her head was lolling like an infant's and
she gagged.

"Hold on, my love, hold on now," a nurse soothed in a loud
voice as she held a small steel pan beneath Addie's mouth. "There
you go, there you go, my love." She glanced at Kyle gripping
onto the door frame with the apprehension of a dog being lured
into an unfamiliar house. "Are you family?"

"Her son."

"Perhaps you can get us a cold cloth from the washroom."

He bolted into the washroom and flushed cold water onto a
white cloth and brought it to the nurse, dripping.

"Perhaps another squeeze," said the nurse and he twisted
back into the washroom, squeezed the thing mercilessly. The
nurse was easing Addie's head back onto her pillow. Her face was
the colour of putty. The shower cap was nowhere to be seen.

"Hold the cloth to her forehead," said the nurse. "How are
you, Mrs. Now? Are you feeling better? I've got the pan right
here—just tell me if you're sick again."

Too loud, the nurse's voice was too loud, but kind, as if she
was coaxing a reluctant youngster to the supper table. She'd hate
it, his mother would hate it, and he was quick to her bedside,
wanting to quiet the nurse. He sat in the chair close to her pillow
and held the cloth awkwardly to Addie's forehead. She turned
into it, so pale, so wretchedly pale. He felt himself go faint. She
groped for his hand and he wrapped his hand around hers and it
felt small and soft like a handful of cotton. Her eyes were closed
and she was drooling and he dabbed it with the cloth and refolded
the cloth back onto her forehead.

"You okay, Mom? You look fine. The cap thing is off
your head."

"Is the nausea gone, Mrs. Now? I'm still holding the pan here. How're you feeling, my love?"

"Shh." Kyle shushed the nurse and silently urged her out of the room. Then he looked to his mother's chest, all flat and bandaged, and he clutched the nurse's sleeve so she wouldn't leave.

"I'll be right outside," said the nurse. "Put the pan to her mouth if she gets sick. Push that button if you need me and I'll be back in a flash."

Addie opened her eyes, a pairing of blue.

"Here. Here's the pan, throw up if you need to. I got the pan right here." He held the pan firmly beneath her chin as she spat up, and then he wiped the fluid seeping down the side of her neck. "You're done? All right then, lie back. Got the pan right here if you needs it agin, just let me know, I'm right here," and he crooned some more and kept crooning and he didn't know himself. He heard her sigh; he put his ear to her mouth and heard her sigh again and he felt her coming back to him, coming through the darkness and emerging into the light. She opened her eyes onto his—hope already in them, dawning like the sun through morning shadow. Then a scent all too fragrant twitched his nostrils and he drew back. Bonnie Gillard stood at the foot of the bed, a bunch of yellow daffodils in her hands. She looked from Addie to Kyle and opened her mouth to speak but her lips wobbled as though she might cry.

"She's not ready for visitors," he said coldly but Bonnie stepped closer, offering the daffodils like an entrance fee. His mother tugged his hand and smiled faintly at the flowers.

"They were selling them downstairs. How are you, my love?" Bonnie asked but Addie was drifting again and Bonnie fitted the flowers into a vase and sat on his mother's other side, her eyes level with his, her mouth compressed like a stalwart convict defying the tightening of the rope.

Jaysus. He got up and paced the small room, stretching out his back and shoulders, and then looked about for the first time. Faded green curtains half drawn around his mother's bed. On the other side of the curtain someone was deep-breathing through a heavy sleep. There were no other beds, semi-private. Small blessings.

"Suppose I should offer you my condolences," he said, sitting back down and facing Bonnie.

She fixed her eyes onto Addie's blanket, started fussing with it.

"Must've been hard news to get," he said. "Clar ending up like that."

"Death is always hard news."

"What do you know of it?"

She looked at him. "Know of what?"

"Of what happened to Clar."

She shook her head. "I'll not think of him right now. My mind is with your mother. Someone who's shown me kindness." She went back to fussing with his mother's blanket.

"Where's your car?" he asked.

"In the garage."

"What's wrong with it?"

She gave him an impatient look. "It needs a new carburetor, I think. Not getting her gas or something."

"What garage?"

"What garage? I don't know what garage. You asks a lot of questions. Garage in Deer Lake somewhere. Marlene took her in." She stood up abruptly, pulling back his mother's blanket. "How's her tubes—they draining okay? I helped a friend through this some years ago."

"Don't touch her."

"'Course I will. We've already planned I'll help her with her tubes. You all right?"

Kyle had blanched upon seeing a white tube looking like a fat translucent worm creeping from beneath his mother's bandaged chest, gorged with a pinkish red fluid. A rush of heat flooded his face and he stood up, gripping the bed so's not to faint.

Bonnie looked to him apologetically and he cursed her cunning.

"They're not hurting her," she said. "Just tubes for draining. The cups at the end there—they collects the drainage and it's a healthy thing for it to drain."

He forced himself to sit back down.

"Your car—"

She folded Addie's blankets in place. "I told you, it's in the garage. I got a ride in with Kate Mackenzie."

His senses sharpened; he felt like a dog seized by two scents. "What—when did Kate drop you off?"

"Half hour ago, I suppose. On her way to Port au Choix."

"Port au Choix?"

"I think she got people there. Don't nobody know much about Kate, and by Jesus I envies her that," she added, her tone mirroring victory on Kate's behalf.

Addie stirred, her eyes fluttering awake, and Bonnie smiled, gripping the bed railing with hands that were chapped and red-knuckled from hours of shaking crabmeat out of shells, her nails chewed like his. "How are you, my love?"

Addie fluttered back to sleep and Kyle rose. "There's always somebody who seen something. *Count* on it."

"Who *thinks* they seen something," said Bonnie evenly. "That's only the half of anything, that is—seeing something."

"Did Kate say when she was coming back?"

"Said she'd pick me up around suppertime if I wanted. But I told her I was staying the night. Sleep out on the road if I got to, but I'm not leaving her." She gave him another bold stare and then her red-boned hand touched his mother's silken fingers and he was struck by the loyalty in which Bonnie Gillard stationed herself by his mother's bedside.

"Kyle." Addie's voice was feathery soft but stronger.

"I'm here. I'm here," he said, but she was looking at Bonnie. Her brow wrinkled with concern and Bonnie gave a slight nod of reassurance and they both turned to him. He watched the brazen communication going on between them and was about to get up and march the Gillard woman out of the room and choke the truth out of her but was stalled by a nurse pushing back the curtain, dragging a trolley of metal instruments.

"Are you awake, Mrs. Now? I'm going to take your temperature. How are you feeling?"

"Go home now," Addie whispered to him. "See to your father. Bonnie will stay with me."

He shook his head, then averted his eyes as the nurse pulled back his mother's blanket.

"That looks good," said the nurse. "Looks good, Mrs. Now. We'll check the other one."

"They're filled," said Bonnie. "Perhaps you can watch me change one? Make sure I do it right?"

"Hold on, now. I'll loosen those bandages."

"The surgeon," whispered Addie. "He said he left me a little cleavage."

"That he did, my love," said the nurse. "He always leaves a little near where your top button comes undone."

Kyle backed out of the room, out of that secretive place of women, and headed for the elevators.

He drove through the brightening afternoon light. Blue patches of sky widening through thinning cloud. His window was partly down, cold air rushing past his brow. His thoughts were too spastic to follow and he sped faster down the highway with an eye on the rearview for cops. He slowed, passing the restaurant at Hampden Junction and thinking he'd catch a cup of coffee, but released the brake and kept going. Twenty minutes later he cruised through Bayside and passed Clar Gillard's house, its windows dark and curtains drawn. The Lab was sitting on the front steps, his ears perked towards the door as though waiting to be let in.

Coming to Bottom Hill, Kyle hesitated. A cup of coffee, he'd go home for a cup of coffee, then drive down to the Beaches and work a few hours with his father. Turning off the pavement onto Wharf Road, he braked, a speedboat cruising just offshore catching his attention. It was Hooker in his old man's boat. And Skeemo sitting at the bow. Wasn't right for the boys to be cruising the shallow waters of the mud flat. Farther out he saw several more boats, two just off the wharf from his house. Last time he'd seen this many boats on the water was during squid jigging season last year.

He drove past the gravel flat, eased around the turn in the road where the incident with Clar Gillard took place, and then braked hard. Ahead he could see yellow tape fluttering in the breeze. The wharf and his house were cordoned off. To the side, near the shed, was a parked police car. Hooker had spotted him from his speedboat and was now heading towards him, the arse of his boat spitting foam. Kyle threw the truck into park and got out, standing on the rocks and dropping to one knee as Hooker cut his motor and drifted in way too fast.

"What the hell's going on?" yelled Kyle. He leaned forward, grabbing hold of the nose of the boat and pushing it sideways to keep it from bouncing off the rocks.

"Where you been at?" Hooker asked.

"With Mother in Corner Brook. What's going on?"

Skeemo moved forward. "They found a swatch of Clar's shirt hooked on your wharf, buddy. Just below the water mark. Right by your door. He was stabbed on your wharf. He was stabbed and either fell or was pushed over and caught on a nail going down."

"Hey? How the fuck's that? His truck was on Hampden Wharf."

"Yeah, so what the fuck, hey? Cops already searched your house. And they had Syllie down Deer Lake for questioning this morning."

"Like that got them somewhere. Our wharf—how the—" Kyle went silent. Bonnie. She'd been sitting with his mother. He'd been going for Bonnie Gillard. "What time did he get killed?"

"Don't know. They got a police boat out there and divers looking for the knife," said Skeemo. "Here they comes, then." The cruiser parked by the shed had kicked into life and was now pulling a U-turn and coming towards them. Kyle looked to Hooker, who was still sitting in the boat, unnaturally quiet, eyes fixed on the police car.

"What's with you?" asked Kyle.

"Nothing, buddy. Keep her cool."

The cruiser hauled alongside, two policemen getting out. One of them Canning and the other much younger—clean-shaven, big eyes, small nose. Looked like an oversized sixth grader.

"How's this going to work," said Kyle, going towards Canning, "the house ribboned off like a fucking crime scene?"

"Mind parking your truck, sir? We're taking you to Deer Lake for questioning."

"*Sir!* Yesterday I was your *son*. And yeah, I bloody mind. Where we all going to sleep tonight? Unless you found something in your search—"

"Get in the car, Kyle," said Canning. "We'll talk at the station."

"What, we can't talk here?"

"The car, sir." It was the new cop.

"Constable Wheaton," said Canning by way of introduction.

Kyle glanced at Hooker and Skeemo bobbing just off shore and stepped up to Canning, voice low, urgent.

"My mother just had surgery. My father, he needs to know how things went. Can we talk driving to the Beaches? He's on the job site—where you spoke to us yesterday."

"Send a message with your friends."

"I can't tell my friends. She's keeping it private about her operation. She has cancer, it's bad."

"Send a message that she's okay," said Wheaton. "Get in the car."

"Look, I just need to make sure the old man's all right. And what the hell, where's he going to sleep? You can't bar us from the house."

"Get in the *car*, sir," ordered Wheaton once more. He held open the door of the cruiser, beckoning him inside.

"Christ, my mother just had serious surgery and I can't go tell the old man she's all right?"

"Don't worry, bud," Hooker called out. "We'll go see Syl. We'll tell him she's okay."

Kyle faced his friends with a fierce look. "Any fucking chance of privacy here?"

"Relax, bud."

"Go on, b'y," said Skeemo. "We'll see to your old man. Meet you for a beer after."

"Don't open your fucking mouths."

"Tell you what," said Hooker. "We needs to blab, we'll go yodel to the dead on Miller's Island. Arse."

Kyle bent to get into the police car. "Don't put your fucking hand on my head," he ordered Wheaton.

"Hey, Ky," Hooker yelled, "meet you at the bar! I'll wait."

Inside the cruiser Kyle stared resentfully at Hooker and Skeemo picking up speed and foaming their way towards the Beaches. Everybody in the whole stinking outport would know about that operation before the night was done. He stared hard at the backs of the cops' heads, his jaw hurting from grinding his teeth.

———————

Forty-five minutes later they drove off the highway into Deer Lake, where everyone from Hampden, Beaches, and the rest of White Bay went to see a doctor, fix their teeth, pick up groceries and shoes, and all else. He'd passed the cop shop hundreds of times. This was the first time he'd entered its white wooden doors.

They led him down a short hall and into a square room. He recognized the scene from cop shows. Only this one had no two-way mirror. And the chairs were cushioned and a coffee pot was percolating on the little square table. As Wheaton poured himself a cup, Canning beckoned Kyle to one of the two chairs at the table. Kyle sat and rubbed his face and stretched out his back. He was tired. He thought about asking for a lawyer but he didn't know fuck about getting lawyers.

The door opened and Sergeant MacDuff shuffled in, white shirtsleeves rolled up, top button undone, wattle sagging, belly sagging, pants sagging. Looked like a half-stuffed laundry bag.

"Evening, boys." His eyes crinkled into smiles as though they were sitting in some kitchen sharing tea and muffins. Taking the seat across from Kyle, he flipped through his notebook, settling on a clean page. "Sorry to hear about your mother's troubles." He held up a reassuring hand to Kyle's surprised look. "Chatted with your father this morning. He was concerned."

"You're so concerned, haul that fucking tape off our door so's he got a bed for the night."

"Let's work on that, son. Let's go back to the day Clar Gillard blocked the road to your house. Tell me what happened."

"Check buddy's notes there," said Kyle, indicating Canning. "I've told him everything."

"Now you'll tell me, Kyle. I need to know in exact detail what happened during that altercation between your father and Clar Gillard."

Jaysus. Kyle dragged both hands down the sides of his face. He sat back and told again about Clar blocking the way while playing fetch with his dog and his father pushing Clar's truck off the road.

"Your father had a heart attack—when?" MacDuff said, riffling back through his pages.

"Three years ago. What's that got to do with anything?"

"Would've been a lot of strain on his heart, pushing that truck."

"Seen him straining harder than that."

"He must've been mad."

"Seen him madder. Expect Saint Peter had a temper. And his mother and the sweet baby Jesus too if his arse was rubbed raw. You thinking it was my father now who knifed Clar?"

"What words were exchanged between the two?"

"None."

"None? Are you sure?"

"Yes, I'm sure. Clar got in his truck and drove off."

"When did you see him again?"

"At the bar."

"What time was that?"

"About eleven, I suppose. Like I already told you, I had a few, I needed air. I went outside and he—Clar—looked to be waiting.

He never spoke, just punched me in the jaw, and I woke up in the ditch a few minutes later."

"Then what did you do?"

"I started walking home. Got picked up by Kate and sat by her fire for a bit. She always has a fire going."

"What time did you leave the fire?"

"Around midnight. Hooker drove the old man up in his truck and I went home shortly after and took a nap on the wharf and the old man came home and woke me up. Around half-past twelve."

"You were drunk, half asleep. How would you know the time?"

"Saw the clock on the stove when we went inside. It was the only thing lit up. The clock. Big yellow numbers. Twelve-thirty or twelve-forty. One or the other."

"Why didn't you drive your father home from the bar?"

"Forgot him. Was stupid. Took a blow to the head and wasn't thinking."

"Why didn't your father leave the fire and go home with you?"

"Wasn't finished his beer." He rubbed his eyes tiredly. The room was stuffy. MacDuff wiped at his brow, half moons of sweat damping the underarms of his shirt.

"Kate Mackenzie. What time did you say she picked you up?"

"Jesus, you're kidding me, right? I've told you that a dozen times."

"Tell me again."

"Eleven-thirty-five."

"Is that a.m. or p.m.?"

Kyle stared blankly. "Trick question, right?"

"Answer the question, sir." It was Wheaton who spoke. He and Canning were standing on either side of MacDuff like matching mannequins.

"Eleven-thirty-five *p.m.*"

"What time did you say you left the bar to go outside?"

"Look, we've covered this."

"What time did you leave the bar, *sir*?" It was Canning now.

"I don't *exactly* know, *sir*. Around eleven is what I've figured."

"When were you punched by Clar Gillard?"

"Soon as I stepped outside."

"What did you do then?"

"I was knocked out."

"How long were you out?" asked Wheaton.

"Don't know."

"Minutes? Hours?"

"Minutes. Band was still playing the same song when I woke up."

"When exactly do you think Kate Mackenzie picked you up?"

"Like I haven't already answered that? Man, the time's not going to change. It already happened."

"What time did Kate Mackenzie pick you up?"

"Eleven-thirty-fucking-five *p.m.*"

"How're you suddenly clear on the time?" asked Canning.

"The clock on her dash."

"When did you first see your father after that?" asked Wheaton.

"About fifteen, twenty minutes later. About midnight."

"Where?"

"At the fire on the flats."

"But he was passed out in his truck down by the bar."

"Hooker drove him up from the bar."

"How do you know what the time was?"

"What the time was when? What the fuck are ye all talking about?" Both Canning and Wheaton were leaning towards him now, staring hard into his eyes as though practising some ancient Asian art of lie detection based on the size of his pupils.

"How do you know what time he drove home that night?"

"What time *who* drove home?"

"Your father."

"I don't know. Did ye all do Dale Carnegie? Because you're all starting to sound and look alike."

"You just said midnight."

"I said *about* midnight—who the fuck cares what time it was. He showed up at the fire about midnight and then he showed up at the house around twelve-thirty or twelve-forty, like I said."

"There's blood on the doorknob of your house. How did it get there?"

"*What?* I dunno—oh right. My jaw was bleeding." He looked at MacDuff who was easing back in his chair, scribbling in his book. "Is that what this is about? My mouth was bleeding from where Clar punched me. I was sleeping and drooled over my hand. Must've got on the knob. Hey!" He flicked his tongue around the inside of his mouth, searching for a cut. Couldn't find one but stretched his mouth open anyway. "Here—have a look. You wanna see the scab, man?"

Both cops stared at his open mouth. MacDuff kept writing.

"Tell us about your father and Bonnie Gillard," said Canning.

"What about them?"

"The nature of their relationship?"

"The *nature*—what's that mean?"

"Are you aware of anything going on between your father and Bonnie Gillard?" asked Canning.

"Are you fucking nuts?"

"You got a short fuse, sir."

"You got a filthy mind, *sir.*"

"Your father and Bonnie Gillard were seen in your father's truck around ten the night of the murder."

"So what? He was giving her a ride."

"Ride where?"

"Ask them."

"We're asking you, sir."

"How would I know?"

"You just said he was giving her a ride. A ride where?"

"Where the hell did he pick her up? That's what we do around here, you see someone walking and you pick them up."

"Did you see Bonnie Gillard that night?"

"No."

"When did you last see her?"

"She was at the hospital, sitting with my mother."

Canning flicked a look to MacDuff and Kyle kicked himself.

"When did she get to the hospital?" asked Wheaton.

"I dunno."

"What time did you see her?"

"I dunno."

"Were you there when she showed up in your mother's room?"

"Yes."

"Around what time was that?"

"I dunno."

"Why don't you know?"

"Cuz I was taking care of my mother. Cuz I didn't give a fuck about Bonnie Gillard or the time."

"You don't give a fuck about Bonnie Gillard," said Canning, "and yet she sits with your mother during this private time?"

"What's your question?"

"Why don't you like Bonnie Gillard?"

"I neither like nor dislike Bonnie Gillard. She's my mother's friend."

"Is she your father's friend?"

"No."

"Did you see your father with Bonnie Gillard the night of the murder?"

"No. Why don't you ask Bonnie Gillard where she was? Why don't you ask her sister where she was? Ask anybody in the whole fucking town where she was. Somebody always knows something. You haven't got that figured out yet?" Christ but he was mad, mad at the whole fucking works of them, and Canning and Wheaton kept bearing down on him like dogs, barking out questions they'd already asked and he snapping back answers, *Yes, I seen Father earlier that night, we does what we always does, drives around for a bit—I drives and he drinks. Yes he was drunk and passed out. Yes I parked the truck behind the club. Yes, he was passed out and it's what he does, he drinks and passes out and we'd gotten hard news about Mother that night and he was drunk, stoned drunk, and he should've been home with Mother and that's what you should be nailing him with, getting drunk when he should've been home, and not following some shit story like—like . . .* He faltered, his throat raw, his heart pounding, his face on fire. Gawd-damn. His mother all hacked up in the hospital and they hunting up some story about his father and Bonnie Gillard. He should tell them about the car, about her bawling in his mother's house, but now he couldn't tell them nothing about that because they'd want to know *when* he found the car and *where* his father was when he found the car and they'd know he *wasn't* with his father like he said he was and smothering Jesus, he had himself all sewn into his own lie. He stopped talking. He simply stopped talking and stared at the cops. They stared back. They were waiting. Waiting for what? Him to break like some arsehole scene from some arsehole cop show? "We done here?"

MacDuff flipped back through his pages, tutting like an old woman, sweat gathering on his brow like he was coming down with something. He put down his pencil and gave a tired smile.

"We're sorry about the timing, Kyle. We put off talking to you earlier out of respect for your mother's hospital procedure."

"Yeah? You're touching my heart. Who's driving me home?"

"This way, sir," said Canning. Kyle pushed past MacDuff, who was looking sadder than a lost cow, and followed Canning down the hall to the door.

"We'll be calling soon," said Canning, showing Kyle out. "Evening, now."

"What—you kidding me? No one's driving me home?"

"Sorry, sir. We don't taxi people."

"*Taxi?* You haul me forty miles from home and I'm to *walk* back?"

"There's a bus in the morning, sir."

"You got a bed for me somewhere? Oh, right, you're not a hotel service, either." He went outside, kicked at the door closing behind him, hurt his foot. Bastards! He limped to the highway and looked west towards Corner Brook—there was lots of traffic; it'd be easier to hitch a ride and spend the night in the hospital sitting room. But he had to see his father. What the hell had they done to his father this morning with their arsehole questions?

He stuck out his thumb pointing east. Ten, fifteen minutes passed and a scattering of cars. He was shaking from the cold and shaking from rage. A trucker swept past, nearly blowing him off the road. Jaysus. He walked half a mile west to a gas station and lucked into a ride with a closed-mouthed old fellow from Jackson's Arm. Eb Langford. Second cousin to some uncle on his father's side. They rode in silence—Kyle too tired to talk and Eb having never strung two sentences together in his life. They took the cut at Hampden Junction and ten miles later came to a split in the road: one leading another twenty-five miles to Jackson's Arm, the other leading ten miles to Hampden. It was dark, darker

than old jeezes, and more bears around these parts than gulls snatching at roadkill. When Eb pulled over to let him out, Kyle offered
him twenty bucks for the extra ten-minute drive to Hampden.
He was met with the same stony eyes as Wheaton and Canning's.

Fucking Langfords. Low-life fucking Langfords. Wouldn't give
you a rhubarb stalk if it was rotting in their yard. He got out of the
car and started walking. The woods bordering the roadside were
black, the road a greyish hue before him. His blood was pumping
hard, motoring his step and keeping other stuff from creeping in—
like the shadows of darker things up ahead against the already darkened skyline. Another thirty minutes and there'd be stars and a rind
of moon. He pricked his ears for bears and the night pressed around
him like a great, smothering blanket. And silence. Fucking silence.
Where the saints reside. Where God is. A blessed thing. A scary
thing, a thing of peace. He hated silence. Nothing made more
noise than silence, hovering before your face like a pent-up scream.
Dead people. That's who were silent, dead people. Stillness. That's
what he remembered most about Chris, his *stillness* in that coffin.
His sealed mouth and sealed eyes. And the stillness of his face, no
matter all that sobbing and suffering going on around him. Except
for Sylvie. She wasn't sobbing. She was as silent as Chris. Her face
the same pallor. He'd wanted to touch her, but couldn't. She
must've felt him thinking of her for she looked up at that instant,
meeting his eyes, and he closed his. Closed her out. Couldn't look.
Couldn't bear what her eyes might tell him. *Christ,* there he was
again, stuck inside his head and thinking about *things,* all those
things his mother and sister were wont to talk about and he would
have nothing to do with. He picked up his step and hurried as he
always did from Sylvie, from silence, from the whispers wriggling
like insects through his ears, forever driving him out the door and
down the road to the bar where there was noise and people whose

loud chatter shushed his tiresome whispers and tiresome thinking about *things*. He walked harder, pushing through the dark, pushing through the night, pushing through the rest of this day where so much had happened and was happening still.

The throbbing of a truck sounded from behind, yellow headlights sweeping over him. Dougie Gale. Getting back from his cabin down Rushy Pond and with his wife and youngsters in the cab with him. Kyle shook with relief, climbed aboard the back, and roared out *"The bar!"* Ten minutes later he was kicking at the tire of his father's truck parked outside. Hooker's car was next to it. He went in. He needed a drink—gawd-damn, he needed a drink.

The bar was almost empty. Curses from the corner where the old-timers jabbed pegs into a crib board, air blue with smoke from their homemade rollies. Julia leaned over the pool table, ponytail coiling like silken rope onto the green felt. Fellow from Bayside chalking up his stick beside her. She missed her shot and cursed. A few of the boys from Sop's Arm were sitting at the back of the bar and Hooker was sitting amongst them. He shoved back his chair upon seeing Kyle and Kyle rapped the bar for the bartender who was feeding quarters into the flashing face of a one-armed bandit. He scooped a handful of nuts from a bowl sitting on the table and shucked them into his mouth, near choking as Julia appeared before him. White T-shirt, low-hung jeans. She tucked her foot between his on the rung of his stool, cue stick staffed beside her.

"How's everything, Ky?"

"Holding your cue too tight," he told her, brushing nut crumbs off his mouth.

"You think?"

"Cue jerks when you holds it too tight. Screws up your aim."

"You giving lessons?" Her smile was saucy. Her eyes lazy as she scanned his face. Big grey eyes, clean and healthy.

"Your break, doll," called her pool chum and she winked at Kyle and turned, her ponytail sweeping his face with scent. He scooped another handful of nuts into his mouth, salty and crunchy. He finished off the bowl.

"What's up?" said Hooker, taking the stool beside him. "Couple of whiskies," he called to the bartender who was still sitting and feeding the bandit, "when you're not too busy, that is. Arse." He turned to Kyle. "How's she going, bud?"

"See the old man?"

"He went off awhile ago. Tried getting him to Father's place for the night, but hell, when Syllie gets like that."

"Figures."

"I tried to keep him here."

"Yeah, don't worry, I knows where he is."

"He come in for one, and then walked away from it. Whaddya think of that? Had it poured and stared at it and then walked away. I followed after him, but he faced me down. Swear to jeezes, he would've clocked me if I took another step. Sorry, bud."

"Did he say anything? About what the cops asked him?"

"Nothing. Not a word. But he was dark around the gills. He was after going through something." Hooker paused, looking worried. Hooker always looked worried.

Kyle spat out a bit of nail from where he was chewing on his thumb. "What's everybody saying?"

"That it's weird Clar was on your wharf. But they thinks Bonnie Gillard done it. Except they don't know how she'd get the strength to knife down Clar if they were in a fight. Unless she surprised him with the knife."

"Who else the cops questioning?"

"Everyone they sees on the road."

"They take anybody else in?"

"Don't think. Nobody knows where Bonnie is."

"The cops knows now. I'm after telling them she's at the hospital."

"That's where she's at, with your mother? Good one. Never thought of that. By the way, word's out about your mother's operation. And it weren't me or Skeemo, you got that?"

"Yeah. Sorry."

"Arse."

"Me today, you tomorrow."

"Yeah. Always somebody wagging their chin. Joanie Jenkins was in visiting her mother and seen Andrew Stride in there. He works in X-rays or something. You can't keep nothing here, bud."

"Yeah, well, that's it now."

"Anyway, buddy, listen. I got something to tell you, all right? Fuck." Hooker blew out a hot breath of air. He reached for the shot of whisky that wasn't there. *"Anybody working in this hole?"* he yelled at the bartender.

"Calm 'er down, bud. What's going on?"

Hooker fixed his eyes on the drink the bartender was pouring. He reached for it as the bartender landed it none too gently before him. He took a gulp, calling for two more.

Kyle's mouth went dry. "What's the matter? What's going on?"

Hooker took another gulp. Something softer than a spring leaf touched Kyle's hand. Julia. Touching his hand goodbye as she was passing with her pool chum. Her eyes the glistening grey of wet beach rocks.

"I haven't told one cock-sucking soul about this," said Hooker. He leaned towards Kyle, speaking quietly. "The second I tells you, it's gone, got it? Out the window. Got it?"

"Got it."

"Good, then. The night of the killing, I found Syl down on

Hampden Wharf in his truck, parked next to Clar's. He was soaked from the waist down. He was in the water that night."

Kyle nodded. He remembered waking up on the wharf, his father standing there, his pants damp, stiff. "So? So, what? Perhaps he pissed himself. You think of that, he pissed himself?"

"His boots were soaked. A horse couldn't piss that much. He was in the water. It don't mean nothing. He was drunk, staggered on the beach into the water or something."

"That's what he done then—went for a piss and staggered. Fell into the water. Or perhaps he heard something and tried to see. It was foggy. Leaned too far and staggered—anything could've happened. I mean, did anybody see him?"

"Haven't heard nothing. Might be nobody seen him. She was thick, buddy, the fog was thick, but she was thinning in spots. I drove down, could see a bit with the fog lights on."

"How come you were there?"

"Word circled the bar Clar punched you out. I went looking and seen both trucks parked on the wharf. Syllie's was running—likely he was trying to dry off. He was out of it. Empty forty-ouncer beside him. He never spoke, his eyes were open, but it was like he was comatose. Can't figure how he drove, drunk as he was. Unless he got drunk while he was there. I parked my truck and got in his and drove him up to the gravel flat hoping Kate had her fire going and you'd be there. Kate said you'd just left. I had a beer with her and left Syllie sleeping in the truck. Kate said she'd keep an eye on him." Hooker opened his mouth to say more, hesitated.

"What?"

"I ain't never going to say this agin, you got that?"

"Just say it."

"He said something about Clar being dead."

"Jesus."

"He didn't do it."

"Jesus. Jesus, fuck."

"It don't mean nothing. Syllie ain't got it in him. I'm only telling you because you should know that, and it don't mean dick, but I thought you should know it."

"What, then? What the fuck, then?"

"Think about it. Clar was on your wharf. If Syl done it, he wouldn't have got aboard his truck and drove down to Hampden Wharf and parked by Clar's. Unless he was wanting to get caught. In which case he would've just phoned the cops himself. Said it was self-defence or something. And if he followed him along the beach and done it, he wouldn't have come back to his truck and passed out there. Not if you killed somebody. Naw!" Hooker was shaking his head. "Syl wouldn't knife nobody. He hasn't got it in him. And it don't matter dick what I seen because I just forgot it. If anybody else seen, they'd be yakking before now. All right, buddy? We got it forgot, all right?"

The old-timers in the corner scraped back their chairs, their cards a mess on the table, hollering to the bartender to tally up.

"Right, buddy?"

Kyle nodded.

"Right, then. Let's do some figuring." He inched his stool closer to Kyle. "Clar parked on Hampden Wharf. He's figuring nobody can see because of the fog. He climbed around the cliff to your wharf—for what? What was he up to? This was after punching you out. Must be Syllie he was after. Why else would he go to your wharf?"

Bonnie Gillard. He was after Bonnie Gillard, not his father. Kyle opened his mouth but closed it again. They weren't his words to speak. They were his mother's.

"Your mother—did she see anything?"

"She got too much going on."

"Yeah, sorry. She's all right, is she?"

"Yeah. She's going to be fine. Look, I gotta go. See to the old man."

"I'll give you a ride."

"Appreciate it, but I'll walk. One thing: Kate coming up with an alibi for all of us that night. Was that your doing?"

"We both come up with it. Next morning I was up to your house before the cops came. And you and Syl were already gone. I talked to Kate—didn't tell her about Syl being on the wharf or anything. Just that he was drunk behind the wheel and we both come up with the story. She said she was going down Beaches for a drive and would fill you in. Which was good because the cops showed up right after I left, talking to her. Then they hauled me over by the post office—picking up a parcel for Mom—and I seen Kate driving past. On her way to tell ye what we worked out." Hooker grinned, proud of himself.

"Lying to the police. You don't need that kinda trouble, Hooker."

"None coming. Syl was drunk and passed out behind the bar. I drove him home."

"Right. And Kate—why's she lying? Why's everybody lying to the cops about the old man?"

"Because Syllie got enough going on. He don't need extra shit. And we understands what the cops won't." His voice dropped. The old-timers were shuffling to the bar now, arguing about who owned the last round.

"What's ye hooligans cahootin' now?" one of them asked.

"Mind your own beeswax," snipped Hooker.

"I'll be going," said Kyle. "See you later, bud."

"Sure. Hey, Ky?"

"What's up?"

Hooker took on a pained look, then shook his head. "Nothing. Go on."

"Let it out."

"It's stupid. Too fucking stupid."

"Can handle something stupid right now."

"Forget it."

"Spit it out, b'y, what's going on?"

Hooker shrugged, wiped at his mouth. "Fucking Roses."

"What about her. What, I gotta choke it outta you?"

"I think she likes you."

Kyle sank back on his stool.

"I knows you're not after her, man—don't get me wrong—aw, told you this was stupid. It's just—I dunno. The way she was fawning over you at the dance."

"You nuts? You fucking nuts?"

"Yeah, I'm nuts."

"She's playing you, fool!"

"Yeah, I know. I know. Aw, hell, this is bad."

"Yeah, it's bad. You're getting soft, all right? Soft in the head."

"I hates my head. Hates my fucking head."

Kyle slapped Hooker's shoulder. "It's all right, buddy. Women does that to you. All right? I gotta go."

"Sure, you go. See to your old man. You knows where I am, right?"

"Take 'er easy, hey."

"I loves you, man."

Kyle thumped Hooker's back and followed the last of the old-timers out the door. The moon was out and a smattering of stars. He looked over at his father's truck. *He was soaked. He was in the water. He knew Clar was dead.* He started walking. End of the road he turned left up Bottom Hill and crested the top and started down the other side. He was tired, bone tired. The moon offered scant light on the underbrush crowding the roadside and he judged from habit the opening to the shortcut and started down the choked path, to hell with squeamish fears. A smell of rot and he more felt than saw the ground sinking away to his right and the charred flooring of the Trapps' burned-out sawmill, the smut-blackened skeleton of a corner post rising like a crucifix over some apocalyptic ruin. A loose piece of wood dangled from a half-collapsed beam like a charred effigy, its creaking in the stirred air sending chills down his neck. The path steepened, trees walling each side. He grasped at prickly branches, easing his way down, and was soon breaking through the woods behind his house.

The windows were unlit. He crept along the side. A gull cried out, its shadow fluttering across the lemon track of the moon over the sea. Wavelets fretted against the piles. Something shuffled down on the beach rocks and he drew back, near yelping as a black shape leapt onto the wharf. Clar's dog. Eyes burning yellow with moonlight. It stood staring at him, head down, tail down, whining deep in his throat.

"Go," Kyle ordered in a throaty whisper. "Get home."

The dog whimpered and flopped on all fours, looking up at him like a dejected child. Kyle crept towards the front of the house, pricking his ears. Drafts of wind snatched at the yellow ribbon that flickered like candlelight amongst the shadows. No cop cars. But he'd take no chances. Slipping to the back of the house, he hissed at the whining dog again to get home. He pushed open the window to Sylvie's room, remembering too late his bruised ribs and near crying out as he levered himself across the sill. Dropping onto the floor, he picked himself up and slipped off his boots so's not to soil his mother's clean floors, and then cursed as he stepped into a puddle of water.

"She'll shoot you," he said, walking down the hall. "What, you couldn't kick off your boots?"

His father was sitting by the window at the kitchen table, a cigarette burning in the ashtray, his lungs rattling like a croupy youngster's. He was looking out over the water, his face carved in ridges by moonlight.

"We'll be thrown in jail if we gets caught in here." Kyle hauled out a chair and sat beside him. "She come through it fine. She was sitting up when I left, ordered me to drive home and take care of you."

"When's she coming home?"

"Another day or two. They don't keep them long these days. She got them tubes in her. We'll go see her in the morning."

His father lifted his smoke to his mouth, scorched tobacco burning red through the dark.

Kyle jiggled his foot. "You're going to see her, right?" His father's collar chafed against his neck. He supposed it was a nod. "Get the footings finished today?"

"Ready for pouring. Harvey Rice gave us a hand. Some of the boys."

"Good, then. They said they might. You had a time of it then. In Deer Lake with the police?"

"Doing their job, I suppose."

"They talked about the blood on the doorknob, right? What did you tell them?"

"Nothing."

"It was mine from where Clar hit me. Loosened a tooth or something. I drooled over my hand when I was sleeping and must've got it on the doorknob."

Sylvanus butted out his smoke.

"I seen Bonnie Gillard here that night. Sitting here and talking with Mother."

He felt his father stiffen. "When was that?"

"Before you got home."

"What else did you see?"

"Nothing. That's it. Was she still here when you got home?"

Sylvanus pulled another smoke from his pack resting on the table. His hand was shaking. He struck a match, an awful light burning in his eyes. He took a deep suck and hacked, smoke skittering from his mouth. Kyle gnawed on his thumb. His father was frightened, he could smell it like dung from a horse. *How did you know Clar was dead, why were you in the water . . .*

"So, was she?"

"Hey?"

"I asked if Bonnie was still here when you got home."

"Never seen her. You?"

"I told you, she was sitting here with Mother. What the fuck's wrong with you?"

"That's it now."

"That's it now, what?"

Sylvanus took a deep drag on his smoke. Kyle shifted with unease. Felt like he was sitting with an unyielding stranger before a forced supper.

"So, you never seen her?"

"What was she doing?"

"When I seen her? Nothing. She was bawling. Mother had her by the shoulders, like she was shaking sense in her. I think she did it."

"Who?"

"Bonnie. Who the fuck do you think?"

Sylvanus butted out his half-smoked cigarette and rose.

"Hold on, brother, we needs to talk," said Kyle.

"Go to bed."

"No, we don't go to bed, we've got to talk." Kyle was on his feet, chasing after his father who was heading for his bedroom. "Look at this!" He'd pulled the keys to Bonnie's car out of his pocket and dangled them now in front of his father. But it was too dark to see. "Bonnie's car keys. I found her car half in the river in past the old park ground. Not long after she left here. Either Clar got her car from her somehow and tried to get rid of it or she was trying to off herself. What do you think? I happened to see it when I was walking to the bar, after I left you in the shed. Keys still in the ignition."

Sylvanus touched the keys. "You tell that to the police?"

"No. I never told nobody, for Mother's sake. I'm thinking Mother's covering for her. I think she tried to off herself and couldn't do it and then come here bawling to Mother about it. I'd like to know when Clar was killed—the timing of it. What do you think?"

"Less we knows the better, I think. Go to bed, now."

"Hold on. Jesus, old man." His father had gone into his room. "Dad?" The room door closed. "Dad, we need to talk."

The bedsprings groaned beneath his father's weight. Kyle stood there, listening. Fighting the urge to push open the door and go kneel by his father's bed and ask straight out what the hell he was doing in the water that night and how did he know that Clar was dead. He lifted his hand to the doorknob, drew it back. He couldn't. Better he didn't know. Didn't want to know.

He went to the fridge, broke off a chunk of cheese, buttered a heel of bread and ate it, washing it down with cold tea from the pot his mother had made that morning. Felt like a fortnight ago. Finishing off the bread and cheese, he went to his room and fell across his bed, his body sinking beneath its own weight into the comfort of the mattress. His ribs ached. Silence ruled the house. The first night his mother wasn't in her bed.

SEVEN

—————

H e startled awake, a thump on his door. The room was dark. "Get dressed," his father called.

He hauled himself up. Christ. He was still wearing his clothes. He pushed open his door and smelled soap coming from the bathroom, his father already showered. It was morning. Jaysus.

He fished clean clothes from his drawers, showered, and then helped himself to the bacon and eggs his father had left for him in the pan. Sylvanus was sitting at his spot by the window.

"You want toast?" Kyle asked him.

"I'm done."

Kyle poured coffee and sat by his father, chewing a piece of toast, the two of them watching through the window as light broke through the eastern skyline. It spilled over the water and crept up the side of the wharf where the last remnants of night hung like sin over the gump where Clar Gillard had likely taken his last breath. Sylvanus shoved back his chair, his boots on, and pushed his arms through his coat as he peeked through the curtains by the front door.

"Leave through the back," said Kyle. He half rose, forking the bacon and eggs into his mouth. Then he drained his coffee cup and hauled on his coat, following his father down the hall. The *burr-ring* of the phone cut through the house. They both looked back. It rang again, its sound urgent in the morning quiet.

"Might be your mother."

Kyle went back, lifted the receiver and said *hello*. It was Sylvie. Her voice clear, as though she were standing next door.

"Ky? Are you there—can you hear me?"

His mother's words came to him. *It's fine she don't know, let her have her holiday.*

"Ky?"

"Hi Sylvie."

"How are you, bugger? How's everybody?"

"Fine. Where you at?"

"Some café in Stone Town. Zanzibar. How are things? Is Mom there?"

"No."

"Where is she then?"

He heard the change in her voice. She knew the time. Their mother would be home unless something was wrong.

"Ky? Where is she then?"

He looked to where his father stood in the doorway, head slightly raised, listening.

"Ky, what's wrong? Is something wrong?"

"She's in the hospital."

"The hospital—why? What's wrong with her?"

He hesitated. "Cancer," he said finally. "She has cancer, breast cancer." He felt a jab of satisfaction as he spoke the words. Then he heard her cry of fear and was sickened. "It's okay, she's fine," he quickly added. "It was a small lump and now it's gone. She don't want you coming home, she told us not to tell you. There's nothing you can do."

"They operated? Did they take off her breast? Ky, what did they do?"

"They—yes. They took off her breasts—"

"Breasts?"

He nodded. Then said yes out loud, feeling the sweat building on his upper lip. He glanced at his father again, who was looking at him with surprise. Sylvie's voice had fallen into the background with a wail and then Ben was on the phone.

"What's happening, what's going on, buddy?"

"Tell her Mom's fine. She'll be home in a couple of days. She didn't want Sylvie to know."

"Right. We're on the next flight out. Hang 'er tough." The line went dead.

Kyle cradled the receiver. He should have told her about Clar Gillard instead. He shouldn't have even answered the phone. "I shouldn't have told her," he said. "But I had to. Mother's not here— she would've figured out anyway that something was wrong, right?" He turned back to the doorway but Sylvanus was gone.

He hurried to the back room, climbed out the window, and started up the choked path after his father. Hearing a soft mewl, he looked back: Clar's dog was sitting on his haunches near the gump, staring after him. He turned from its grieving eyes and remembered Sylvie's those times she tried talking with him after the accident.

He walked fast past the rotting, stinking sawmill, thrusting through the night-wet brush and breaking out onto Bottom Hill with cold, wet knees. At the top of the hill he looked down upon the darkened windows of Hampden, at the yellow ribbon cordoning off the wharf and Clar's truck. He looked to the violet house, Julia's room window softly lit—he'd seen her leaning out of it once, blond hair streaming down like some mythical damsel.

He turned onto the dirt road leading to the bar, glimpsed his father's back vanishing over a rise. He topped the rise and dragged his feet as he neared the bar, remembering the night Sylvie came out through the barroom door to where he was standing, his back against a car. She was upset, telling him that Chris had bought a ticket to Alberta and wanted to fly out with her the next morning. *Why wouldn't he?* he'd wanted to shout at her. *Why wouldn't he when it's the path you showed him?* Chris came out of the bar a few moments later, his face twisted with a scared smile. He'd never seen Chris scared before. Never, ever. He beckoned Kyle to follow him home. Julia had come to the door and was watching after Chris too, hand pressing against her chest as though holding back a heart beating too hard.

Sylvanus was sitting in the truck now, waiting. Kyle climbed in behind the wheel, switched on the ignition, and started them towards the highway. He looked at his father whose hands were gripping his knees and not the more accustomed whisky bottle. His face was sullen and hard. Whatever remnants of the tender, mischievous man Kyle had known as a boy, and that might have survived Chris's death, were gone now. Shed like old skin since the night of the murder.

"Don't open your mouth to your mother about Sylvie calling," said Sylvanus.

"Good one. And when Sylvie shows up?"

"Too late for fretting then."

"Fine."

"Make sure you don't."

"Why would I blab?"

"You blabbed where Bonnie was."

"How'd you know that?"

"Your mother phoned last night. The cops were after being there, talking to Bonnie."

"Right. They wasted no time."

"Surprised they never found her before now."

And you, do they know about you being in the water . . .

They spoke no more. At the hospital Sylvanus walked down the ward a step behind Kyle. Steel trolleys squeaked past. Slippered feet. Pale faces watching from doorways. A nurse with a tray of silver instruments rushed out of his mother's room and behind her a stout old priest with a sprinkle of dandruff on his black-clad shoulders. Kyle stood aside and his father stepped into Addie's room, shoulders hunched as though he were heading into nasty weather. Kyle stepped in behind him. She was propped up with pillows, eyes closed, face unnaturally pale. Bonnie was leaning over her, speaking softly, fingers assured as she fixed something into place on that bandaged chest—the tubes, no doubt. She pulled down the coverlet and he and his father hauled back from the doorway, their faces taut as drawn elastic.

Bonnie saw them standing there and patted Addie's hand. "You've got company, my love."

Addie opened her eyes and Kyle saw in them her fatigue and then her worry as she took in theirs.

"We're doing fine," he said too quickly and thumped his father's back, jolting him farther into the room. "He couldn't get here fast enough."

"I can see that," said Addie, her voice surprisingly clear. She smiled, raising a bony wrist encircled by an ID bracelet. "Well come in, sit."

"Sit here, Syllie," said Bonnie, indicating the chair behind her. "I'll go get some coffee. Can I bring back something?"

Sylvanus shook his head and took the chair. Kyle gave her a scant glance and sat at the foot of his mother's bed.

"She's been a godsend," said Addie.

"Good," said Kyle. He looked at his father, who muttered something too guttural to be understood. Then they both looked at Addie—her IV, the bandaged chest beneath the blankets. Their eyes fell, landlubbers on seas they couldn't fathom.

"Sylvie called," blurted Sylvanus. Kyle snapped him a look of surprise.

"My, how is she?" asked Addie. "You didn't tell her, I hope." Sylvanus looked to Kyle.

"Kyle?"

"Well, uh—"

"My, Kyle, you knows you didn't tell her."

"Now, Addie," said Sylvanus as she tried to come forward on her pillow.

"I had no choice," said Kyle. "But I told her you were fine and that you said not to come."

She lay back, disappointment soaking her face.

"Well, what the frig was I supposed to say? She asked for you. And it was six this morning. She'd know something was up if you weren't home."

"Jackson's Arm," said Addie tiredly. "You could have said I was down Jackson's Arm. With my sister." Her eyes came more awake. "You didn't tell anybody else?"

"No. Nobody knows. Only that you got stuff going on."

"Thank God for that. I'm surprised they're not all here. I couldn't stand it if they were."

"Might be nice, having your sisters here," said Sylvanus.

"I wants nobody around me, times like this. I'll not argue it, Sylvanus. Is Sylvie coming home? You told her not to come, I hope?"

"That's what I told her, not to come," said Kyle. "I never thought about your sisters—never come to me. And he never offered nothing." He looked accusingly at his father, who was sitting like a lump. He tried to avoid his mother's eyes. She was watching him, watching his face too close, and he fumbled for more words to defend or apologize and couldn't think why he'd want to do either.

"Go. To the cafeteria," she said. "And buy Bonnie breakfast. Will you do that for me?" Her tone was quiet with disappointment and he rose irritably to his feet. She hadn't always felt so protective about Sylvie; they used to fight like dogs, she and Sylvie. *Always sneaking around, your sister is, like she's trying to catch me stealing from her,* Addie would complain, and Sylvie would whine to him in turn, *Always looks like she's the one who's snooping.*

It's because they're just alike that they fights, his father told him. It's because she don't love me, Sylvie whispered. They're too close to pick it apart, my baby, dear old Gran told him as he fed vanilla ice cream into her gummy mouth. And then they did pick it apart, his mother and Sylvie. On the oil-drunken earth of Alberta over the broken bones of Chris. The day Sylvie left for those oilfields and took Chris with her, their mother went into a silence so cold it froze her face. He understood then that Chris was her favourite and that they'd fought because Sylvie wanted to be. When his mother flew off to bring back Chris's body he'd thought she'd return home alone. He remembered again that moment when his mother stepped off the plane, holding Sylvie's hand. They reached for him, his mother and sister, with those strong joined hands, Chris a mangled shadow in their eyes. And he had run from them both.

Everything smelled like boiled cabbage inside the cafeteria. Bonnie was sitting to the other side of an open counter displaying fruit and green Jell-O. She was holding a cup of coffee and looking out the window. His irritation grew. He poured himself a coffee and went to her table. She didn't see him coming, caught, as she appeared to be, in her thoughts or the washed-out image of herself in the window. The corners of her mouth drooped, striking a picture of utter sadness, and it irked him further. Everything about her irked him. He hated that she'd placed herself like the angel Gabriel at his mother's bedside.

He pulled her keys from his pocket and laid them on the table before her. She drew back, startled. He thought she'd get sick she turned so pale.

"Found your car."

She took a minute and then raised her eyes to his. He was surprised by their calm.

"I told the police where to find you," he said when she didn't speak. "I'll tell them about the car, too, if you don't tell me what's going on."

She gave a half-hearted shrug, then looked back out the window with the apathy of a traveller who's known too many dead-end roads.

"Who put it there?"

"I'll not talk about it."

"Yeah, you will. You got my mother caught up in this."

He sat across from her and she looked at him, examining his face with a remote curiosity.

"Best you tell me what's going on before I talks to the police."

"I'm not asking this for me."

"Bullshit. It's not just Mother you got dragged into this." He pointed at the keys. "I'm concealing evidence now. Either you talk or I talk."

She lowered her head, rubbing at her temples. Then looked back at him. "Would you keep it quiet for a while?"

"I can't say that."

"I needs a few more days of quiet. God knows, they got enough to talk about."

"What happened after you left our house?"

"Promise you'll tell no one. Least, till your mother gets released. I don't want the police coming here while your mother's recovering."

"You'll not bargain my mother with me no more."

She gave him the bemused look of a wearied parent. "What's that mean?"

"I seen you sitting at the table with Mother that night."

She sat forward. "You best keep that to yourself."

"Tell me what happened."

"When you swears to keep your mouth shut. Else I'm gone home and you can sit with your mother, helping her through this." Her eyes were fixed on his, her mouth so tightly pressed it would've taken a crowbar to pry it open. "Right, then," she said to his slight nod. She settled back, facing her reflection. "He was waiting halfways up Bottom Hill. He was parked crooked. And he was hanging out the door—head near touching the ground. What do you know, I fell for it. Thought he'd had a heart attack or something. So I got out of the car and ran to him. And he grabbed me by the arm and that was it. He had me."

"What did he do?"

"Threw me back inside my car." She rubbed her forehead. He noted a bruising beneath her hairline.

"Then what?"

"My head hit the dash. Stunned me. He drove us hard through the park. Couldn't get my balance, he kept hitting me." She folded her arms, hugged herself. "And he tried to drive us into the river. Well, not himself." She gave a tight grin. "Only me."

"He was trying to drown you?"

"He wasn't thinking about a car wash."

"How did you get out?"

"He got out first. My door was against a tree. He started rocking the car—the river was right there, a foot away. I was screaming. I seen the water starting to hit against the front of it. Then I remembered the second set of keys. I always carry a second set—not the first time he stole my car. I got them in the ignition and lowered the back right window. He was still rocking the car. I climbed into the back seat and out the window— he must've seen me. The car was still rocking when I hit the ground and I just up and started running through the alders. He never chased me. He can only take it so far." This last was added in a quiet tone.

"So far?"

She nodded. "Then he comes to himself. Sin. Sin he got to do things like that."

"Sin? He tries to drown you and you feels sorry for him?"

She stretched her little finger towards the keys, caressing the cut edging with a nail more chewed than his, then scooped them off the table, dropping them into her purse.

"Well, then? Why? Why would you feel sorry for him?"

She shrugged. "Who wouldn't? He never had nothing, did he? Money. His parents had money. Least we had love." This last word a whisper, as though it weren't hers to speak. She looked to him defensively. "Dad might be a drunk but he's a nice drunk. Cries over the scriptures when mother reads them. Kneeled with us every night when we said our prayers. Not what you wants to hear about Jack Verge, is it?" she asked him, and he flushed like a snoop caught at the door. "Don't feel bad. Not what anybody wants to hear. That's why I feels sorry for Clar. Nobody listened to his prayers. There was a hole where his heart should've been."

He tried to turn from her, but couldn't, a horrid fascination grow-ing with her words. Her eyes were dark, murky, stoked with grief. He sat back, shifted his glance around the cafeteria, looked back to her.

"So why'd you leave it there? Your car. How come you didn't get somebody to haul it out?"

"I'm after telling you, they all got enough to talk about for a while. Can't believe no one's seen it yet but you. Tell the truth, I don't know if I ever wants to see it again." She lifted her purse off the chair and rose.

"What were you doing back at our house that night?"

"Needed someone to tell it to."

She started across the cafeteria and he followed. "Just a second. The police said you were in the truck with the old man that night."

"Syllie picked me up on Bottom Hill, gave me a ride to Bay-side. That's right, to Clar's place. Imagine that." She stepped through the cafeteria doors, but then drew back. "One of us got company."

His stomach kicked. Constables Wheaton and Canning were coming through the foyer. They paused at the sight of Kyle and Bonnie and then started towards them, smiling like two chums pleasantly surprised on their way to supper.

"Say nothing to them about Father being here," Kyle said to Bonnie. He nodded politely as the constables stood before him.

"We'd like your company back at the station, Mr. Now," said Canning. "You'll excuse us, ma'am?"

"Yes, I will," she said. And then stepped boldly before them. "And the next time you wants to talk to me, phone up to the room and I'll meet you outside. Don't barge in upsetting Mrs. Now like you done the last time."

"Roger that, ma'am." Wheaton touched his finger to his hat. She lifted her chin with a sniff. She walked away, Kyle watching with a deepening sense of her unfamiliarity.

"Hey," he called to her, expecting her to snip *Hay's for horses.*
He held out the truck keys as she turned. "Best do mother's shop-
ping for her. Tell her I'm gone home with one of the boys, checking on the cement." She took the keys, and with another snooty
look at the policemen, strode off.

"Ready, Mr. Now?"

———————

At the police station he was ushered into a smaller room than
before, asked to sit in one of the two wooden chairs, and then
left alone with the door ajar. He got up and paced, his stomach churning like an agitator in an old washing machine. A
door opened and closed down the hall. A phone rang, a woman
snapped hello and then cradled it noisily. A babble of voices grew
near, paused outside his doorway, and went quiet. He resisted the
urge to peek out.

Keep calm, he ordered himself. What do you know? What do
you *not* want them to know? Think about what you've already told
them, tell them what Kate said: eleven-thirty-five p.m. She picked
him up at eleven-thirty-five p.m. and he sat at her fire and Hooker
drove his father up to Kate's around midnight and then he went
home and before that his father was passed out in the truck behind
the bar all evening. That's all he knew. That's all he'd say.

Sergeant MacDuff hurried into the room with a file under his
arm. "Kyle," he said warmly. "How's your mother?"

"Sends her regards."

"Nice woman. Sorry about her troubles. We'll make this
fast—I imagine you're wanting to get back." He wore glasses this
time, with heavy frames that kept slipping down his nose. He kept
pushing them back up and grunting irritably.

"Lost my contacts," he said conversationally.

Kyle looked past him for Wheaton and Canning, but Mac-Duff was closing the door. He sat, pulled some papers from the file, and crinkled his eyes reading them. "Right. Right, a few things here. Right." He looked at Kyle over the rims of his glasses. "Kate Mackenzie. How well do you know her?"

"We've shared a few beers."

MacDuff went back to his notes. "Says here she showed up in Hampden about a year ago. What does she do there?"

"Not much. She plays guitar. Sings nice songs. Writes them herself."

"Where did she come from?"

"Never said."

"Never said?"

"No."

"Strange, don't you think?"

"Never thought about it."

"A stranger walks into town. Buys the shack next door and sets up house and shares nothing of herself with her neighbours. You don't question that?"

"Actually, it's a nice cabin."

"How does she support herself?"

"Never asked."

"You curious?"

"Nope."

"Outport folks are pretty friendly. They like knowing who lives next door. Don't you think it curious when a stranger picks a small, friendly place to live a private life?"

"You're thinking Clar Gillard tipped his hat to all hands strolling about, sir? Jaysus! Should meet Uncle Jake sometime. He'd rather see you drowning than swimming. Aunt Trude

Pynn hasn't stepped through her front door in fifty years. Cousin Max likes dragging his nail clippers down his sister's back. Kinda makes Kate read like a well-flipped comic book. And the next time you're driving through, say howdy to the teachers and the minister and the doctor and old Mr. Stonehouse down Fox Point—all come-from-aways who keeps their curtains closed and door locked from sun-up to sundown. Stop reading them tourist books, Mr. MacDuff. Ain't nuttin' strange about a city girl comin' to roost along shore."

MacDuff's face drooped into humourless lines.

"Darn, now I made you sad."

MacDuff pulled off his glasses and wiped patiently at his eyes.

"I come from an outport of twelve houses, Kyle. And six of 'em didn't talk to the other. Squid rolled, capelin struck, and we grew up on crabs, not lobsters. And strangers never cruised into town and bought a shack and lived there year-round without a reason to." He put his glasses back on and sharpened his smile. "Kate Mackenzie. She was seen with Bonnie Gillard in her car the night of the killing. What do you know about that?"

"Nothing."

"Had you known they were together that night?"

"No."

"Later that night when Kate Mackenzie picked you up walking home, did she say anything about Bonnie Gillard?"

"No."

"What was Kate Mackenzie wearing?"

"Hey?"

"That night she picked you up, what was she wearing?"

"What was she *wearing*? How the fuck would I know?"

"Think, Kyle, the night of the killing, she picked you up."

"Eleven-thirty-five p.m."

"What was she wearing?"

"I don't remember."

"Was she wearing clothes?"

"Yes, sir. She was wearing clothes. Dark clothes."

"Coat?"

"It was dark."

"And yet you noted the time."

"Eleven-thirty-five. The clock was lit on the dash. Right in front of me."

MacDuff rapped the table with the gentle knuckle of an old uncle. "Think for a minute, Kyle. Her hands were on the wheel. Was she wearing mitts or gloves?"

"I never noticed."

"What were you wearing?"

"Jeans, T-shirt, coat."

"That was fast recall."

"Except for funerals, weddings, and swimming, it's all I wears."

"Were you wearing gloves?"

"No, sir."

"Mitts?"

"No, sir."

"What was your father wearing?"

"Jeans. T-shirt inside a button-down shirt and heavy jacket."

"Mitts?"

"Doubt it."

"Why's that?"

"Don't wear them in snowstorms, doubt he'd be wearing them in springtime."

"When your father came home that night, where were you?"

"Outside the house—sleeping by the gump."

"What time did he get home?"

"Twelve-thirty. Or, forty, thereabouts."

"How do you know the time he come home if you were asleep?"

"He woke me up. And we went inside and I noticed the clock lit up on the stove."

"Who opened the door?"

"What—I don't know, who the hell cares?"

"Who opened the door, Kyle?"

"I did. I opened the fucking door."

"You swear to that?"

"If I was on the stand I might."

"You want us to put you on the stand?"

"I swear to it, all right? I opened the door."

"Might he have opened it before you woke up? Found you missing and went looking for you?"

"Doubt it."

"Why?"

"Because I'm potty trained, sir. He don't come into my room during the night no more."

"The blood on your hand. When you woke up you said you had blood on your hand. Where did the blood come from?"

"Yeah, I think we covered that. Clar clocked me in the jaw. He broke a tooth through the inside."

"Can I see?"

"Uh?"

MacDuff leaned forward, peering at Kyle's mouth. "Open it. Let me see."

Kyle flicked the inside of his jaw. There never had been a cut, and his lip hadn't been cut either. Must've been a sore gum or something that had bled.

"Sorry. It's gone."

"Gone?"

"Healed."

"You cut your jaw three nights ago and it's healed?"

"What, you never gargled honey for a cut jaw? Amazing healing properties. And yes, sir, I know this ain't no fool's game, but my jaw was cut and you had your chance to see it but you turned it down. And now it's healed. What more can I do for you?"

"Somebody got murdered on your turf, Kyle. We need to know who did it."

"*You* need to know who did it. I don't give a fuck. The man was an arse."

"An arse. Right." MacDuff took off his glasses, laid them on his notes, and wiped at his eyes again. He got up as if to shake himself awake, circling behind Kyle. "Murdering an arse will net you thirty years, Kyle. Was your mouth bleeding before you went to sleep?"

"I woke up drooling. I drooled blood from a cut jaw."

"Who opened your front door to let you into your house the night Clar Gillard struck you?"

"I opened the door."

"Where was your father?"

"Behind me."

"Did you see the blood on your hand before you opened the door?"

"Yes. When I woke up I seen the blood on my hand."

"Did you wipe it off?"

"No, seen the old man standing there and never thought no more about it. What's the fucking big deal?" He twisted sideways, unnerved by MacDuff standing so close behind him that he could hear his breathing scratching past his nose hairs.

"Think back, think back to that night. You were sleeping. You woke up and your father was standing there. What did he do?"

"He done nothing."

"If he done nothing, he'd still be standing there. What did he do?"

"Christ." Kyle dragged his hands down his face, trying to think.

"You stood up. What next?"

"What next?"

"Think back."

Think back—think back—he was lying under the tarp, he pulled himself up and got the spins. Near fell off the wharf. His father caught hold of his arm, led him to the door. And opened it. His father. His father opened the door.

"What do you remember, Kyle?"

"The dog. The dog was there, whining. Drives me nuts, that fucking dog. I got up, pushed past the old man and opened the door and went inside. Now can you tell me what the fuck got you hooked on *who* opened the door?"

"It was Clar Gillard's blood that was on your doorknob."

The words reverberated like eddies from a dropped rock. Two thoughts surfaced, one following the other and each grappling for his mind. He hadn't felt fear before because he hadn't done it and there was safety in that. And Bonnie Gillard. She hadn't shown fear either; when the cops had accosted them back at the hospital she hadn't been afraid. She didn't do it. Bonnie Gillard didn't kill Clar. That thought suckered like a leech onto his brain whilst another slipped from some distant mooring and sank cold in his heart. *He was in the water, he knew Clar was dead, he opened the door that night, and Clar Gillard's blood was on the knob. It was his father. It was his father who killed Clar Gillard and his mother was covering for him and Bonnie Gillard was covering for them both.*

"What's going on, Kyle?" MacDuff's voice was like an ice pick chipping at his neck. Sweat started down his forehead, and as it trickled onto his lashes he raised his eyes and saw the black nose of a camera tucked behind the door facings. They were watching him. They were watching him up close and he smelled his own fear like a bloodhound smells supper.

He got up and faced MacDuff. "Nothing's going on. I didn't kill the bastard and it don't matter who did, they done humanity a favour. Ask his ex-wife what he done to her. Tied her to a chair and sprayed her with oven cleaner. How's that for a sick bastard?"

"You think she killed him?"

"Da fuck you care what I think? What do *you* think?"

"I think there's a lot of secrets going around, Kyle. And we think you know some of them. Like, how did Clar Gillard's blood get on your doorknob?"

"He was up to no good, is why. He was on our wharf. Likely he tried the door."

"Was it locked?"

"No. It's never locked."

"Then why didn't he go in?"

"Maybe he seen through the window I wasn't there. What the hell do I know?"

"Clar Gillard already punched you in the jaw. Why would he be waiting at your door for you to return?"

"You're asking *me* why Clar Gillard would do something? He was nuts. Maybe he wanted to clock me agin. Maybe he thought I was dicking his girlfriend."

"Maybe he thought your father was?"

"Even Clar Gillard knows the difference. Tell you what. If any of them secrets come to mind, I'll give you a call. Right now I got nothing you don't already know. Mind if I leave now? There's cement waiting to be poured and I'll not say no more till I got a lawyer. Unless you're going to charge me with murder, I'll be on my way."

It was instinct, not balls, that made him say that. If they thought it was him, they wouldn't be wasting their time questioning him about others. He went for the door. He waited for Mac-Duff to order him back, half wishing he would. He twisted the knob, went out, and started down the hall. No footsteps came after him, no one hollered for him to come back. He took the wrong hallway, walked past a receptionist behind a glass partition and two scrawny teens sitting outside, sneer-like smiles as they waited for roll call. Another short hall and he was in the foyer and then outside, legs trembling, hands dug into his pockets, shoulders hunched against a chilled wind.

EIGHT

H e crossed the highway and stuck out his thumb, heading
west towards Corner Brook. Sylvanus would still be there,
sitting with his mother, and he needed his father, he needed bad
to see him.

A green Chevy drove past, heading east towards Hampden. It
honked, pulled over, and the window lowered. Ambrose Rice,
Ben's father. Kyle hopped back across the highway and ran towards
the car. A dark grizzled head poked through the passenger side
window. Suze, Ben's mother.

"Recognize that muck of hair anywhere," she called out. "Just
like your father."

"How's she going, Suze? What're you up to, buddy?" he asked
Ambrose, lowering his head to better see him.

"Get in," said Suze, "we gives you a ride. Your mother would
have a copper kitten if she knows you're hitchhiking."

"Thanks, but I'm on my way to Corner Brook."

"Then we'll drive back to Corner Brook. We were just visiting with your mother. Imagine that now, she keeping all this to
herself and your poor old father going along with it."

"Yeah, I gotta go see him, you guys go on, now."

"Your father's on his way out," said Ambrose. "Said he had to check on you and the boys with the cement."

"He's on his way out? You're sure?" Kyle straightened, looking back down the highway.

"That's what he said then—might already be ahead of us. Had to pick up some things for Addie in the drugstore."

"I'll take a ride home, then." Kyle squeezed into the back seat amidst a pile of stuffed grocery bags and tried to focus on Suze's yakking as Ambrose hauled them back onto the highway behind an eighteen-wheeler screaming past.

". . . he got some lot on his mind now, your father do. Hardly spoke all while we were there and that's not like Syllie, hey Am? And to think, not one of you calling me about your mother. But that's Addie—always to herself. Never knew a thing till Roger Nichols showed up from Corner Brook yesterday, looking for a box of crab legs. And I blames you, too," she said, twisting sideways, grey eyes snapping back at Kyle.

He mumbled something apologetically and Ambrose winked at him in the rearview mirror and he kept seeing his father opening the house door that night, *Clar Gillard's blood on the doorknob.*

". . . and what's Bonnie Gillard doing there? Motioning me outside your mother's room and telling me to say nothing about your house being taped off and all that. Like I was going to barge into Addie's room and bring it up. Near bit me tongue off. It's Bonnie Gillard herself what's worrying me. All that stuff going on and she acting like she don't have a care in the world. They says she done it. That's the word down home. I hope she's not bringing her troubles onto your mother because that crowd can suck blood from a turnip, they can. Drains the energy right outta me just looking at the mess around her father's doorplace. Jack Verge.

Not fit. And he the first one up every morning, then, with the smoke coming from his chimney so's everyone thinks how hard-working he is. Stun thing. Most likely he's not gone to bed yet. Still sitting and drinking at the breakfast table. And your poor father! Sitting by your mother's bedside and holding her hand like she was his young sweetheart . . ."

. . . next morning his father wouldn't drink, had thrown that bottle of booze out through the truck window . . .

"And that Kate what's her name—you know her, Kylie? Sidling off down the hospital hall with Bonnie Gillard—"

"Kate was there?"

"Like thieves they were. You wonders what's so important they stole off like that, having their chat and your poor mother watching after them, right concerned."

"What were they talking about?"

"I never heard—they kept far enough to themselves, whispering like two crooks. Where we taking you, my love? You can't go home. How long they going to keep your house sealed off? And where's your mother going to go when she gets out of the hospital—and Sylvie?"

"Don't know. We'll figure it out." He shut out Suze's prattling and stared out the window at the passing belt of green. The clouds parted, a shaft of sun striking gold through the trees. Winter finally ending and yet here he sat, paining like an arthritic limb before the mother of all storms about to descend. And for the first he could remember he felt like something adrift, no pier to tether himself to.

"Look. Look there," Suze cried out. Sitting on the guardrail beside the junction turnoff to Hampden and Jackson's Arm, arms wrapped around himself for warmth, was Trapp. Skinny as old fuck and with ruffs of tawny hair clinging to a gaunt, pointy face. He rose as Ambrose braked, turning off the highway onto the

Hampden Road, and came towards the car. Glassy green eyes staring into Kyle's with such intensity that Kyle drew back.

"Don't you stop, don't you stop!" Suze was shrieking at Ambrose. "We're not giving him a ride, he can rot on that stump before I ever gives him another handout. Don't you stop, Am."

"You gone silly?" yelled Ambrose as Suze grabbed at the wheel. He sped up, pushing her aside, and Kyle looked back, watching Trapp staring after them. The same slump to his shoulders that he'd worn the second last time he'd seen him, sitting on the bank outside the bar and talking with Ben. Or, listening. Trapp hadn't been talking. Just slumped there, head hanging as though it were too heavy to hold up, and Ben, his arm wrapped around Trapp's shoulders, hugging him, hugging and talking hard and Trapp kept slumping further inside himself.

Suze's voice was rising unbearably. "He's heard Ben's coming home, that's why he's poking around now. He got poor Benji drove crazy, he have. Too bad it wasn't he that got shot and not his dog—"

"Sufferin' Jesus."

"I means it, yes, I do mean it, Am." She looked back at Kyle. "That's how it started, back when Trapp's dog bit Benji. And Benji always felt bad when that sick father of Trapp's shot the dog. He's still making up for it. And I don't care if Benji was teasing the dog—you can tease a dog and not have your leg bit off. And he was strange, Trapp was. And he's who caused your poor brother's death, too. Poor Chris. Don't shush me, Am. Benji told us enough. Trapp wasn't doing his job properly on the rig, too busy fighting with everybody, and then when he seen the rig about to blow—"

"Shut up!" yelled Ambrose. "Bloody well shut up. She don't know no such thing, Kyle."

"Benji told me straight."

"Ben was drinking and shouldn't been talking."

"And that's when the truth comes out, when liquor got your tongue."

"By Jesus, the devil must have yours, then. Blaming a man for something like that just because you don't like him."

"And what's the reason I don't like him? Because he's so nice? You must be foolish, my son, because the reason I don't like him is because he's an arse. Just like Benji said."

"Ben treats him like a brother."

"Brothers hate each other. Ask Cain." She twisted around back to Kyle again. "And your poor sister, wonder she never got killed, too. She was there, seen it all, she did. First one to his side, she was."

Kyle was opening his car door now. "Pull over, Am. Pull over." They'd just driven past Bayside and were coming upon Bottom Hill.

"I never meant to say anything. Oh, my, Kyle. He never suffered, it was too fast and he never suffered. Oh my, what have I got done now?"

Kyle was out of the car before Ambrose rolled to a stop. "Go on now, thanks for the lift. Don't worry," he said to Suze. "Go on now and we'll see you when Ben gets back." He started walking. Walking fast down Wharf Road. Walking fast from Suze—*your poor sister, seen it all, first one to his side* . . .

He hopped the yellow ribbon cordoning off his house and then went up to the door and stopped, staring in through the window. He saw them there, his mother, father, Chris, Sylvie—all of them. Their faces hung like ghosts around the empty kitchen. The yellow plastic ribbon *tic-ticced* in the gusting. He clasped his hands behind his head and walked in circles like a mangy dog. His father, he needed to see his father.

The tide was just starting in. He hopped off the wharf onto the scrap of beach and started climbing around the outcropping, grasping onto the cold granite rock, short-cutting it to Hampden.

He came to the ragged inlet that had cradled Clar. He wondered at the innocence of wavelets splashing and playing where Clar's sightless eyes had stared up at him. Then he sat, cupping his knees in his hands and seeing Chris's warm brown eyes full of light. He watched the seaweed floating on the water, watched again as it settled onto the vacant eyes of Clar Gillard, and wondered if light had ever entered those dark orbs or if he'd been a darkness even unto himself. Doing as he, Kyle, was doing. Fleeing down side roads and detours and never stopping to think that yesterday can never be fled, that its ills and thrills work hand in hand in shaping the morning's path.

The water started swelling into the inlet, the wavelets lapping a little too hard at his boots. He pushed himslef up from the rocks to leave and paused. Peered more closely towards the rugged back wall of the inlet. About six feet up, just above eye level. A little star within the crevice of a rock. Sunlight bouncing off steel. He found footing on a ledge and hoisted himself closer. He saw the handle of a knife, its blade buried. A knife used to fillet cod in the fish plants. His heart kicked with knowing—the knife that had ended Clar's life. Sure as hell, it was the knife. He leaned closer and his heart kicked harder and kept kicking, near rupturing his rib cage. It was *his* knife. Kyle's. The knife that his father always used. Nicked in the handle from where he, Kyle, had pinged his axe off it once.

Blood pounded in his ears. The water lapped harder at his boots. He looked madly around the inlet for somewhere to hide the knife. Why hadn't the cops found it? It was right there, easily seen. How hadn't they seen it?

Because it couldn't have been there. Couldn't. They would have seen it. Someone put it there. After the cops had finished searching, someone had returned and stuck in the knife. There hadn't been a storm. No wave could have flung the thing ashore and wedged it this high onto the rock. He looked up. It was a thirty-foot drop from the top of the cliff.

He pressed his hand against his still kicking heart. He extracted the knife and slid it down the inside of his coat sleeve, crooking his elbow to keep it in place. He climbed around the outcropping and onto the grey pebbly beach girdling Hampden, looking up at the houses against the wind-blown sky. A revved chainsaw ripped through the air, smell of cut birch. A missus hanging a mat over her clothesline. Another coming out of her basement with a load of splits. They both stopped, looking down at him, watched.

He bent his head, took a scuffed path through the weeds and up onto the road, coming face to face with the old fellow with the hitched-up pants and glasses. Dobey Randall. His eyes cut stark clear through his lenses at Kyle. They were poignant with knowing, as if he'd seen everything that had just happened. Kyle walked away from him, his step quickening with panic. He kept himself from breaking into a trot past a gathering of men and young boys on the wharf near Clar's ribboned-off truck. Their voices lowered as he passed. Felt like he was in a movie scene and all eyes were on him; the director would yell *Cut* any second now, everyone would break into chatter, all would be normal again. A rough voice called out.

"Your father working today, then?"

"He's in Corner Brook. How's she going, Pete, b'y?"

"Not bad. Your mother's good, then?"

"Yeah, she's good. You sees Father, tell him I'm down Beaches."

"Needing a hand down there?" asked Stan Hurley.

"Naw. Got the boys with me, Lyman and Wade."

"Give you a ride, I suppose."

"Naw, be someone along soon enough."

The knife slid down his arm, the tip pricking into his wrist. He gripped the cuff of his sleeve and straightened his arm. Heard a car coming down Hampden Hill. The shiny four-door manual Chevy, straight off the lot, bucked like a rabbit and choked to a stop alongside of him. Julia. Driving her father's new car. The passenger window rolled down. She lowered her head, staring scantways at him. Clear blue eyes, hair clamped in a messy bun, stray feathery strands tickling her face.

"Chance a ride?" she asked.

He got in, the knife sagging to the back of his sleeve. He dug his hand into his pocket and closed the door.

"Going down Beaches?" she asked.

"Yup. Yup, I am. How far you going?"

"All the way if you'd like."

He forced a smile to his stiff jaws. He held on to the door handle as she started the engine, rode the clutch too hard, stalled her.

"Self-taught?"

"Yup." Another twist at the ignition and the car vaulted forward, grinding first gear into a nub and then jumping into second and much too soon into third and they were bucking down the road. "Dad sees this, he'll kill me." She laughed. "But that's how he done it—stole his father's standard and learned on a hillside."

"We're riding a stolen car?"

"Borrowed. Not like he don't know by now. Half the outport's harping on the phone by now. *She stalled her going downhill, b'y. Can't think what she'll do going uphill.*" She laughed again. Her mouth the prettiest pink he'd ever seen. "You always so serious?" she asked him.

"What? No. No. Just busy, is all. Nice day, eh?"

"How's your mother?"

"She's fine."

"Glad to hear that. Nice woman, your mother. We always chat at the post office or in the store."

"Yeah. We like her, too."

"Right. Anyway, she's interesting. Quiet without being quiet, you know what I mean."

"I do."

She gave him a contrite look. "We all knows about her operation."

"Figures."

"That bothers you?"

"No. No, I don't mind."

"She does?"

"She's like that."

"You Nows. Floated up the bay all those years ago and you're still strangers."

"Jaysus. That bad?"

"Your sister hardly talked to any of us going to school."

"She's shy."

"And you?"

"Me? Uh, no. Nope. Hell, I'm about. You're the one who's gone."

"Changing that soon enough."

"How's that?"

"Not quite figured, yet. Everybody's beating a path to Toronto or Alberta or Saskatchewan. Not me. I'm the one who's gonna make it here."

"Doing what?"

"Figure something."

"Your folks'll like that."

"Right. The old man pales whenever I mentions it. Wants me making it big in da big city, like Mary Tyler Moore."

He smiled.

"You? What's your plan?"

"Still figuring it."

"There it is. Closed-mouthed Nows."

"Takes after Mother."

"Yup. She don't hand out invites, either."

"I'll tell her to invite you for tea."

She laughed. "Roses said you were daft."

"Roses is a thorny bitch."

"She can laugh, though. Don't think I've ever seen you laugh."

"Huh, maybe later." He grabbed the door handle to keep me from jolting forward as she yanked the gear stick from fifth down to third, starting up Fox Point, tires biting into the dirt.

"Oops, forgot fourth," she said and laughed at the concerned look on his face and he wanted to touch the creamy taut column of her throat as she tossed back her head, laughing harder. "Why are you so *serious*?" she asked, turning to him.

He smiled. Couldn't help himself. Felt like he'd slipped through a crack from gloomy skies into liquid sunshine.

"Stop chewing your nails."

Jaysus. He dug his hand into his pocket.

"An ouroboros moment?" she asked.

"A what?"

"The snake. Feeding off its own tail while growing a better one."

"Yeah, that's it—regrowing myself. In bits."

"Well, you starts with your head. Then the rest takes care of itself."

"Perhaps. Or perhaps you just lose your head."

"How many headless gurus do you know?"

There was an undertone to her banter. He lowered his window, too stuffy to breathe. "Cripes, slow down, here." They were driving through the Beaches and a dozen youngsters flew out onto the road in front of them, hollering and yodelling. Bath towels tied around their throats, hanging cape-like down their backs. Bandanas with cut-out eyes around their heads.

Julia hauled the stick into neutral, slowing to a crawl. Kyle yelled out the window, *Won't be enough of ye left to pray over, you gets struck.* He rolled the window back up. "Look at that little devil," he said to Julia as the eldest—one of the Keatses—waved a silver plastic sword at him with one hand and gave him the finger with the other.

"The finger? He gave you the finger? My God, what is he, ten? Eleven?"

"Been giving me the finger since he was four," said Kyle. "Rimmed or warped, that one."

"Oh my lord, brazen little bugger." She honked her horn and laughed and he loved how she was always laughing and he hated driving past the last house and her pushing the stick into neutral and coasting to a stop.

"Too hard on the brakes. Ought to gear down."

"Yeah, I'll figure it." She leaned against the wheel, watching him, smiling.

"Yeah, see you later, then."

"Just a sec." She reached for him as he was opening the door and too late he twisted away, her hand already enclosed around his forearm, her palm against the bone-hard handle of the knife. She pulled back, shocked. There wasn't a man, woman, or child in all of White Bay whose hand wouldn't intuitively know the feel of a trimming knife. Fear chased across her face with dawning clarity as she stared at him.

He cursed. Sat back in the car, closing the door.

"Say nothing," she whispered.

"I found it."

She nodded.

"I can't talk about it right now," he said. "Maybe—well, when it's all done with."

Her hands gripped the wheel. He moved to reassure her and she shrank against the door. He gaped at her incredulously. "You're not scared of me? Holy Jesus. Look, I didn't do this thing. There's stuff going on—Christ, I don't even know myself what's going on."

A sharp whistle sounded from the beach. His cousins. They were off by the shoreline, having a smoke. He held up his hand to them and Julia pulled the stick to reverse.

"Listen," he began, but she interrupted with a shake of her head.

"You can't talk now, I get it. And you shouldn't. I have to get home."

"I'll—I'll talk to you. Later."

She nodded. Her mouth, her face, all concerned. She wouldn't look at him. He got out of the car, closed the door, and stepped back. She sat quiet for a moment, then looked up at him. She gave a slight nod and he put his hand to his heart in gratitude.

"Hol-ee jeezes!" Wade had come up behind him, watching as Julia rode the clutch hard, burning through the gears as she drove back up the road. "That her father's new car?"

"Come on, let's go to work." Kyle walked onto the dark raw earth of the site, looking at the dug trenches for the footings, already encased with honeyed two-by-twelves and carpeted with beach rocks. Lengths of rebar were laid out, ends interlacing and tied with steel wire. Mounds of sand and gravel and bags of cement mix stood next to a wheelbarrow by the eastern corner. Everything tidied, strips of plastic anchored down with rock. Waiting for a clear sky and his father to come and start mixing the cement.

"How's Aunt Addie?" asked Wade.

"She's fine, just fine. Looks good, buddy. Lot of work done."

"That's your father. Hard man to keep up with when he gets going."

"Hooker and Snout came and give us a hand," said Lyman, joining them.

"They're gone back to the plant. Working this evening," Wade added. "Heard you got hauled in agin. Awful stuff, hey, b'y?"

"Questions, Jesus. Don't know why they thinks I got the answers. Come on. Let's mix cement." He started towards the wheelbarrow, the knife sagging heavier in his coat sleeve.

"Hey? But we got no mixer," said Lyman.

"We'll mix it ourselves. In the wheelbarrow." Kyle looked skyward. The cloud was thin. "Won't be raining for a while. We'll have the footing poured by then."

"What about Uncle Syl? Who's going to do the mixing?"

"Your brother, nutcase. Graduated Boudine High, suppose he can handle a bag of cement."

"You sure?" asked Wade. "Uncle Syl mightn't appreciate us going it alone. And without a mixer."

"What's the matter, forget your recipes?"

"One part, two parts, three parts. Mix, sand, and gravel. Let's get at her, then. If that's what you wants."

"That's what I wants."

"Fine, then. Go get the hose," Wade said to Kyle. "And you get them spades over there," he ordered Lyman. "Over there, stun arse, next to the wheelbarrow. Never mind, I gets them myself. You run up to Vic's and get her rake."

"A rake?"

"Just go get the fucking rake. Come on, let's get at her," he said to Kyle and shifted the wheelbarrow closer to the bags of cement. "I've never done it without a mixer. But I suppose it's the same mix, hey, b'y?"

"Yes, b'y."

"Now, let's see here—for a wheelbarrow full, we'll need two bags of mix."

"Where's the hose?"

"Tucked over there by the bottom of the hill. Set her up this morning. Running her from Billie's Brook up there."

Kyle went over to where the rubber hose coiled like one of Julia's snakes near a clump of dried brush and hauled the end of it back to the wheelbarrow.

"Here, give it to me, I hoses down the wheelbarrow first," said Wade. "We'll start pouring there, the east corner. Go check it, make sure she's ready." He stuck one of his fingers into the opening of the hose, jettisoning a spray over the wheelbarrow. Kyle went to the east corner, letting the knife slip from his sleeve into his palm. He checked that Wade had his back to him, then bent to brush away the small pebbly rocks beneath a strip of rebar. Quickly, he dropped the knife, covering it with the pebbles. Then he stood, looking down to make sure it was fully concealed, and walked back to Wade.

"Looks good. Let's get her started."

"Grab that bag of cement. Hold on, now. We puts the water in the wheelbarrow first, cuts down on the dust when you add the mix. Open the bag from the end, there. Hold on now, we gets the water in—not flowing very good. Slower than Lyman.

"All right, start measuring the water. We measures the water before we pours the mix. Get that bucket, there. Has to be same amounts every time else it'll look all patchy. Get the spade, start mixing in the mix. Rake is better, if bonehead ever gets back."

"How's this? I think it's good . . . add the sand?"

"That's right, add the sand. Grab the shovel. Slow—mix it in slow. That's the way. Now then, shovel in the gravel. Okay, start mixing."

"Right. All right. There she goes, mixing just fine," said Kyle. "How's your father?"

"Contrary as Mother."

"Don't change."

"Got hisself a shack built down Big Island. He's the only one there."

"That should do him."

"You'd think. So contrary he built another shack right alongside it. And he made the rule he's not allowed in there. Imagine that now, his own rule. Gives him something to complain about."

"Go on, b'y."

"Swear to Jesus, that's what he done. Here comes poke. What took so long, dicked the dog?"

"Dick you."

"Here, give me that rake."

"Move over, I does it myself." Lyman stuck the prongs of the rake into the mix in the wheelbarrow and started raking. "Bit more water, she's drier than the Pentecost." He raked slow and easy. Folding and blending till it looked like a load of mouldy cottage cheese. Kyle lifted the handles of the wheelbarrow and pushed it to the eastern corner as Wade started shovelling the thick mix into the casings.

"Get over here, Lyman. Grab the trowel, Kyle, man. Hold on, now. Hold on. All right. Start levelling. Smooth her out."

Kyle followed behind Wade, flattening and smoothing the cement with the rake. Lyman followed Kyle, smoothing it with the trawl. They poured and levelled and smoothed till the wheelbarrow was emptied and a good length of footing filled. Kyle checked where the knife was buried beneath the cement, resisting an impulse to bend down and mark the sinning spot with a cross.

They mixed another batch of cement and Wade poured, Lyman levelled, and Kyle smoothed. He kept looking for his father; no sign. The wind took a turn into a southerly, the air warming on Kyle's face. A meagre shaft of sunlight limped across the site and one of his cousins muttered *What the jeezes is that*. They mixed up another batch, and then another and another. Batch number eight and Kyle's back started stiffening. He took off his coat, switched from raking to pouring and then back to smoothing. The sea grumbled along the shoreline. Gulls squawked. It had begun to darken when Wade touched his shoulder.

"We better get it covered—can't trust it won't rain before morning. Expected Uncle Syl before now."

Kyle looked up the road for the hundredth time. He took the hose and sprayed clumps of drying cement off the wheelbarrow. Lyman cleaned the spade and rake and they all took a hand in covering the poured cement with strips of plastic. It was nearing six when they finished, Kyle's stomach rumbling. Couldn't remember what he ate last.

"Where's your car?" he asked Wade.

"Ask Lyman. He rear-ended a feller on the highway. Just past Deer Lake."

"*Rear-ended* somebody on the highway? How'd you manage that?"

"Don't know. He was three car lengths in front of me and I looked at something on the dash, and then I was up his arse. Cops took my licence."

"What for?"

"Said the car wouldn't safe."

Jaysus.

"Should start our own company," said Wade. He was standing next to Kyle, looking back over the freshly poured footings. "One side left and she'll be finished. Get the floor poured tomorrow if the rain holds. Not bad work, hey? What do you say, Ky? Start our own company? WK Contracting."

"Kinda like just the K."

"Right. Pours his first load and thinks he's boss." He thumped Kyle's shoulder and mock-kicked his brother's butt.

"Like the old man, always up to no good," Lyman complained. They strolled off the site and up the road through the Beaches. None of the youngsters were in sight. A few minutes after they passed the last house, Harry Saunders, with his wife and boys and two mutts all crowded inside the cab of his truck, pulled over. Kyle climbed in the back, his cousins beside him, and after he smacked the roof of the cab Harry drove them up the road. Two light poles before the government wharf in Hampden, Harry half rolled to a stop, the cousins jumping out. Kyle clung to a spare tire as the truck started forward. He looked back at his cousins walking up the hill towards a stand of birch and the weather-beaten hovel they lived in. This past winter had taken a nasty swipe at the dwelling, scarcely a piece of felt left on the tar-blackened roof. He watched his cousins go through the doorway and then look back, lifting a final hand of farewell towards him, and he felt the heart beating strong inside that hovel. He could tether himself to its portal in any storm.

At the crest of Bottom Hill he thumped on the cab, hollering his thanks to Harry, and jumped out. No sign of his father's truck. He cut through the roadside entanglement of dead knapweed and thistle and half slipped, half strolled his way down the muddied shortcut through the woods, holding his breath as he always did whilst passing the rotting sawdust and fire-charred remnants of the Trapps' sawmill. Hated that fucking beam hanging and creaking.

Coming down to the back of his house, he stopped. The dog. He was sitting by the gump, string of drool hanging from his mouth. He flapped his tail like a beaver and whined. Eyes wide and hopeful. It was hungry.

"Nobody looking after you?" he asked irritably. He peered around the corner of the house. Crept up to the front, looking down the road. He saw no cops or anybody about and went to the back, crawling in through Sylvie's bedroom window. Expected to see his father sitting at the table. No one there.

He keyed open two cans of corned beef and emptied them onto the cutting board. Forking one, he threw it out the window and the dog was on its feet, chomping it full before it hit the wharf. Jaysus. He tossed out half the contents of the other can along with a heel of bread and then closed the window. He sliced the remaining bully beef over two thick slices of bread, slathered it with mustard, threw in a couple of pickles, and bit into it whilst stripping off his clothes for a shower. After towelling himself dry, he crawled into his bed for a nap. He'd go look for his father later. Perhaps he was drunk agin. He fell into a fatigued sleep, thanking the Almighty for the opium of work.

NINE

—————

His dreams plagued him. But it was still early evening when he woke up and dressed. He checked his father's room. No sign of Sylvanus. He dragged out the phone book from beneath the coffee table and called the bar, then Hooker. No one had seen him. Perhaps he should call Corner Brook, he thought, but that might get his mother worked up. Must be on the booze agin, guaranteed.

He climbed out the back window, cut up through the woods to Bottom Hill, and then circled back down the road and onto the gravel flat. Kate's car was parked by her door. A light was on behind her closed blinds. He strolled down to the beach, teased a fire out of a swatch of dried seaweed, and teepeed it with driftwood from the supply Kate was forever gathering in her morning forages around the riverbank. Ten, fifteen minutes later, she opened her door. Hair battened down by a toque, grey braid trailing, fingerless mitts. No guitar. First time he'd ever seen her coming across the flat without her guitar. She raised her hand in greeting and sat on a half-burnt log and gave a tepid smile. He looked through her fire-blazed lenses to the green of her eyes and saw no light there. He saw nothing of that sense of expectancy she always held out for him. He saw only sadness. Her face drawn like shrunken hide.

"What's up, Kate?"

"The moon, Kyle. Always the moon. How's your mom?"

"Doing fine. Guess you already know that."

"Matter of fact, I did poke my head in this morning. You don't mind, do you?"

"Why would you ask that?"

She shrugged. "You've been protective. I understand that. Hear you got pulled in by the police again."

"They were more curious about you this time. I'm getting jealous."

"Wanting to know what I was wearing, right?"

"Right."

"Right. Already told them. And what you were wearing too. And your father."

"What the fuck's that all about."

"Don't know."

"That alibi you cooked up. If not for it, I think I'd be in the slammer now."

"They're fishing in the dark. They don't know who killed him."

"How'd you know I'd need an alibi?"

"I didn't. Just something Hooker and I came up with, that's all."

"It gives you an alibi too, Kate."

"Sure does." She smiled. "Thinking I killed him, Kyle?"

"Thinking you might know some things I don't. Cops said you were driving Bonnie Gillard around that evening."

"I was."

"Mind if I ask you about it?"

"Don't know if she'd want me talking about her stuff."

"She's already told me things." He hesitated. "I came across her car by accident in by the river. She told me about Clar trying to drown her. She tell you that?"

Kate nodded. "It was a rough night for Bonnie."

"Got a lot rougher for Clar."

"It did."

"So, what's up, Kate. What was she doing with you?"

"Not a whole lot to tell." She picked up a stick, idly stoking the fire. "I was getting some things from the car and thought I heard something. In the bushes. Thought it might be a fox. Heard it again. And a sound, like a cry. I went looking and there she was." She drew an unpleasant face. "She was looking pretty bad, crouching in the bushes. Her clothes were muddied. She was shaking, scared. Looking up at me like a little girl, scared her momma was going to smack her for being dirty. I took her hand, and I led her inside my house."

"Scared of her momma? Shouldn't she be scared of him?"

"Sometimes we got to change things up, Kyle. So's we can live with them."

"Everyone thinks she killed him."

"She didn't."

"How do you know that?"

"She would never kill him."

"*Never*—? Jaysus. Am I missing something here? At the hospital she looked like she was grieving. He's been torturing her for years. I don't get it. He tried to drown her and she's grieving him? She sick in the head?"

"You're sounding mad, Kyle."

"Yeah I'm fucking mad. He tried to kill her and she got us all mixed up in her shit and, what, they're best friends now?"

"You said it. That's just who they were, best friends."

Kyle's mouth opened but no words came out. He was like a barrister, staring with contempt at his own guilty client.

"Takes a bit of figuring out, Ky. She was Jack Verge's daughter. She had nothing but poverty. It smelled off her. Nobody chose her

for a best friend. She might've played the same games with everybody else in the schoolyard, but she was always the last one standing. Nobody ever picked her. Then he picked her."

"Sad fucking day for her."

"Wasn't back then."

"She's not a bony arse kid on a swing no more. She got
money, a new car."

"Don't matter what she got. In her head she'll always be poor.
Like she'll always be poor in *your* head. Perhaps she'd get over it if
everybody else would and stopped blaming her for it. If there's
one thing worse than being poor as a youngster, it's having everyone believing it's your fault." Her words were sharp but without
hostility. Kyle felt himself flush. He felt something else, too. Felt
like she'd just given him a piece of herself. *A stranger walks into*
town . . . shares nothing of herself . . .

"We all have our songs, Kyle."

"Sing me yours."

She looked away, mouth closed.

"That bad?" he asked.

"Felt like it at the time." She looked at him, firelight flickering
shadows across her face. "Suppose it wasn't too unlike Bonnie's. I
grew up poor, too much drinking. Not that I knew we were
poor. There were only four or five of us families living in that
cove, everyone the same social standing, so to speak. We were
always fed, warm clothes. Then we moved to a bigger outport and
I can hear the whispers now. *She's some poor, dirt poor, not a pot to*
piss in. Funny. I didn't know what poor meant. I asked my mother
one day." Kate smiled, "*It ain't poor if it's a thing you choose.* That's
what Mama said. I went back to school feeling shame for them
that mocked me. That's the strength of a mother's love, Ky.
'Course, that can turn too." Her face knotted. She rooted at the

fire. "Love keeps us going, my friend. Even what Clar Gillard offered as love."

"Didn't take Bonnie far."

"Perhaps that's all she felt she had, that and hope. Hope that he'd be nicer. You never think things are going to get worse. And then when they do, well—you keeps thinking they'll get better soon. Hope's a powerful thing. It's what takes us into the next world, hopes of a better life. I've written songs about hope. Shadows of hope, promise of hope."

He was reminded of his mother, her tireless fortitude. Kate, seemingly aware of his having shifted, touched his knee, pulling him back.

"There's always hope, Kyle."

"Where's Bonnie's, now that he's gone?"

"She'll find it again. She's just got to grieve it first, her lost hope."

"You grieving too, Kate? That why you moved here?"

Her reply, if she would've given one, was interrupted by a truck rumbling down the road and turning onto the gravel flat, two dulled beams of light bouncing and tilting towards them.

"I'm off," said Kate, rising. "Take care, Kyle."

A young fellow from Bayside was driving the truck, a bunch of his friends in the back, laughing, hooting, looking for a party.

"Hey, Ky, your old man's house on fire?" one of them called. "He near ran us off the road back there."

"Back where?"

"Going up Bottom Hill."

"Horse to the barn, b'y." Kyle waved them goodnight and started walking across the lot. He hesitated as he got to the road, looking right towards Bottom Hill, then turning left down Wharf Road, not giving a damn who saw him. The lights were out in the house, and he'd expected that—but not to find the door locked. Jaysus. He hadn't known that door *could* lock, or that there was even a key.

He rapped on the door and peered through the window. His father wasn't to be seen. He started towards the back of the house and Clar's dog rose from beside the gump with a sharp yap. "Jesus, b'y." His legs had weakened with fright, near toppling him over the wharf.

"Get home," he snapped. "Get the fuck home." He raised the window, hoisted himself across the window bench and teetered, falling face first into his father's boots. He cursed, got to his feet, and went down the hall, pausing at his father's room door. "Dad? Dad, you in there? You home?"

He cocked his ear to the door, heard the bedsprings creaking like bad ball joints on a worn-out clunker. "What, you in bed already?" He listened. No snoring. His father never slept without rattling the rafters. "Dad?"

Christ. He rested his head with weariness against the door-jamb and then went to his own room. He hauled off his clothes and got into bed and listened to a lone gull lamenting the night. He drifted, maybe slept, and was jarred awake by the shrill yap of the dog. A voice. Low, mumbling. He lifted his head off the pillow, heard nothing. Lay back down. Kept listening, silence scratching at his consciousness like a burr against a naked shin. Kicking aside the bedclothes, he hauled his pants back on, wrapped a blanket around his shoulders, and went to the kitchen. The light was on over the door. He went outside, chilly night air running like ladders up his arms. The shaft of the overhead light fell across the dark shape of his father's legs as he sat by the side of the house in Chris's old spot, his feet lodged against the base of the gump and the dog sprawled out beside him. He couldn't see his father's face, just his legs and his hand stroking the sleek black head of the Lab.

"What, you got a mutt now? Where the fuck you been?"

"Muffler fell off the truck," said Sylvanus, his voice tired, gut-tural tired. "Waited with your mother while they fixed it."

"You could've called."

"I did. Ten times."

"Yeah. Well, that's it now. I was working all day. Me and the boys poured the footings. We done the mixing in the wheelbar-row. Grunt all you wants now, she looks good." He bent down on one knee, trying to see his father's face. Saw nothing but the glint of an eye. Smelled the whisky-free air. Felt his fatigue. The weighted hand stroking the dog's head.

He drew the blanket more closely around himself and sat down beside him. "How come you never said nothing about Bonnie Gillard then, in the truck with you the other night?"

His father shifted, shrugged. "Nothing to tell, I suppose."

"Nothing to tell?"

"She was walking in the road. I gave her a ride."

"To Clar's house. He tried to drown her just before. She tell you that?"

"She told your mother."

"He near reamed her car in the river, with her in it. And she goes to his place after. That make sense to you?"

"As much as any of it. Go on to bed now, Kylie. Get some sleep."

"Sleep! Jesus. How you going to sleep with all this going on?" He hesitated. "I was talking to Hooker. He found you on the wharf that night, parked next to Clar Gillard's truck. You remem-ber that?" Sylvanus didn't speak. "He said you were pretty drunk. He drove you up to the bar and parked behind it. He—he said you were in the water that night. When he found you on the wharf, you were wet. He said you knew Clar was dead."

The gnarled hand stilled upon the dog's skull.

"So, how did you know?" asked Kyle.

"When did Hooker tell you that?"

"Last evening."

"How come you said nothing till now, then?"

Kyle fell silent and turned his head away.

Sylvanus grunted, shifted his face into the light, and then his eyes widened with disbelief. "My son, my son." His big hands, all weathered and chapped from hand-lining cod and chopping wood, gripped Kyle's shoulders, then softened into a caress. "You thought I did it? Kylie, you thought I did it?"

"You didn't?"

"No. Christ, no."

Kyle had been leaning forward, his stomach twisted. He sank back now against the house, his fear oozing from him into the dark night. His father settled back beside him.

"What else did Hooker say?" asked Sylvanus.

"Not much. What do you know of that night?"

"Not much. I woke up at the fire. Thought I drove up to the bar. What else did he say?"

"Nothing else, I told you. You were in the water and you knew Clar was dead. How'd you know that?"

Sylvanus lapsed back into silence.

"Old man, you got to tell me. I been through hell with this."

"It's not over yet, then."

"What's that mean?"

"Nothing. Go to bed, now."

"I'm not going to fucking bed. Did you go after Clar? You seen his truck and went after him, right? Pay him back for the graveyard thing?"

"I was thinking that." He dropped his head, scrubbed a hand through his hair. "I should never have left, never have left her. Sin. Sin I left her."

"Sin! That's for fucking well sure. Jesus Christ, old man, why did you leave? I left you with her, she was all by herself and you left her. What the fuck!"

"Should never have left."

"What did you see?"

"Go to bed now, Kylie."

"I'm not going to bed. Why was your clothes wet? You seen Clar parked on the wharf and you went after him, right? What happened? When you parked next to his truck, what happened? Old man, I'm not leaving till you tells me."

"He wasn't there."

"Wasn't where? In his truck? Where was he, then?"

"I heard his dog, up by the cliffs."

"So you went after him?"

"Knew he was up to no good."

"What happened?"

Sylvanus shifted some more, shook his head. "I don't know, Kylie. I was too drunk. Kept tripping. Falling down."

"Did you catch up with him?"

"No."

"You didn't catch up with him?"

"No, I told you. Too drunk. Too gawd-damned drunk."

"What happened then? You seen something. What did you see?"

"I can't tell you. Go on to bed."

"Can't tell me what? You seen it, didn't you? Christ, did you see it happen? What did you see? Will you fucking tell me?"

"I seen him falling. That's all. The light was on over the door, wouldn't have seen him otherwise. Too foggy."

"Who was here? You saw what was happening here on the wharf? Our porch light was on?" He tried to remember if the porch light was on when he had gotten home that night. Couldn't. "Tell me, who was here, what did you see?"

Sylvanus's breathing was harsh. He twisted a finger inside his collar to loosen it.

"Gawd-damnit, Dad, what did you see?"

"Leave it there for now."

"No. No, I can't leave it. No fucking way. Was it Bonnie Gillard? Who did you see?"

"Thought I heard somebody, thought it was you, first. Must've been a gull."

"It was Bonnie, wasn't it?"

"No. I seen her."

"Who else was here? Who the fuck else, why won't you answer me? Jesus, what're you, drunk? You're freaking me out. Tell me who was here."

"I don't know."

"Bullshit. Tell me! I'm not giving up till you tells me. What was she doing—what was Bonnie doing?"

"She was bawling. She was over there, end of the wharf. She started running. I seen her running towards the house, bawling. I heard him, then. Clar. Awful scream. That's when he fell backwards, into the water."

"Did you see who did it?"

"No."

"Who else did you see? Who else could've been here—" His thoughts broke off. "No," he whispered. An absolute stillness took him. He thought he heard her voice then, his mother, calling his name, calling him foolish. Perhaps if he listened harder and longer and could be stone-still, he would hear God's voice persecuting him, persecuting his father, thundering hell's fire down on them for thinking such thoughts.

"She didn't do it. You didn't see her do it. Did you? Did you see her?"

"No. I said no."

"Then you don't know. You don't know nothing. He done it himself, maybe. They does that. Maybe she—Bonnie—done it and ran down to the end of the wharf. And then—perhaps the knife was already in him and it took a while. For him to fall over. Anything could've happened. You didn't see her. Right?"

His father shook his head.

"You swear?"

"I slipped on the rocks. I was too gawd-damned drunk. Couldn't get up, couldn't get here in time. If I'd got here—if I wasn't so gawd-damned drunk."

"You went back to the truck. Why didn't you come here instead? Why'd you run off?"

"Don't remember. Don't remember getting back to the truck. Remember being on my knees, couldn't get up. Seen the dog jump in after Clar. Seen him dragging Clar straight towards me. Hard to see, the fog. I seen your mother, then. She come and took Bonnie's arm. Telling her it was all right. She never had to be afraid again."

Kyle sank back, shivering.

"Can't have her knowing I seen. Case it went to court."

"But you didn't see nothing. You didn't see her do it and you don't have to testify against your wife."

"Don't remember nothing after I seen your mother. Don't remember getting back to the wharf. Nothing. Woke up at the gravel flat in the morning."

Kyle started to rise. "We have to talk to her."

"No." His father pulled him back.

"Yes. Yes, she got to know we knows, case she needs us."

"She decides that. She decides when to tell."

"But I needs to know. I needs to know right now—I can't handle not knowing and she might be needing for us to know."

"No. You'll keep it to yourself like I done."

"I got to talk to her."

"No! Gawd-damnit, no! We says nothing till she talks. Addie's not stupid, and whatever she's figuring, we lets her."

"What about Bonnie? She got her into this. I'll make her talk."

"You'll not go near her, either! You hear? *She* decides. *Your mother*. If she done it, it was self-defence. How come she's not saying that? There's something going on there. I can't figure it. But I knows enough to leave her with it till she makes her move. She's not stupid. And she's not scared. Whatever happened, she's not scared of it and she's holding on to it. For now. So we holds on to it too."

"No, she's not scared. And if she's not scared, she didn't do it."

"I don't know, Kylie. I don't know." His father's voice was wearied. He made to get up but sank back down. He shifted forward, wrapping his arms around his knees. He peered through the dark, his body taut, as though seeing in the distance the remnants of his old house that had once been strong and true and needing to get there again. He turned to Kyle, his voice deep with conviction.

"We wait. We lets her play her hand. I owes her that, all I put her through. When she gets it figured, she'll tell us. *She* decides when to tell us. You got it? *She* tells *us*. Else we might fuck up something she got going."

Kyle tightened the blanket around his shoulders to stop his shivering. He wiped at his eyes, tired. His father rested beside him. For once he was glad for the dark. It hid the fear shrinking his face. It let him sit close to his father, their shoulders touching, and he felt like a boy again, feeling his father's warmth, his strength. It comforted him. He searched through fear's pockets for hope. He needed hope now. He needed his father to have it so's he might catch it like a gawd-damn germ. Hope's contagious like that: if one believes, then another might.

A spattering of rain against his face and he worried about the footings, if they were covered good enough, and near laughed. Such small things.

"Come on," said his father. "Let's get some sleep."

———————

He was lying across his bed, still swaddled in his blanket and his belly cramping, when his father rapped on his door. The rain had cleared, a strong wind squalled at his darkened window, and the greenish neon numbers of his watch said five o'clock. In the kitchen his father looked a shaggy hulk hunched over the table. Looked like he'd been there all night staring out the window. He lit a cigarette, smoke still curling from the butt in the ashtray.

"Working on lung cancer, hey, b'y."

"That's it now."

"Right. Just what Mother needs." He made himself tea by the stove light shadowing the kitchen. He bit into a piece of bologna left warming in the pan for him. He sat, looked at his father.

"What's we going to do?"

"Go down and finish off the footing, I suppose. Check the mess ye got made. You take the truck and go get Sylvie. Her plane's in around six."

"I figure Suze will be there, picking up Ben. I imagine she'll take Sylvie to see Mom. I'm going to work."

"I told Suze you'll be picking them up."

"Why'd you tell her that?"

"Just what your mother wants, Suze by her bed. Tongue like a logan. Go. Do like you're told."

"I wants to finish what I started yesterday—I'll phone Suze."

"We'll bloody phone you if we needs you. Now go get your sister."

"Haul back them eyebrows, old man, before they tangles in your nose hair. Jaysus."

"Truck's parked upon Bottom Hill. There's a bag of stuff in it for your mother. I bought it in the drugstore. Make sure you brings it to her. She's coming home this evening."

"This evening? Already? What the hell we going to do, the house ribboned up like Halloween."

"I'll rip the gawd-damn stuff off if I got to."

"Oh, here we go. Another round with MacDuff coming."

"That's it now."

"She don't need you getting thrown in jail."

"You not gone yet?"

"Mind if I put on my boots? How you getting down?"

"Drive with the boys."

"Cops took their licence."

"You not gone yet?"

Jaysus. He went to the back room and skimmed out through the window, scratching his face on the pane and cursing. It was still dark. He felt for the path with his feet and started up the steep hillside muddied from the rain. Couldn't see a thing in this sunless vault, not a fucking thing. Wind scudded through the bush, wetting his face with tree water. He felt the woods falling away to his left, heard the creaking limb from the rotting carcass of the old sawmill, heard water suckling through its bones. And something else. He paused mid-step. Something rustled the bushes behind him. Too strong to be the wind—a fox, perhaps. He kept walking, then stopped. There it was again, a shuffling—no fox, too loud to be a fox. A fucking bear? He started to run. He slipped, fell face first into the dirt. He scrabbled to his knees and stared through the dark. Above him the branches shifted with the wind against the meagre bit of dawn emerging through the heavens. More shuffling, right next to him now, and he cowered, feeling the air shift around his face. He was on his feet, his heart thudding with terror. He thrashed up through the woods and then the brush and onto Bottom Hill. The truck was a dark shape across the road, flagged by a pale star breaking through the cloud. He ran towards it, clambered inside, and locked the doors. He revved the engine and flicked on the headlights. He looked towards the path and strained to see. There was something there, swear to Jesus, there was something there. He shoved the gears into reverse and backed up and turned so's the headlights fell across the mouth of the path. Nothing. Grey clumps of foliage. Darkened woods behind.

Putting the truck in gear, he booted it down the road and drove through Bayside towards the highway, shivers spiralling down his back. He flicked on the heat, drummed on the wheel. He couldn't keep from shivering, thoughts shooting through his head like comets. It could've been a bear, this was the time for them, crawling outta their fucking caves, looking to eat. Jaysus. He wiped at his nose, tried to sit back, relax. He was all twisted inside. More from his talk with his father the night before than a stupid fucking bear. His mother. Clar Gillard. Bonnie. What happened? What the hell happened? He couldn't bear it, couldn't bear another thing, and now he had to pick up Sylvie. Last time he was at the airport it was to pick up Sylvie. And Chris was in a white box behind her.

He wiped at his face, hand cold, shaky. He jacked the heat on high. Driving across the second bridge near Faulkner's Flat, he saw too late the small reddish disc glimmering at the side of the road. Moose. He jammed on the brakes, tires screaming, rubber burning as he skidded towards the black bull lumbering across the road, antlers wide enough to hang bedsheets. Damn, gawd-damn. The tires bit into concrete, the truck's rear end swinging sideways and the hind wheels thudding into the ditch, seat belt digging into his bruised ribs. The moose stood to the side of the road, looking back at him.

"Get off the road, you fucking moron!"

The moose sauntered into the woods. Jesus, oh Jesus. He rested his forehead on the cool hard plastic of the steering wheel. He didn't know how long he waited there. Watching light sieve through dawn's dusk. Greg Bushy drove by, stopped and chained the bumper of the truck to his trailer hitch and hauled him back onto the road.

Forty minutes later, Kyle pulled into Deer Lake airport, the smell of jet fuel and car exhaust rankling his already nettled stomach. Inside the small, one-gated terminal, the baggage carousel creaked to a stop, a few suitcases grouped to the side of it, couple of odd souls strolling about. He learned from the striped-blouse attendant behind a ticket counter what he'd already figured: the flight had landed fifteen minutes ago, and was readying again for takeoff.

He went outside, looking about the mostly empty parking lot. She'd taken a cab. Knowing Sylvie, she wouldn't have waited longer than five, ten minutes, her urge too great to see their mother.

He called the hospital, asking for his mother's room. He might as well drive back home and work on the house with his father.

No answer in her room.

He walked about the deserted terminal for five minutes, then called back. No answer. Another ten minutes and he called again, cursing the wasted time. No answer. They're in the family room, he thought. Sitting down, yakking. He'd go home, then. They didn't need him now. He'd give his mother's stuff to somebody else driving in, always somebody driving to Corner Brook.

He got in the truck and drove back out the airport road. Nearing the highway, he braked, signalling left to head east, homewards. His mother's bag of stuff shifted. It slid onto the floor and like the waters of the Atlantic being pulled by a celestial ball floating through the heavens, he, too, felt himself being pulled westward onto the highway by some invisible force. Hell, bloody hell. He drove hard, blasting his horn at a three-quarter-ton rust-bucket creeping along the highway. He pulled out and cut ahead of it and was mad, mad as he'd ever been and couldn't say why. At his mother, he supposed, for what she'd done or hadn't done that night on the wharf. And his father, for what he hadn't done, but could've. And at himself for freaking out back there in the woods over whatever the hell it was that spooked him. And then near hitting a moose and missing Sylvie and his mother would have something to say about that. If she could think of anything else these days but fucking Clar Gillard.

He found a parking spot near the hospital door. Inside he elbowed past a bewildered looking group asking for directions to the blood clinic. First time in the hospital, he figured, and all gathered around a splinter of an old woman dozing in a wheelchair. Jaysus. The whole horde gotta escort Granny for blood work. Outside his mother's room, he was motioned aside by an unsmiling young nurse.

"She has a small infection. We've given her antibiotics. She's been sleeping a lot."

"She's all right, though?"

"She's fine, but we mightn't let her go home this evening. We'll keep watch."

He searched the sober-faced nurse for more but she was hurrying off. He listened at his mother's door; there were no voices. He nudged the door open, stepped slowly inside. She was alone, sleeping. He stood by her bed, looking down at her thin form beneath the sheets. Her face was anemic, spiritless, and each deeply drawn breath seemed punctuated by weariness. He felt the cold steel of the bed's safety bar beneath his hands and no longer trusted that the cancer had left her and no longer trusted that she would be fine. Her eyes fluttered and her hand reached for his.

"You didn't get your sister."

"I near hit a moose on the way, ended up in the ditch. She's here, though?" He spotted a bulging knapsack resting by the bathroom wall and a small canvas bag.

"Kylie."

"I'm here."

"It wasn't her fault."

"Whose?"

"Your sister's."

"What? Her fault for what?"

"Chrissy's dying."

"What? Jesus, Mother!"

"That's what your father does, blames himself."

"Mother, I don't blame Sylvie."

"I sees it on your face. It robbed your father, his blaming did. He blames himself for getting sick. Eats at his heart." She smiled up at him, her eyes the softest he'd ever seen them. She touched his knuckled hand. "It's not time that ages you, my baby. It's life."

"All right, enough of this."

"He can't be in your heart if it's filled with blame. Your father, now. He carries death in his heart."

He wiped at his face, couldn't look at her. Her fingers clutched his hand, forcing him to her, her eyes bluer than the heavens and with a depth that had nothing human in it, like a wormhole through to eternity.

"Go. Find your mercies," she said urgently. "Before you harden into something ugly. Make peace with your sister." She turned aside, her eyes closing, whether in sleep or dismissal he couldn't know.

"Jesus, Mother. What got you thinking like that?"

Her eyes opened again onto his, so brutally clear. A week after Chris's funeral and he'd snapped at Sylvie for some small thing as their mother stood on a chair, hanging curtains. She stepped down from the chair, staring at him with the same brutal clarity, and stood beside Sylvie, the curtain rod held aloft like Orion's sword. He'd backed away from those knowing eyes as though he'd been caught slugging back wine from the holy chalice. And Sylvie. Just standing there, silent, fighting to keep erect her bowing head when he wanted it further bent with shame.

Kyle moved back from his mother's bed. He circled the room, jammed his hands in his back pockets, and kept circling. His mother's breathing slowed a little; she was sleeping. He cut out through her door, hurried past the elevators and took the stairs, near leaping from landing to landing. Coming into the lobby, he bolted outside and was grateful for the wind scraping cold across his face. He hooked the truck keys from his pocket, stopped, then ducked behind a white van. Sylvie was getting out of a brown Buick parked a couple of car lengths away, just to the other side of the truck. She was balancing a couple of coffees on a cardboard tray and a brown paper bag greasing up the side from buttered muffins or bagels. She had lost weight. Her arms were reedy, her legs so thin she looked knock-kneed like their father. She'd always been concerned about looking knock-kneed, and as though hearing his thoughts she glanced down, like she was always doing, checking her knees, and he felt a rush of affection.

She trotted past him so close he saw the colour of her eyes— brown eyes, Chris's eyes. She'd watched the light leave them, she'd sobbed to him, stumbling drunk from the bar one night. She hadn't told anyone else in the world that she'd watched the light leave his eyes, watched them die like the flame in their old gran's lamp after the wick burned dry. And when she curled her arms around Kyle's neck, craving comfort from her awful secret, he shoved her away and ran, widening his own eyes to draw light, widening them so big they watered, his vision running like rivers and he swimming through them into a sea of dark.

He watched the hospital doors close behind her and his face burned. Burned with the shame of wanting her to hurt further. He climbed into the truck, backed out of the space, and sped towards the street. Then he braked hard, thinking he saw her in his rearview. She had stepped back outside and was staring after him. No. No, it wasn't her. A car blasted its horn behind him. He accelerated, checked his rearview—it *was* her! Watching him speed away. The horn blasted him again; he hit the accelerator and then instantly jammed his brakes to keep from rear-ending the arsehole in front of him. He hauled out and passed him, gunning uphill to a cacophony of horns blasting from all sides. He drove harder, checking his rearview; she was gone, she couldn't see him. *Make peace with your sister, make peace with your sister.* Damn. Gawd-damn. He slapped the steering wheel and then slammed on the brakes, tires smoking as he skidded to a stop, watching another gawd-damned moose lumbering across the highway. Speed bumps. Newfoundland gawd-damned speed bumps.

He pulled off the highway, fighting for calm. His face was wet. He wiped it, surprised. That he could harbour such secrets from himself, but not from those they hurt the most.

Man. Oh man, he was fucked.

He was almost at Hampden Junction when he remembered something. Trapp. He'd forgotten. That same night Sylvie wept on his shoulder down by the bar. Trapp had been watching them through a window. His white face staring at Sylvie, his eyes the false light of a jealous moon. A curious thing, he remembered now. Strange thing to have forgotten, that.

TEN

———

Nearing the gas bar and restaurant off the highway near Hampden Junction, he saw Julia getting out of her father's car, fair hair fanning down her back as she headed inside. He flicked on his blinker and pulled into the parking lot. Inside the restaurant he took a seat at the counter, nodding at Rose coming out through the kitchen door, wearing bright red lipstick and a checked apron over black pants and a white shirt. She tucked her cropped brown hair behind pink-shelled ears and brushed at bangs a mite too long.

"Hey," she said.

"Hay's for horses."

"Aren't you a smart boy."

"The company I keeps."

"We been noticing. Must be training to be a cop, are you? All the time you're spending with them."

He tried for a flippant answer, couldn't find one. Searched her face for meanness.

"Joking," she said and grinned. "Sorry about the stuff going on. Hear your mom's doing fine."

He nodded. "New job?" *Where's Julia . . .*

"Evenings. Some weekends." She patted a bulge of change in her apron pocket. "Few more truck drivers and I'll soon have enough for next semester. Figured out what you're doing yet?"

"Working on it. Can I get a bowl of soup?"

"Coffee with that?"

"And wrap up some butt chops and chips for the old man. Make sure it's a fatty chop."

"Use a bit of fat yourself. Getting skinny. And you needs a shave." She went off. He swivelled on his stool, rubbing his bristled jaw, looking about for Julia. The place was crowded. Smelled of partridgeberry pie and french fries. A swinging door opened into the kitchen and he glimpsed Julia talking intently to Rose. She spotted him and her eyes widened with the surprise of a caught youngster. A waitress came through with two coffees, the door swinging shut behind her. He hadn't time to think before Hooker hustled inside from the parking lot, bringing a rush of cold air with him.

"Need to talk to you, buddy," he said. He nodded towards a couple of folk from Sop's Arm sitting in a booth nearby and then beckoned Kyle to the door still opened behind him. "Let's go, buddy."

"What, we can't talk here? I just ordered soup."

"Later. Let's go!" Hooker was back outside and Kyle reluctantly followed, a last look towards the kitchen door for a glimpse of Julia.

"Get in," yelled Hooker, climbing inside the truck.

"What's going on, bud?"

"Get in and start her up. We'll talk behind the gas bar. Hurry up, man, let's just fucking go." He looked anxiously towards Hampden Road as Kyle started the truck and circled behind the building.

"What's going on?" he asked, shutting off the engine.

"You tell me." Hooker was staring at him with wide, perturbed eyes. "You tell me what's going on. What's this about the knife? The cops dug it out of the cement down on the site. They're out in Hampden looking for you. They'll probably be here any minute."

Kyle dropped back his head. His breath left him. She'd told.

"Ky?"

He hadn't thought she'd tell.

"What's up, man?"

"Go on home now, Hook."

"Go *home*? When you answers my fucking questions I'll go home. What's going on, bud?"

Kyle shook his head.

"Tell me about the knife."

"What did you hear?"

"Nothing. The plant shut down and I was just at Hampden turnoff and the old fellow, Hurley, was there, heading for his cabin. He told me."

"Told you what?"

"That the cops dug the knife outta the cement."

"How'd they know it was there?"

"I don't know, he didn't say."

"How'd you know I was here?"

"Hurley told me—he was just here gassing up—who gives a shit! What the fuck, man, what's going on?" Hooker was leaning towards him, taut as a forestay in a storm.

Kyle gazed out the windshield at the trees trembling in a timid wind. He felt a sudden give in Hooker's thinking, heard a slight groan.

"Oh, man. Oh man."

"Go home, Hook."

"No. No, I don't believe it. I can't believe it."

"It's not what you're thinking, go on home, now." Kyle reached for the keys to start the truck and cursed as Hooker grabbed his hand.

"I'm not leaving till I knows everything."

"Some things, buddy, you don't want to know."

"I already knows the worst."

"No, you don't. The old man didn't do it. Now bugger off and leave me alone with this."

"I knows what I seen that night."

Kyle dropped his hand from the keys and snatched at Hooker's coat flap. "You don't know fuck," he snapped. "What you saw that night didn't happen. It didn't happen, remember? You swore it didn't happen and I'm holding you to it. It didn't happen."

Hooker pushed Kyle's hand away. He withdrew into a huddle in his corner of the truck. Kyle laid his head back again. He rubbed hard at the back of his neck and suddenly stilled. He stared unseeingly at the windshield. Then he sat forward, rested his head for a second on the steering wheel, and reached for the keys.

"I have to go," he said to Hooker, starting up the truck. "And you've got to let this one happen."

"Let what happen? What're you doing?"

Kyle twisted sideways, backing the truck towards the parking lot.

"What's going on? Tell me, man. Let me help."

"Not this one. You can't doctor this one, brother. Okay?" He hauled over to the side of the gas bar and parked.

"There they are!" said Hooker. A police car had come into view on Hampden Road. It slowed, Wheaton and Canning's morose faces staring at the truck.

"All right, Hooker. Get out now. Want your word on this one, okay, buddy?"

"Piss off."

"I want your gawd-damned word!"

"Fuck you, you'll not tell me who to talk to." Hooker was out of the truck and slamming the door. Kyle got out behind him, yelling, "Hey, tell Julia it's okay, all right? Tell her she done the right thing by telling, you tell her that?"

The cruiser pulled alongside and Canning stepped out. As might a doorman from some fancy digs, he opened the back door of the car, gesturing for Kyle to enter.

Jaysus. "Don't put your hand on my head," he snapped at Canning, bending to get into the car, and cursed as Canning put his hand on his head, pushing him inside.

"Ky! Ky, wait."

Julia was running from the restaurant with Rose and Hooker trailing behind her. Canning closed the car door and held up his hand, blocking Julia from the car. She shouted past him at Kyle. He saw her mouth moving but couldn't read her words, didn't want to see them, didn't want to hear them. *You did the right thing, girl.* Canning got in the car and Rose held Julia's arm as they drove off. Kyle kept looking ahead. His neck ached to look back. He wanted to look back hard. His neck twitched and then he couldn't help it. They were standing by the side of the highway. Hooker had his arm draped around Rose and Julia, all three staring after him. They looked so dear.

And now, with the two silent cops in the front seat and the grey strip of highway unfolding before them, he was suffused with sudden loneliness. Canning turned towards Wheaton with a murmuring of words. Wheaton tilted his head to catch them. Shaved necks chafing stiff collars. The whir of wheels on asphalt. Rumbling of the motor. Static crackling from the two-way radio, wind hissing through a slightly cracked side window. It all sounded too sharp, nothing harmonizing, leaving him feeling at odds with everything. As if he was walking in someone else's shoes again. Come to think, he'd been feeling that way ever since the phone rang three years ago with the news of Chris—that everything about him was surreal. And becoming more surreal with this new plan that was birthing itself inside of him. His old friend, fear, crept in. To be this removed was to be dead. He thought of his father, his aloneness with the bottle. And his mother. To have lost her son and then watch the rest of them in their isolated pods of grief. And what now, when she got word of this new thing he was about to do? When his father got word of it?

In this moment when he'd never felt so far removed from himself, he suddenly wanted to go back. Not to the way it was before Chris's accident—that was too utterly lost to them all. To the way it was just a week ago: his mother clinking china in the kitchen, his father sitting at the table, sizing up the weather, and he biting into a thick slice of bread slathered in peanut butter and bakeapple jam, the smell of birch wafting from the woodstove.

And he'd been starting to like mornings, too. Wasn't much, but he'd been feeling some sort of awakening inside of him, as with the awakening of the day. No doubt by midmorning every-thing started feeling heavy again. Like the sweet greens of spring darkening by summer's end. But it would've happened. Time erasing things, growing new things. He could see it now looking back, new ways starting in. Julia.

Gawd-damn Clar Gillard. Gawd-damn his brutal winter's breath, killing everything just starting to seed again. Shame on himself, too, and his father. Too isolated in their loneliness to feel the good still left to them. Shame. Shame what they'd brought onto his mother. Perhaps none of this would be happening if they'd helped her celebrate the living instead of pining for the dead. And he thought of Sylvie. How he'd run from her. Leaving her to carry alone that lasting memory of Chris and the light leaving his eyes. Shame. Shame he kept himself isolated in his yearning when they were all yearning for that one thing taken from them.

At the police station, he followed Canning to his old room. This time he turned and smiled for the camera. MacDuff dragged his feet through the door, wiping his nose with a wad of tissue, eyes red-rimmed from a head cold. He smiled sadly to see Kyle and shuffled like a geriatric to his chair.

"Suppose days like this you wished you smoked," said Kyle.

"Still watching your cop shows?"

"Naw, they gets boring after a while."

"That's the difference in real life, son. Nobody gets bored sitting where you are right now." He stuffed his wad of tissue into his back pocket and sat. "Tell me about the knife."

"Why don't you tell me."

"You got it backwards, son. I do the questioning."

"And I choose which ones to answer."

MacDuff looked up with rheumy eyes. "Are we bargaining, here?"

"Might. Else, I get a lawyer and he does the bargaining."

"Why don't we talk first? Maybe there'll be no need for a lawyer."

"How's that?"

"Obvious. What most cop shows have in common: nobody knows what the other knows. Makes for good television but not real life." MacDuff twisted a sad smile. "We help each other, Kyle. And we get through this tired mess."

"Good, then. You tell me what you know about the knife and I tell you what I know about the knife."

"Perhaps you can tell me why you want me to go first?"

Kyle smiled to catch himself a moment. He couldn't say as to why; there was no real why. She had told. He wanted to hear it from the police that she'd told and how and why. His mouth felt wooden as he opened it to speak, his tongue dry as sawdust.

"I buried the knife to hide it. I stuck it in Clar Gillard."

He saw the barely detectable look of surprise on MacDuff's face. He heard a door close somewhere outside. He felt himself swing like the limb on the old sawmill. Too late. He was on the other side of fear now. He felt proud. Chris had given his life to save his family and now he was giving his. Too much hurt, everybody was carrying too much hurt. He'd carry it for a while.

"You sure this is where you want to take it, Kyle?"

He gazed at the old cop, his scraggly bit of hair slipping across his sweaty head. He should be home in bed. He should be retired and fishing along shore somewhere, nice cabin to fry his fish. *Perhaps I could tell him everything. He's got no heart left for pain either, can tell by the disquiet in his eyes. I could tell him everything and he'd make it right. Lay it all down, let the old fellow mould it with his big warm knowing hands and mould the law to serve the family's cause.* Christ. He felt himself growing faint. He needed to get outside his head—too many voices. He was starting to feel nauseated, not knowing which one to listen to.

"Tell me what happened, Kyle."

"Gillard came looking for trouble. He had my knife. He must've got it in the woodshed; that's where I kept it."

"Keep talking."

"We wrestled for it and he dropped it—he must've been drunk, else I'd be dead. I managed to get it and he came at me and I didn't mean to. It was an accident. Self-defence. Everyone knows the guy's a prick. He would've killed me. He's been waiting to kill all his life, whether by plan or accident. Perhaps he was even hoping it'd be him who got killed. Sonofabitch. He just wanted to take someone else with him when he went down. Cowards are like that."

"You're not a coward, are you, Kyle."

"I don't know about that."

"You're acting pretty brave right now."

"I'm not acting, sir. Like we said, this ain't no TV show."

"Why did you bury the knife?"

"So's you wouldn't get it."

"If it was self-defence, why wouldn't you just face it?"

"Thought if I put up a bit of a fight, it would all go away."

"Why'd you stop fighting?"

"You got the knife, you got me."

"Here's what we know about the murder weapon. It was done with a knife with a long, slender blade. Like the knives used for trimming fish in the fish plant. Everybody who ever lived in an outport owns or has access to one of those knives. Most of them got four or five collected over the years from the plant. Why would we think your knife was the murder weapon?"

"Who else was caught burying their knife in cement this past couple of days?"

MacDuff hauled his tissue out of his pocket and blew into it loudly. He wiped at his reddening nose and pocketed the tissue, sitting back. "You learn things about people in this job, Kyle. Becomes a gawd-damn psychologist after a while. Some things here are not adding up—you're a fighter, but you just stopped fighting. You should be stinking of fear, but you're smelling like the hero."

Kyle laced his fingers, fidgeted with his thumbs, and stared back unblinkingly at MacDuff's long, searching look.

"Why did you bury the knife?"

"Obvious, isn't it? I didn't want it found."

"Why go through so much trouble to hide the knife and then confess so easily?"

"I already said. You found the knife, you found me."

MacDuff was staring at him as though he were something broken that needed fixing. Kyle struggled to keep his face straight. Think. Think. There was something off. "What more do you need to know?" he demanded. "Why did you bring me here?"

"We brought you here to talk to us, Kyle. Somebody was killed on your front step. Some things you can't help knowing. Perhaps we're looking for those things—the ones you can't help knowing."

"Might often be the case. But you just got your man. Case closed."

"Why do you think Gillard came after you a second time? He already punched you out."

"I'm thinking it felt so damn good, he just wanted another smack. Things don't have to make sense to Clar. It just had to feel good."

"What things are we talking about, here?"

"He was stoked about us confronting him the day he blocked the road."

"It was your father who confronted him."

"I was driving the truck. Good enough for Clar."

"Not adding up. He'd just suckered you. Why would he go to your house looking for you?"

"Perhaps it was the old man he was going for. But it was me that come home instead. He had me knocked out; perhaps he didn't think I'd be home so quick."

MacDuff pulled his notepad before him. Flipped back through a few pages. Kyle kept his smile, his mind working furiously. *Think, think.*

"When did Kate Mackenzie pick you up?"

"Eleven-thirty-five p.m."

"When did you leave the bar?"

"Around eleven."

"That gives you thirty-five minutes to be punched out, walk home, kill a man and, what, go for a walk around town before taking a lift with Kate Mackenzie?"

"I took the shortcut home—cut down through the woods. Takes five or ten minutes from the bar. That would've gotten me home around eleven-fifteen. Clar was already there and it was fast. Too fast—I can hardly replay it in my mind. He was there by the edge of the wharf—"

"Who was by the edge of the wharf?"

"Clar Gillard. It was dark, I didn't see the knife—"

"Who else was there?"

"Nobody. Just me and Clar. He come at me and I got lucky. I was more trying to duck him than hit him. He must've been drunk. He dropped the knife—it fucking near stuck itself in my hand. And I grabbed it. I come up and he threw himself at me. I was more like—trying to push him off me. But I had the knife. I didn't mean to, but I must've struck him with the knife. I don't remember feeling it—it was too fast. I give the shove and he went over the wharf. It was then I felt wet on my hands, too thick for water. I couldn't see but I knew it was blood.

"The dog was barking. I was scared it was going to wake up Mother. I leaned over the wharf, but it was too dark to see Clar in the water. The dog was already on the beach by then, and running out in the water. I jumped down on the beach and started running towards the cliff."

"Why did you run in that direction?"

"I don't know. I freaked out, wasn't thinking. Guess I thought Clar would be swimming that direction, making for home. I never thought he was dead—just hurt or something. I whistled for the dog; I could hear him in the water. It was foggy, I couldn't see. Then I got scared, thinking it was Clar and not the dog. That he was coming after me again. I started back for the house. But then I thought about Mother. She had so much going on with her operation and I didn't want her getting upset. I had blood on my hands and perhaps on my clothes, I couldn't see. I dunk my hands in the water and then ran back the other way. I scrabbled around the cliff to Hampden and booted up the back road towards Bottom Hill and was just coming down the other side when Kate picked me up."

"What did she say to the blood on your clothes?"

"Twas none there, checked soon as I got home. But I made sure in the car I was sitting so's it wouldn't show if there had been. She wouldn't have noticed anyway because I was so razzed up and telling her about Clar striking me outside the club and after that we just sat by the fire, had a beer." *Slow down, slow down, slow the fuck down.*

"Where was Kate coming from?"

"I don't know, never asked. Too much going on. Couldn't get my head around any of it. I remember just staring at her dash, at her clock on the dash, talking mostly gibberish. She thought I was drunk. Most I remember is the clock on the dash."

"And the time was?"

"Right. Eleven-thirty-five."

MacDuff had listened with his head down, as though saving his ears from any distractions. When Kyle finished, he lifted his eyes like an old asthmatic horse labouring for breath. He scratched irritably at his scrag of grey hair, patted it back in place, and looked with impatient eyes at Kyle.

"How long does it take to get from your house on the wharf to the wharf down Hampden?"

"About ten minutes if you're pacing yourself."

"Was the tide in or out?"

Kyle hesitated. He felt the trick, he felt it coming. Think. Think. His father had been wet.

"The tide was starting to rise."

"It didn't slow you down none?"

"Adrenalin was pretty high. I was fast as a cat scaling that cliff."

"Yet you couldn't see where to put your feet it was so foggy?"

"It was starting to thin. I could see some things clear enough."

"Did you see Clar's truck on the wharf?"

Kyle hesitated. "It wasn't that thin."

"Did you see it?"

"Just the shade of it."

"Then you must've seen your father's parked alongside of it."

The glassy-eyed old fucker, Dobey Randall. He'd seen the truck and told the cops, guaranteed. Guaranteed, the glassy-eyed old fucker.

"I didn't see the old man's truck."

"It was there. Why did you lie?"

"About what?"

"You said your father was parked outside the bar all night."

"He was. Most of it."

"Why did you lie?"

"I thought he *was* parked behind the bar all night. Till Hooker told me differently."

"Why did Hooker lie?"

"Hooker was looking for me. He found the old man drunk and drove him up behind the bar."

"He said he found him behind the bar."

"Father was drunk. He didn't want to say my father was drunk."

"So he wouldn't have been drunk if he was parked behind the bar?"

"He wouldn't have been drunk and driving. Everyone parks behind the bar when they drinks too much and don't wanna drive home."

"Hooker risks being accused of obstructing justice in a murder investigation rather than risk having your father lose his driver's licence?"

"You don't know Hooker, sir. He needs to be taking care of people. He's always taking care of people, especially my father."

"Who was at the fire when you arrived there with Kate?"

"No one."

"You indicated that the fire was already burning when you arrived there. Was it?"

"Wouldn't be a fire, sir, if it weren't burning."

"Who lit it?"

"Don't know. Somebody lights a fire and sits for a bit. Piles on the driftwood before leaving, and someone else comes by—the eternal flame. Perhaps Kate lit it herself before driving off."

"When did Hooker show up with your father?"

"Bit after midnight."

"Where were you?"

"Sitting by the fire. Check your notes, sir. I went home shortly after and was sleeping outside the house by the gump when the old man showed up about a half hour later."

"Why didn't your father go home with you?"

"Was finishing his beer."

"You said he was passed out."

"He woke up."

"Why wouldn't he go home with you?"

"Just told you, he was finishing his beer. Don't matter, we always staggers home when we wants and he come home around a half hour later and yeah, I'm sure of the time, the clock was lit up on the stove when I went in. Twelve-thirty or forty, something close to it."

"Are you lying, Kyle?"

"No, I'm not fucking lying. You wanted to know who killed Clar Gillard, and now you know, so what more do you want?"

"The truth?"

"You got the truth."

"A convenient truth."

"What the hell does that mean?"

"Clar Gillard was killed at eleven-thirty-five. He was heard screaming. You were sitting in Kate's car. By your own admission you just cleared yourself of murder."

Kyle struggled to keep the surprise from his stricken face. Felt like he'd been running through the dark and was suddenly sprung into sunlight on the edge of a cliff. "Must be a mistake," he said quietly.

"What kind of mistake?"

"I must've read the clock wrong. Or maybe the clock was wrong. I was pretty freaked out—I must've read the time wrong. Who heard him scream? Must have been that old fellow with the glasses, Dobey Randall. He's always walking the roads, stun as a grouse, you can't trust nothing he says."

MacDuff pushed himself up from his seat, tucked his notebook inside his pocket, and started towards the door. Then he paused. "Oh," he said, "you can stop bumbling around your house at night and turn your lights on now. House is no longer under investigation."

"Why's that?"

"We've found the murder weapon."

"MacDuff!" Kyle stood up. "I just made a confession, sir. Perhaps I should get a lawyer?"

"Lawyers work on keeping their clients *out* of jail, Kyle."

"If I walk out that door, I'm on the run. This is a one-shot deal."

"Only cowards run, son. You've not shown that." The old cop put his hand on the doorknob. "Wish I had more of a Columbo parting, here. But Kate Mackenzie picking you up at eleven-thirty-five makes for a good alibi where you're concerned." He looked with sudden thought at Kyle. "It gives her an alibi, too. Where did she say she was coming from?"

"She didn't."

"Was she at the bar?"

"No, sir."

"It was foggy. Not the kind of night one goes for a drive, don't you think?"

"I've not thought about it, sir."

"What was her mood when she picked you up?"

"Her mood?" Kyle shrugged. "Like I said, I was too distracted to notice anything."

"What did you talk about?"

"I don't remember. Nothing much."

"Her hands—do you remember if she was wearing anything on her hands?"

"No, b'y. I don't. You suspicious of Kate, now?"

"Everyone's a suspect, till they prove they're not. And your father—do you remember if he was wearing mitts or gloves the night of the murder?"

"Told you that last time we talked: No. He was not."

"That'll be it for now." He went outside and Kyle stood staring after him. He was playing a game. He was a cop playing daddy, playing sympathetic friend. Implicating his father, implicating Kate.

Kate. What the hell had she seen? *It gives you an alibi too, Kate.* She'd smiled. *Thinking I killed him, Kyle?*

Rubbish. MacDuff was playing him. Setting him after Kate. Why? What did he know? What did she know?

He sat back down, then remembered where he was and quickly got back up as Canning entered the room to escort him outside.

———

He hooked a ride on the highway with a trucker driving east. At Hampden Junction he bade his thanks and climbed out of the rig, heading for his father's truck in the restaurant parking lot. The kitchen window swooped open and Rose poked out her head.

"You still want those chips and butt chop for your father?"

He gave her the thumbs up and went inside. A tentative search through the few faces sitting in their booths with platters of chips and gravy.

"You want a can of Coke or something else to go with that?" Rose was sliding a brown paper bag along the counter next to the cash register. He went and stood in front of her, eyeing the kitchen door. Rose's face was closed tight.

"Looking for someone?" she asked.

"Nope." Whiffs of fried onions watered his mouth and he was suddenly weak with hunger. He straddled a stool and ripped open his father's butt chop and chips and dug in with his fingers. "Fix up another one, will you, Rose?"

"Here, b'y. Be civilized," she said, putting a plate and cutlery before him. "Want a beer?"

"Coffee."

"Slice of pie?"

"Two."

"Kind?"

"Coconut cream. How come you're being so sweet?"

"Hoping for a tip."

She came back with a mug of coffee and two slabs of pie on a plate. "You want some pie for your father?"

"Sure." He speared half a dozen chips into a puddle of ketchup and vinegar and then into his mouth. After he'd cleaned the plate he started in on the coconut cream pie, licking his fork clean. He felt someone watching him and glanced over his shoulder. The whole gawd-damn place was sneaking looks at his back.

He finished off the pie, laid twenty-five bucks alongside the cash, grabbed his father's bag, and started for the door. Rose was piling dirty dishes onto a tray. She snatched a glance at him, a peculiar look on her face.

He paused, hand on the door. "What's that for?"

She feigned not hearing, studiously wiping down the table.

He went over to her. "What the fuck was that look for?"

She brushed at her bangs with the back of her hand and stared at him. "They're saying you done it."

He glanced around at the bent heads, the suspended forks. "That's what I just told the cops," he said loudly. "That I done it." He swung out the door and Rose came after him.

"She wants to talk to you."

"Tell her to pick a number."

He boarded the truck and drove the thirteen miles to Hampden without seeing the road.

ELEVEN

At Bottom Hill he faltered, looked towards the gravel flat and Kate's cabin. He needed to see her. Something wasn't sitting right. Kate wasn't sitting right. He drove down onto the flat and pulled up before her door. Her car wasn't there. The dog was sniffing around the back of her cabin, whining and fretting. He gave a sharp bark at Kyle and went back to his sniffing. Kyle swung the truck around and drove off the flat and up Bottom Hill. Fucking MacDuff. Stirring up a curiosity about Kate he'd never felt before. Nor wanted. He liked Kate just as she was, someone from away who had no connections to any of the goings on around Hampden. In a place where everyone's aches and pains and passions and peeves were as familiar as his own undershirt, it was nice having a friend with no baggage that needed unpacking.

Cruising down the other side of Bottom Hill towards Hampden, he caught sight of Julia leaving the post office and hurrying towards her house, blond hair riffled by the wind. She saw the truck and stopped and he kept going. The spectacled old fellow stood on the roadside, thumbs hitched inside his suspenders, ogling him as though he was Cain returned.

"Get off the road, you nosy old fuck!" yelled Kyle, blasting his horn. He clipped down the hill, then slackened speed as he drove along the shoreline towards the Rooms. He felt like he'd lived ten days since crawling out of bed this morning. A southerly wind chopped the sea, warming the air a bit. On the far side of Fox Point he saw Wade and Lyman shovelling sand from the side of the hill into the back of—if he wasn't mistaken—his uncle Manny's truck.

Uncle Manny. His father's brother from Jackson's Arm. His favourite uncle. He felt a lump of warmth in his belly. Good. His father had company. Uncle Manny always made things better. He tapped his horn to his cousins, hoping to drive on past, but Wade dropped his shovel and was pumping his arms like a windmill for him to stop. What the hell. "Don't have time to talk, buddy," he said to his cousin, coasting to a stop.

Wade leaned his forearms across the rolled-down window, his face all tender with concern. "Can't help but wonder what's going on."

"'Course you can't. Everybody's wondering what's going on." Kyle laughed. "*I'm* wondering what's going on. Hell, I'd give my two right limbs to know."

"It was one of the Keats kids that told. He's a brazen brat, that one."

"What? What did you say?"

"Mutt-faced Keats. Rob. He was up in the woods, spying. There was two or three of them up there but he's the ringleader. I made his brother tell me. You was part of their game. Luke Skywalker. Leave it to Keats to be Darth Vader."

She didn't tell.

"Anyhow, b'y, don't look so serious. Like I told the cops— always something falling out of our pockets into the cement. Buried me wallet, once. We got it all filled in agin where they broke it up for the knife. See you later now." Wade drew back, then slapped the side of the cab with a finality that invited no further comment from Kyle, no matter the curiosity in his eyes.

"Thanks, buddy," said Kyle. "How's the old man doing?"

"Whose—mine or yours?"

"Start with yours."

"Contrary old fucker."

"Tell him about the spark plugs!" Lyman yelled.

"Keep digging!" Wade yelled back.

"What about the spark plugs?"

"Nothing, b'y. Nothing. The old man come up from Big Island last evening and out sawing up firewood with his chainsaw and cocky over there sneaks out and takes the caps off his spark plugs and stuffs in some tissue."

"Jaysus."

"Ha, ha. Old man comes back from a piss and hauls on the cord till his face is blue, can't get a gig. Ha ha. Never cursed, did he?"

"He's going to kill one of ye."

"Naw, he blames everything on the religious fellow next door." Wade thumped on the cab again. "Go on now. Don't worry about your father—Uncle Manny's down there with him. Good as tonic, Uncle Manny is." Wade drew back in. "Gotta watch Uncle Syl, though. Working like a dog, he is. Head down and going at it. He's going to have another heart attack. I told him, 'Old man, take a break. Go on down and see Aunt Addie.' But he don't listen. He's waiting for you right now, better get on down."

"All right, buddy. See you in a bit. And thanks."

"Nothing for it. You take 'er easy, hey."

Kyle drove off feeling full of his cousin's loyalty, if not his faith.

She didn't tell.

There were no youngsters on the road as he drove through the Beaches. *Hope you're all down with the mumps.* His father was sitting on the beach talking hard with Manny. They looked up, hearing the truck coming. Getting out of the cab, Kyle paused to look at the site. The basement floor that had been nothing but mud and gravel the day before was now a smooth slab of grey concrete and already trenched for piping. Two days' work. He'd done two days work in one.

His father was coming towards him.

"Don't worry about nothing," said Kyle in a low tone, patting his father's shoulder in greeting. "I buried the knife because I thought you done it. That was before our talk."

"Say nothing to Manny. Nothing."

"Up for a bit of sun, are you?" Kyle called to his uncle. Manny was getting up, stout and jaunty and black-bearded. Grinning eyes peering beneath the rim of a baseball cap worn backwards.

"Sun! Jaysus, that what it was?" Manny called back, doffing his cap towards the now clouded sky. "Thought it was a UFO and called the cops." He put his cap back on as Kyle came up to him and thumped Kyle's shoulder. "Look at them eyebrows, all growed in and thicker than your father's. Christ, the two of ye—full of shit and down a quart. How's she going, bugger?" He cuffed Kyle lightly on the chin and sat back down on the beach rocks.

"Moving along, things are moving along," said Kyle, sitting beside him. "And Mother's doing fine," he said to his father. "Good news is, the house is no longer under investigation. We can go home. And by the way, they knew all along we were staying there." He looked to his uncle Manny. "Suppose you heard about that stuff, too?"

"Shocking, b'y. Shocking. All ye've been going through and not a word from none of ye." He threw a surly look at Sylvanus.

"Me and the wife been at the winter house down Cat Arm and never heard a thing till we come back up and Matilda went to the post office and got an earful from Suze."

"You knows Mother, now," said Kyle. "Only told us in time to get a ride to the hospital."

"Matilda's gone on down Corner Brook now, helping her get packed to come home."

"She mightn't be home this evening," said Kyle. "And this other stuff, Christ. Something you sees on TV, hey?" He looked up to a fixed stare from his father.

"What do you mean—*mightn't be home this evening?*" asked Sylvanus.

"She got a small infection. They got her on antibiotics."

"How come she never phoned then? How come nobody phoned?"

"I was there, I suppose. The nurse told me."

"The nurse told you. Did you talk to the doctor?"

"They weren't there. No need getting worked up, she was looking fine."

"A gawd-damned corpse looks fine when they puts rouge on them. Did Sylvie talk to the doctor?"

"Sylvie was getting coffee. I never seen Sylvie. I near hit a moose and missed her at the airport. Sit down, b'y. How's the clan, Uncle Man?"

His father's hand came down heavily onto his shoulder. "You comes back from the hospital," he said, eyes black as a crow's, "and you don't know how your mother is, or if she's coming home this evening, and without seeing your sister?"

"I told you, she's fine. Think Sylvie'd be off getting coffee if she wasn't? And Bonnie was there," he fibbed. "Mother's wanting for nothing, Jesus, b'y. Here, get your paw off me." He shrugged off his father's hand, watched the thick hairy fingers curl into a fist the size of a youngster's head. "Sit down. Getting worked up over nothing."

"Don't mind that, infections," said Manny. "Happens all the time in hospitals. Goes in with sore ribs, comes out with sore elbows. No worries about that stuff."

"Yes, b'y," said Kyle. He patted the rocks beside him. "Sit down. All right? Take a load off."

"Yes, b'y, sit down," said Manny. "Like a stormy wind."

Sylvanus tried to smile, his jaw appearing too stiff and he too dammed up for any stream of chatter. Lowering himself onto a flat rock beside Kyle, he drew up his knees, his elbows resting on them. A ray of sun struck down into the sea and he stared at it, eyes brutish.

"Taking a piece out of himself agin," said Kyle.

"All right they keeps her for a few extra days," said Manny. "Give her a break from you. Here, have a beer."

"How's everybody, Uncle Man?"

"Fine, by the size of their arses. That's all I sees. The rest of them is poked inside the fridge, stuffing their faces. Eat! Jesus, all they does is eat."

"Wonder where they gets that," said Kyle, eyeing his uncle's rounded gut.

"Ah, baby fat," said Manny, pinching his belly. "Don't be fooled by that—six-pack in there somewhere, hey Syllie? Cripes, the face on him. Bend over, b'y, I boots you in the arse. Here, Kylie, have a beer with Uncle Man." He snapped open two beers, passing Kyle one and looking appreciatively towards Sylvanus's thermos. "He's gone Pentecost, he told me. On the black stuff. Going there myself soon as summer's finished."

"How's work?"

"Crab plant just closed for another month. You might be feeding me next week. Crab fishery going the same way as the cod—too many licences, too many boats, everything overfished. Thought we learned something from fishing all the cod outta the water. Hey b'y," he said to Sylvanus.

Sylvanus snorted, face to the choppy sheet of blue before him, wind tugging his thick thatch of hair.

"Hey, b'y, what're you saying?" Manny persisted.

"We don't learn nothing now. That's what we learns."

"Naw, you don't say."

"Same gawd-damned thing happening over and over. Good thing they got their science."

"Hah, that gets him going," said Manny, nudging Kyle. "Bring up politics and that gets him going. Right on, b'y. Somebody should teach them adding and subtracting. You takes all the fish outta the sea and how many left back to spawn? Nothing, sir. Now, how hard is that to learn? You done good, Syl, b'y, getting outta the fishery. Not just greedy governments and companies. We fishermen plays it blind, too. We wants the dollar. You done better than we, staying on shore and not trading your nets for the factory freezers. If we'd all stood up like you done years ago, we might still have a fishery."

Sylvanus grunted. "Only thing I changed now is me address. Like the rest of ye."

"Listen to him. Not down on himself, is he?" said Manny.

"Can't give him nothing," said Kyle. "Mother says he thinks he's God, responsible for everything that happens."

"Jesus, b'y," said Manny. "You moved from the fishing when you were starved out. Never give in first shot like we all done. You were right, brother. We jumped on the first boat out and them boats kept getting bigger until we had them Jesus factories sitting out there and siphoning off the spawning grounds. But you stood your ground. Long before the arse was out of her, you stood your ground."

Not aching for a drink, is he, thought Kyle, watching his father take a swig of tea from his thermos and spit it back out. He swung his arm around his shoulders and gave him a sloppy, sideways hug.

"Can't argue that one, can you, old man. You stood your ground."

Sylvanus gave the disheartened grunt of a father over a foolish son.

"Grunt all you wants now," said Manny. "You had your honour. That's what you did, then. You had your honour. Right? Right, my son?"

"Right," said Sylvanus gloomily. "Nice hat she was till a gull shat on it. Lot of good it done me after that."

"Hear him?" Manny asked Kyle. "Hear the like of him? Cripes, you can say what you wants now, but they didn't have you jumping through the hoops like they done us. You seen it coming before we all did. We let ourselves be mollycoddled. Took the big pay stubs. By Jesus, you might've fought through hard times sometimes, but you always had your worth about you—and you deserves that. You didn't barter that like we done. Now we all knows. Too late to do anything. It might've took the heart out of you, working in them woods the way you done. But there's them who think you're the stronger one for taking that stand."

"What good is that now, if you can't do for your family?"

"Not just spuds you feeds a family with." Manny punched Kyle's shoulder. "He didn't get his smarts from sucking turnip greens. You done good, damn good. Not your fault God poked around in your life. That's about the one thing now, that's not predictable—the hand of God. You can't go getting down and blaming yourself for stuff you got no control over. And you can't lose hope, either. You got to trust some things. And that goes for you too, young feller, you never loses hope."

"Hope." Kyle gulped down the word with a mouthful of beer. "That's the word for the day, is it?"

"The hell with hope, then. Take heart from what you already got. You got your boy here," he said to Sylvanus. "And he still got you. And he's gawd-damned fortunate to have you. Not going to take that from him too, are you?"

The sun shuddered through the clouds. Sylvanus turned from its light and stood, kicking his thermos aside. "Get in the truck, Manny. Drive me down Corner Brook."

"Cripes, yes. Get the Jesus outta here. Sitting and bawling when Addie's most likely packing to come home. Where's them young fellers with me truck? Jesus, they got the bottom beat out of her, most likely."

"We'll take mine," said Sylvanus. "Kyle can drive yours till we gets back this evening."

"No gawd-damn rough riding either," Manny said to Kyle. "The wheels could fall off her any minute. Here, come here." He wrapped short strong arms around Kyle and cut off his breath with the strength of his hug. "You remember what I says. You're the fortunate one. You still gets to be with us for a bit longer. The other one—well, he's watching on, somewhere. But we gets to live the riddle a bit longer. Hey, b'y? That's good, isn't it?"

"That's good, Uncle Manny." Kyle stood back and his father came before him, his big arms engulfing him in another hug. He grasped tight to Sylvanus, feeling that warm good heart pumping against his, pumping hard, pumping love, and then he was roughly pushed aside and he stood there, wrapping his arms around himself as though he were cold as his father walked away. He and Manny got into the truck. Kyle kept hugging onto himself, his face wet from a swollen heart as he watched them drive up the road and out of sight around a bend.

He walked around the site, looking about, then walked back to the beach and sat, having no mind for work. He got back up and walked down the shore. A brook cut down through the scraggy underbrush and onto the beach, its flow to the sea encumbered by a kelp-encrusted rock. He watched the brook backing onto itself before rippling over the blockage and felt himself to be that encrusted rock. He scrunched it aside with the heel of his boot and watched the brook flow into the sea, unhindered by thoughts of its own drowning, its immersion a homecoming. He thought of Bonnie Gillard entombed in her red car, screaming with fright as the river rose to greet her. He wondered if Clar Gillard had been frightened going into death. And Chris. His stomach lurched. He shielded his eyes to keep from seeing and then opened them. He needed to know. He needed to know right now.

He got to his feet and walked back up the shore. He walked past the work site, the weathered houses of the Beaches. Curious eyes followed him from behind shifting curtains. Others stared boldly through bare windows, the odd youngster scrambling behind a woodpile or shed at the sight of him. He walked with purpose, passing wet black cliffs sponged with green sods on his left, on his right the one long wave unfurling to his step.

Around a rocky bend his cousins were driving towards him in Manny's truck. Wade lowered his window and called out.

"Just talking to Ben," he said as the truck rolled to a stop. "He's heading to the bar with some of the boys. I told him we'd meet him for a beer."

"See you there," said Kyle, without breaking stride. Going down Fox Point, he cut straightaway off the road, went down the embankment, and then leaped over the white picket fence into the cemetery. He looped around soggy mounds guarded by upright slabs of granite. He came to Chris's, *Taken Too Soon* scripted beneath two clasped hands. He knelt and laid his hands on each side of the tombstone as though they were shoulders and he gripped them hard. He lowered his mouth to a piece of the cold granite, warming it with his breath. *"I'm coming, buddy, I'm coming,"* he whispered.

He heard Manny's truck gearing down to a halt on Fox Point. He got up and looped his way farther across the soggy green of the cemetery, taking a foot-path through the Rooms, the air smoked with hickory from the smokehouse. He walked steadily along the shoreline up to Hampden, his cousins keeping a distance behind. It felt good, their being there. He walked up through the centre of the community, the wind swiping salty across his lips and stirring laundry hanging heavy on the lines. A youngster's wails turned to squawks of laughter behind a closed blind. Farther on, a man's rough command and a sweet, lyrical voice rising in protest against it. Julia. Fighting with her father in the driveway while Rose stood mute beside the new car. The father stomped off towards the house, stopping to wag a thick hairy finger at his daughter, hollering *". . . and if I gets wind of you driving my car once more, you're out on the road!"*

"The hell with him," Rose said to Julia after the house door slammed. "We'll take my mother's car, it's already a banged-up piece of shit."

"Have a word, Julia?" Kyle had come up silently behind them. Both girls started, Julia's face kindling deeper with anger at the sight of him.

"Pick a number, arse," said Rose.

"A private word, Julia?"

"Oh, he's all private now he don't have a room full of people listening. Don't listen to him, Jewels."

Jewels. Kyle looked into Julia's blue moonstone eyes.

"Go see if we can get your mother's car," Julia said to Rose. "See you later on this evening."

Rose threw him a disgruntled look and went off.

"What's up?" asked Julia.

"I apologize."

"You really thought I ratted you out?" Her eyes were dark with hurt and he kicked at the ground with the toe of his boot.

"Too much going on. Didn't get chance to think much."

She stood, slender as a stalk of grass, hair streaming down her shoulders, and he felt like a freak, shoulders hunched, hands knotted. Hair knotted too, no doubt.

"Jewels," he said. "That's nice. Jewels."

"Are you hitting on me?"

"Fuck, no. Don't go hollering for her to come back."

"Fine, then, you're sorry. What more do you want?"

He shifted uncomfortably. "There is something, actually. Not sure if this is the right place for it. Or time." He gave an awkward laugh.

"Go ahead, ask."

He nodded. Turned from her eyes, brittle with cold. "It's— aw, fuck. It sounds foolish now."

"It's the *only* thing now. Ask it." Her voice softened. "Sometimes the questions are tougher than the answers."

He nodded his appreciation. Then he sucked in a lungful of air, glanced at her sideways, and spoke too fast. "The night before Chris flew off to Alberta. You came out behind him when he was leaving the bar. I saw you there. You'd been talking with him?"

"We talked."

"Can I ask what you talked about—I mean, about Alberta. If he said how he felt about leaving?"

She was silent for so long he turned to her fully. Her eyes were softened now, like her tone. "I wasn't his girlfriend, if that's what you mean."

"No. No, I didn't mean that."

"We went to the graduation and hung out some, but nothing serious. The night before he left, well—I guess he was wanting something more. I didn't. Why you asking about that?"

"I—well, that's not what I was asking about. But it's nice to know."

"You feel weird thinking Chris and I were a twosome?"

He shook his head. "I thought he looked scared when he left. Scared of going to Alberta."

"Lord, no. He was proud as punch about that. Couldn't wait to leave. Is that what you thought? That he was scared of going to Alberta? He was scared of leaving me. He thought there might be a chance if he stayed, but that he'd lose it if he left. I did leave it a bit fuzzy with him. But I think he knew that . . . well, that I just couldn't come right out and say no to him. I think that was all right, don't you think that was all right? I've fretted about it."

Somewhere in his heart a small chamber drew light. He looked at her with growing gratitude. "You have a kind heart. Thank you for telling me. Thank you so gawd-damn much."

"If I'd known you thought . . ."

"No. Don't think anything more. It's good."

"What's good about it?"

"Everything. Everything's good about it. I gotta go. You see Ben around?"

"They're at Hooker's. They're heading for the bar in a bit. Might be there yet."

"All right, then. I'll catch you later. Hey, you like fishing?"

"No."

"Take you tomorrow, if you want."

"God. Baymen."

"I'll show you my secret spots."

"Already know them."

"Catch me a fish and I'll teach you how to drive a standard."

"Already knows that, too. It's a clutch thing."

"Right. Right on that. Listen, call me if you wants to go fishing." He went off, step notably lighter, no doubt, to the two cousins sitting in the truck, discreetly parked to the side of Fudge's store, watching. He took a shortcut behind the store and down a grassy hump and crossed a low-built bridge and scaled the hillside that led to the back of the bar. Inside, he sat near the window with his back to the room and waited. He bought a beer and let it sit there. *Unholy it is, drinking over the dead and getting maudlin with your own sorry self.* Words his mother flung at his drunken father once.

His cousins came inside, gave him a wary glance, and sat at the bar, ordering beers. Must've been fifteen, twenty minutes that he sat there, staring at his beer. He heard Ben coming from half a block away. His voice chipper, raunchy like a blue jay's. Bunch of the boys jousting alongside of him and cawing like crows. Always like that with Ben, fellows hanging around him as if he were the Second Coming, all of them talking over and under the other.

They entered the bar noisily, Ben ahead. Longish black curls, broad easy smile. It was how Kyle remembered him those days back on the wharf when he'd come visit Sylvie and Chris, and he, Kyle, was just a kid. Once Ben leaned over the edge of the wharf with him and helped him spear a flatfish with a gaff. Kyle pitched it flipping and flopping onto the wharf, his heart seizing with excitement. Ben gutted it, hands dripping with gurry, and Sylvie shrieking and Chris running for the frying pan. Later Addie fried up the fish with pork scruncheons and Ben saluted Kyle sitting at the head of the table as Fish Killer Supreme.

"What're you at, bugger," called Ben, coming towards him. "How's she goin'." Ben took his hand tight and looked steady into his eyes and Kyle saw that Ben's eyes were clear. No longer shame-cast as when he'd first returned after Chris's accident.

"Good to see you, man, good to see you. Sorry about this morning. Near hit a moose, stuck on the road for an hour. Where's Sylvie?"

"She's coming in a minute. Your mother's getting out this evening, your father's waiting to drive her home. Good to see you, bugger. Look at that stubble. Not like his old man, is he?"

"The spit," said Skeemo. He'd come up behind Ben. Sup, Pug, and Hooker, all of them crowding around Kyle's table, plunking down their beers and scraping back chairs, Wade and Lyman amongst them. *Welcome back, man, welcome back,* they chorused, raising their glasses to Ben. Their smiles fell away as they looked at Kyle, becoming unsure, looking back at each other with loud chatter should their puzzled expressions give them away. Except Hooker. He sat on the edge of his seat, staring at Kyle with the same tension as he might the climactic ending to his favourite TV show.

"Her fever's gone," said Ben, edging his seat closer to Kyle. "She's sitting up, ordering everyone around and demanding to be sent home. Sorry, buddy." Ben gripped his arm, looking into his eyes again. "Sorry you had to go through this."

"Not all bad. Brought the old man around, he hasn't drunk since."

"Go on, b'y, he must be dead. You checked his heartbeat?"

The boys laughed, and Kyle did too.

"What's all this about a knife? What's the scoop on Clar, haven't heard nothing but what Mother's saying. Christ, get strung up you repeats after Mother." Ben laughed, the boys laughed, and Ben toasted them all. "That's the thing with Mother. Something don't make sense, she shapes it till it does and then preaches it as the gospel. God love her, she would've done good at something. So what's the scoop, what's going on, bugger, the Beaches youngsters got one on you?"

"Jaysus, they had me convinced I knifed Clar. Went to the cops and confessed and the cops kicked me out. Not kidding," he said, glancing at Hooker. "They kicked me out. Knife fell out of my arse pocket when we were pouring cement. The little bastards were spying up in the woods, and Darth Vader nailed me for murder." He guffawed, his words easy, his nervousness barely perceptible beneath the jiggling of his foot.

"String 'em up, little bastards," said Lyman.

"That's right, bud," Skeemo hooted, "string the little bastards up," and he clinked his glass against Lyman's and then Ben's. "Welcome home, man. Good to have you back."

"What went down with Clar?" asked Ben. "Mother's after curdling me short hairs."

"He was upping his game for sure," said Skeemo.

"Got worse after Bonnie left him," said Sup.

"That right, now, brother, and just how the frig can bad get badder?" asked Hooker.

"Spraying her down with oven cleaner, old man. Never done nothing that sick before."

"Not that we knows. Nobody knows now what she put up with."

"I say he got worse," said Pug, "else she wouldn't have moved out."

"She was always moving out, numbnuts," said Skeemo.

"And always moving back in," said Sup. "She never this time, though. He was getting worse over time, I seen it in his face. Starting to feel sorry for the bastard."

"That right, now," said Kyle. "And was that before or after he sprayed his wife with chemicals?"

"Not bawling here now," said Sup. "Had a few talks with him, that's all. He had that nice way about him sometimes."

"Yeah, he did. Agrees with you there," said Skeemo. "Way he smiled."

"Last thing I seen before he suckered me," said Kyle. "Didn't look that nice."

"Hey, man, not picking up for the guy, all right? He was one sick fuck!"

"Father says Bonnie drove him nuts," said Lyman.

"*Father says.* Ha ha," said Ben. "Crazy fucking Jake. Still blaming Kitty Wells for killing Hank."

"Perhaps she did. Drove him to drink."

"Drove him to yodel. Ha! And we thought he was singing."

"Seriously, man, who came up with yodelling?" asked Skeemo.

"Someone with their balls nipped on a cracked toilet seat," said Sup. The boys hooted and Sup leaned forward. "Perhaps that's what done it. Bonnie started humming a Hank song, and he got jealous."

"He was fucked before she met him," said Pug.

"He wasn't treated right, man. He was crucified growing up."

"So was Jesus. He didn't roll aside the stone and go trawling for fights, after."

"No b'y, he left that for his Old Man to do," said Skeemo.

"Ha ha, while he snivelled in the desert for forty days and nights," said Pug.

"And his Old Man's been cursing us ever since."

"Cursing who, jingle balls. Clar was fed with a silver spoon," said Hooker.

"Money don't get you everything."

"He could've walked. Starts growing hair in your armpits, you don't need your mother packing your bags."

"Had his noggin kicked too many times."

"He wasn't kicked, where you get that? Old Man Gillard just had to look and Clar shrivelled up. Everybody did. Never had the evil eye, did he, that old fucker."

"That's who he should've tied up and hosed down with cleaner," said Skeemo. "Our father was no effing picnic, but me and Sup, we got bigger than him and frightened the shit outta him one night with a baseball bat. Behaving ever since. Bawled last Christmas when we give him a present."

"What did you give him, black pepper?"

"Pepper you, dickhead! Stick that up your arse, that'll get you hopping."

"Jaysus, there's a thought. I wonder—"

"You knows what thought done now—ha ha, hey b'y?"

"Listen to the philosophers over there." It was Rose and her cousin, Tina. They'd come in quietly and already had beers in their hands, heading for the pool table.

"Got it all figured out, do ye?" asked Rose. "Knows who killed Clar?"

"Heard it was your mother," said Skeemo.

"Heard you're next," said Rose, and Hooker laughed too hard and Rose tossed him a haughty look and started racking the balls. Hooker made to rise and Kyle kicked his leg.

"Make her come to you, b'y. Jaysus."

Hooker gave him a sour look and got up anyway. "Partner up?" he asked, sauntering to the pool table and Rose.

"Sure, b'y, I'll bust your balls for you," said Rose, chalking her cue.

The boys guffawed and Skeemo rose with a pained look. "Sounds like an invite to me."

Ben looked around in awe. "Look at the boys, look at 'em. Few girls walks in and they're all up and gone." He cuffed Kyle's chin. "What about you, bud? Got a girlfriend? Speaking of . . ." He got up, peering out the window. "That's the rental. Sylvie's here."

"Sylvie?" Kyle took a gulp from his drink. He wiped his mouth, held his hands on the armrests for a second, then rose from his chair. "Back in a minute," he said to Ben and headed for the door.

"Hold up, buddy." Ben hurried after him. "Chance for a few words?"

"Later. Need to talk to Sylvie before she comes in."

"Hold on." Ben stood between him and the door. "What's going on?"

"What's not, old man. We'll talk later. Look," he said as Ben backed up against the door, "I've got to talk to Sis. Hey, I didn't do it, all right?"

"Do what? Ben looked stricken. "Knife Clar? Jesus, who's thinking that?" He looked to the boys. "No-o-o, is that what they're thinking? Jesus Christ, what's going on, brother?"

"I gotta talk to Sis, I'll be back in a minute, all right? Look, I need to catch her before she comes in."

Ben drew aside, his hands falling helplessly at the distance separating them. "I'm with you, bud. Whatever the hell is going on. And Sylvie, look, she don't know nothing about you and— and the police."

"Let's keep it that way for a bit. All right, buddy? That's all I can say now. Okay?"

"Thanks." Kyle opened the door and went outside, surprising himself with his assured step.

TWELVE

———

Sylvie was parking the car, her face in profile showing their mother's defiant chin. Fine dark hair brushing her shoulders. She looked up, seeing him. Brown eyes with their mother's clarity that saw straight through to his heart. He slipped inside the car, leaving the door ajar for air. Tried to look at her but couldn't.

She laid her hand atop the back of his and it felt warm. She gripped his fingers and he gripped back, letting her lead him as she'd done those times when they were youngsters and he trod too close to the water's edge and the overhangs and the falls that churned too madly.

"I've missed you, Ky."

He winced.

She put her arm around his neck and rested her cool forehead against his hot cheek.

"I'm so sorry, Sis. I've not been thinking straight."

"You loved him. It was coming from a good place."

"You loved him, too."

"My thinking was no different. We were all screwed up."

"You're just saying that."

"No. No, I wish I were. I liked being blamed. It was my punishment. When I wasn't looking for punishment, I was blaming, too. I blamed Trapp."

He pulled back, looking at her. "Was it his fault?"

She shook her head. "No. It was not."

"They says he fucked up."

"He was good at his job. Things just happen, Ky."

"You tried to tell me before, and I wouldn't listen. Can you tell me now?"

Sylvie sat back. She closed her eyes, pressing her palm against her forehead, still seeing it, still feeling it, and he was incensed at his selfishness.

"I'm stuck, Sis. It's with me all the time. I've sealed him off somewhere. It's like he's fighting to get out and I'm fucked with it, I'm so fucked with it."

"Hey, I know it. I know it, okay?"

"Something always feels foul about the whole thing—you coming home without Ben, him coming three months later with Trapp and the bad feeling around them. And Trapp sneaking around. I just never had the courage to hear about it. Can you talk about it?"

She nodded. "It's when you're alone with it, in your head. That's when I get in trouble."

She wrung her hands and he took one, circling her thin wrist, massaging it with the pad of his thumb.

"It might hurt you," she said quietly. "Some little detail, something new you haven't figured—like pulling the scab of an old cut. It starts hurting all over agin."

He shrugged. "Hurts all the time anyway. Trapp had something to do with it, didn't he?"

She took his hand in hers, held it like a puppy in her lap, stroking it. "Remember how Chris used to go off in his mind all the time, like he was sleeping? Remember once he was eating a crust of bread and he went off, the crust across his mouth like a soggy moustache?"

"His little trances, Mother called them."

"That's where he was when it happened. Gone off somewhere. His magical place, I've always thought it, where his drawings came from. Those crazy magical drawings. The limb of a tree morphing into a bird's claw. Three moons into cabbages on an old woman's hand. Everything spooling from the one thing into everything else. Nothing's separate. And that's where we went wrong."

Her eyes shadowed in the dimming light. "After the accident, we felt him severed from us. It's not so. He's still spooling somewhere. But we're not. We're the ones caught in death. All tangled up in our grief. Not fair to him that we should be all entangled like this. It's not fair."

He nodded and she stroked his hand some more. "That's where he was when the well hole blew. In that place. That magic place. He was already gone."

"What happened?"

"Ohhh, everything, Kylie." She dropped her head back against the headrest, her words scarcely audible. "I don't really understand it. The pipes in the well hole were blown back up through. There were about twenty of them—I'm not sure—all vertical into the ground, one linked to the other. The top pipe had a chain linking it to the rig. Something like that. When the pipes were blown back out of the hole, skywards, the chain snapped. Snake-whipped around his chest. And he never felt nothing. It was so fast he never felt a thing. He was still in that place. It's how he would've drawn it, that bigger thing enclosing him. And that's all there is, my love. That's all he knew."

He closed his eyes. Felt her words eddying around him. Felt them flowing through his heart, pooling there. He opened his eyes onto hers, saw the sadness beneath their calm.

"And you saw it."

"He was lying there when I found him."

"You were the first one to see him."

"I lay beside him."

"You watched the light leave his eyes."

"It felt so soft."

He laid his head on her shoulder. "How did you survive it, Sis?"

"I'm still learning to do that, to look through a moment. Everything was leading up to that accident: Dad's heart attack, my being out West, Chris on that rig when the chain snapped. You can't pick it apart, Ky. Before Chris was even born, things were shaping themselves towards that moment—the fishery going down, Dad meeting our mother. Who can change any of that? Same with Trapp. He was good at his job, the one thing he was proud of. Then, something happened. He froze. Who knows why? Everything leading to that one moment. Just like the pipes coming up from under that ground. A hundred things coming together and Trapp couldn't hold it back. Couldn't hold back those things that froze him. Too many things coming together every moment and we can't hold it back. You see it, Ky? It's never the one thing. We're never the one responsible. And yet we all are. If there's forgiving to be done, it's ourselves we need to be forgiving, for being a part of it all. Clear enough, right?" She shrugged. "Chris knew it. A part of him knew it. It came through his drawings—everything flowing from one thing to the other. His gift to us." She smiled, her words so filled with promise, his heart surging unexpectedly.

"I need to be there, Sis. Where you are with it."

"Let it find you, then. Just . . . let it in. Mother always said we're sainted like Job when we can stand the pain and thrive in the end."

Mother. He turned from her. How the Jesus was he going to tell her about that.

"You must miss him terribly, Ky."

"No more than you."

"I've tortured myself. Thinking about you, back when it first happened, walking home by yourself in the dark.

"Bears, Sis. I'm scared of bears, not the gawd-damn dark. Listen, we have to talk about something."

"It was his fault, barring you in that haunted house."

"What house?"

She grinned. "An old house we liked to think was haunted. He barred you in there—only for a minute. Half a minute—he was just being mischievous. You screeched your head off and near had a fit."

"Sonofabitch. How come that was never talked about?"

"Thought it was. Only time I ever seen Mom mad at him."

"Must be why he let me keep the lights on all those years. Sis, we really need to talk."

"Thought we were. Hey!" Her attention shifted, something in the rearview catching her eye. She twisted sideways, looking through the back windshield. "That was Trapp. I just seen Trapp back there. He was on the highway by the restaurant when I drove out. Most likely he's heard Ben's home."

Kyle looked back, searching the road and up by the woods. "Don't see no one. Why the fuck is he always sneaking around?"

"He never did like attention. He's gotten worse, especially around me. Most likely he seen me and turned back."

"Why? What the hell is his problem?"

"Oh, Ky, we think we got problems." She sat back, keeping an eye on the rearview. "If there's one of us with the clearest claim for guilt about Chris's accident, it's him. He was the one at the controls. He blames himself. He liked Chris. Aside from Ben, Chris was the only other person I've known him to like. He's been taking it pretty hard."

"Yeah, well, guess we know what that's like."

"Yeah. Shame and guilt. Two ugly sisters. And shame's the worst—it don't hear no logic, always too busy damning itself. I'll go tell Ben." She reached for her door handle, then looked at him. "You going to be all right, Ky?"

He nodded. "Let's go in."

"Oh, by the way, who's that Kate woman? She was in Mother's room."

"When, today?"

"This morning. And Bonnie Gillard—what's that all about?"

"What were they talking about?"

"I don't know, I came into the room and they were hovering over Mom like flighty hens."

"You heard nothing? What about Mother?"

"What about her?"

"What was she saying—or doing?"

"*Mothering* them is what it felt like."

"You heard *nothing* they said?"

"Nothing, I told you. Clammed up soon as I come into the room. And she—Kate—near ran me off the road just now, driving out Hampden Road. Who is she?"

"Just a friend. Listen, Sis, I got to run home and wash up. Clothes sticking to me with cement."

"But, Kyle . . ."

"No buts, I'll be back. Tell Ben to order me one." He got out of the car, heading for Manny's truck. "Go on, I'll be back in a minute." When he looked back she was still sitting there, staring after him. "Better get inside," he said, gesturing to the bar. "Good-looking women hanging off Ben in there." He laughed at her scowl and drove off, his face shedding itself of laughter as she faded from his rearview.

———

He drove down the rough, narrow road from the club and swung up Bottom Hill. Coming down the other side, he hit the brakes. Trapp stood by the bushes near the shortcut. Jesus, he was skinny. Pale, scruffy face. He swung around like a cat, hightailing out of sight through the brush. Kyle pulled over, shut off the engine, and leaped out of the truck. He came to the mouth of the path and stopped, listening. Wind showering through the trees. Faint drone of the sea riding against the rock face. He started down the path, one quiet step after another, looking from left to right. "Hey?" he called out. "Hey, man, what's up?"

The grating call of a crow. He went farther down the path, heard the creaking limb of the old sawmill and was soon upon it.

"Hey!" he called out again. "What's up, Trapp, man? Wanna go for a beer?"

Kyle crept past a sunken mound of petrifying sawdust and neared the charred remains of the platform. There was a gap between the foundation and the ground beneath where the creaking limb swayed. As if an animal might be burrowing there. A couple of dead branches lay to the side of the opening. No animal would do that. He went over and bent down, peering inside. A shaft of light from a back entrance tunnelled through, showing a few bits of rags—and a coat. He saw a sleeping bag in there, too. A plastic bag sat to the side of the opening and he pulled it out. A chunk of mouldy cheese, dated from a month ago. Emptied juice packs. Two not opened. A couple of emptied sardine cans. He hunched down, thinking back to that morning when he'd felt something—someone!—skulking behind him in the dark. Trapp. Gawd-damn!

He peered into the burrow again and then stood, looking around. Wind stirred through the black spruce, carrying the nip of a coming evening chill. Lean, bare branches of aspen scratched the air. Sawdust still frozen into mounds and with hearts of ice. Some shelter from the wind perhaps, but little warmth. The limb creaked above, giving him the heebie-jeebies, and he cursed and climbed atop the platform and jumped up, grasping hold of the swinging, fire-blackened joist. It clung on and he wrenched harder till he felt it give and then stood aside as the fucking thing wrenched from its socket and fell at his feet. He brushed the dirt off his hands with satisfaction, wondering why the hell he hadn't laid that thing to rest the first time it spooked him.

He went to the edge of the platform, searching through the woods, listening. Facing east and just beyond a thin ridge of trees was the dropoff over the cliff face below, the inlet that had cradled Clar Gillard's body. He could hear the tide, full in and scraping sluggishly against the cliff. He cupped his hands to his mouth.

"Just wanted to have a beer, is all!" he yelled. He walked back up the path to the truck. He cruised the rest of the way down Bottom Hill and cut onto the gravel flat. Kate's car was parked by her door. Clar's dog trotted from behind the cabin, barking in warning, neck fur bristling.

"Hang 'er tough, buddy," he snapped. Didn't like that fucking dog. "Kate!" he hollered. "You home, Kate?"

Her door was ajar. He hopped onto the step and tapped lightly. It drifted open and he stood back. "Kate?"

He poked his head inside. Her guitar stood on a mat, leaning against a wooden rocker. Bread sliced on the table, a jar of mayo and a chunk of cheese. He looked towards the coffee pot on the stove and saw that it was full, a mug beside it with a hungry mouth. A door led to a bedroom.

"Kate?"

He turned back, looking about the gravel flat and to the wooded west-side hills shadowing black on a flat sea beneath a pearly sky. The river rumbled beyond the old ruins, songbirds twittering through the nearby alders. He looked to the coffee pot again, took a quick step across the room and touched it. Still warm. The dog's muffled growls grew into excited yips. Kyle went outside, rounded the cabin. The dog's rump was in the air, his head down, front paws digging furiously through the burdock and sow thistle that choked the base of the cabin. He'd been digging for some time, had an opening big enough for his snout to reach inside. He drew back as Kyle approached, black eyes burning with urgency, tongue lolling. He held his head high, barked, and then resumed his frantic clawing at the ground. Kyle turned to leave but stopped as the dog wheeled towards him with an excited whine, eyes fevered, and dove its snout back inside the hole. He emerged with a piece of dirtied cloth between his teeth, dropped it to the ground and then circled it, whining and howling. Kyle looked closer. His scarf. It was his scarf. His cashmere scarf that he'd lent his mother the morning she went to Corner Brook with Bonnie Gillard. He bent to pick it up and the dog yapped at him.

"Batter to hell," he muttered and snatched the scarf from the ground. He held it before him; it was shrunken and clumped together in parts. Blood. Dried black blood. Jesus. Oh, Jesus. He dropped to his knees, the scarf laid across his hands like a bloodied infant. He closed his eyes and saw it folded soft around his mother's nape that morning. He had impulsively kissed her there once when he was a boy, surprising her as she knelt in the doorway, tying his laces before shooing him outside for school. He'd been surprised himself by the strength of her scent suffusing his face. Oh, Mother, Mother, the world had felt so big outside and she so strong, kneeling there in that doorway. How safely he had grown in the pools of light filtering through her, the terror of dreams banished by warm milk at her morning table. He held the scarf aloft like a penitence and he an unworthy penitent. *I should've fought harder, made them cuff me.*

The dog circled him, tail between its legs. It was scared and he was scared, too. He started rocking with the scarf in his hands, picturing her coming out of their house through the effusion of yellow from the overhead light, the scarf shawled around her shoulders against the minted cool of that fog-shrouded night. He saw Bonnie running towards her from the bottom end of the wharf and the fog thickened in his brain and he saw no more and understood nothing of how her scarf became bloodied when it was Clar who was killed. He heard only her voice, whispering to Bonnie, *It's all right, you never have to be afraid again* . . .

The dog pricked its ears towards the river and a flock of gulls rose, squawking, their wings lit by slanting rays of the evening sun breaking through cloud. A grey head topped a rise on the far side of the river. Kate. Kyle rose. She didn't see him, and the river was probably too loud to hear the yapping dog. He ran to his uncle Manny's truck and stuffed the scarf underneath the seat. He closed the truck door and stood with his back to it. Kate's head was down as she picked her path across the thinning part of the river, now strewn with boulders. He opened the truck door and took the scarf back out to make sure it was what he'd seen and the sight of the blood made him crazy and he circled the truck holding it, seeing again his mother coming through the house door with the scarf around her neck and Bonnie running towards her from the bottom of the wharf and Clar—where was Clar? And where had she found his knife? He couldn't remember it being in the house, it was always in the shed, and why was the scarf bloodied when it was Clar who'd been stabbed.

He opened the truck door and shoved the scarf back beneath the seat and then closed the door and saw Kate balancing herself with her arms as she teetered across the narrow, rotting foot-bridge. He cut across the flat and walked alongside the muddied ridge by the river, waiting by the concrete ruins as Kate stepped off the footbridge and clambered up a small incline of banked beach rocks. She looked surprised to see him standing there and looked anxiously past him towards her cabin.

"Thought I heard a dog barking."

"Clar's dog. That fucking thing got a name? You left your door open."

"He never needed calling, was Clar's shadow. I've been feeding him. I better get back there, close the door."

"I already closed it." He stood before her and she stood back, appearing calm and yet unable to keep from darting glances towards her cabin.

"Some things I need to ask you, Kate."

She nodded, glanced towards the cabin again. "Can we talk another day, Kyle? Tomorrow?"

He touched his pocket where the bloodied scarf still burned like a phantom limb and shook his head. She lowered her eyes from his and with great effort sat on the ridge of beach rocks. Her hair was loose, feathery about her shoulders. She gathered it in a handful and tucked it beneath her jacket collar like a scarf against the cold and her mouth drooped with sadness as she stared into the fattened river.

He sat beside her. "What do you know about my mother?"

"That I wish she was mine."

"I thought you loved your mother."

"Love has many shapes, Kyle. Some of them can get pretty warped." She rubbed her throat as though her words pained her.

"Starting to feel like a stranger, Kate."

"That worked for a while, not knowing anyone. Gives a person time to hunt one's self down."

"You running?"

She shook her head. "I tried to once. The past shadows us like those birds up there. Cheats our every triumph, and I expect I'm starting to sound tiring here."

"More like Kate writing a song."

She gave a self-deprecating shrug. "Turning days into words. You said that once, and I like that. Guess some days can never be sung."

He jiggled his foot impatiently and she reached out her hand as though reaching for more time.

"It's not a terribly interesting story, or original. My father used to be decent till the moonshine rotted his brain. Started knocking us around like yard ornaments. I cut out."

"Sounds about right."

"Yeah. Except I left Verny behind." She paused. "Vernon. I was fourteen when I had him. His father wasn't much older than me, and he never knew. I was hidden inside the house for most of it. Hidden beneath heavy coats when I went out. He was born early March; my mother took him for hers. Some of our own knew it, but it was never talked about." She looked at him with a twisted smile and he made a move to silence her, to ask only after his mother, but she raised a hand, silencing him.

"Verny was six when I left. He knew me as his sister. And he cried when I was saying goodbye. I always stood between him and my father. I promised I'd come back for him, but I didn't. I married a nice man, and I stopped wanting to go back home. And that is my cross."

"Your husband, where is he now?"

"He was older, much older. He died."

"Sorry, Kate. Guess we all have our cross. Where is he now, your son?"

She shrugged. "I don't know."

"Sorry."

"Yeah, we're all sorry. And I expect you want to know why I'm sneaking into your mother's room at the hospital." She was still gazing into the river, elbows resting on her knees. She was crying when she looked back at him. She took off her glasses, wiping her eyes, and then stood, relieved by the sound of a car coming down the road. "It's your father."

"Can we keep talking, here? What's up with you and my mother?"

"Somebody behind him, they're stopping." She said impatiently, "I need to see what's going on. Who's that behind him?"

He twisted sideways, looking towards the road. His father was pulling over, Manny following. "It's Uncle Manny," he said. "Driving Aunt Melita's car." Manny was getting out of the car and heading towards his truck parked by Kate's. The truck with his mother's bloodied scarf tucked beneath the seat. He was on his feet and running. The dog was squatting on his haunches by the truck door when he got there, ears back, tail down, growling at Manny.

"Watch him. Watch him, Uncle Manny!" Kyle stood breath-
less beside his uncle. Sylvanus was tooting his horn from across the
road, rolling down his window.

"Whose dog? He your dog?" asked Manny.

"Naw, Clar's dog. Get! Get outta here," he shouted at the dog.
"Get! Been hanging around ever since the other night. We all
been all feeding him." The dog lowered its head and tail and then
trotted after Kate, who'd come up behind Kyle and was now
walking purposefully towards Sylvanus.

"Who's that?" asked Manny. "She that strange woman everyone's talking about?"

"Suppose, b'y." Kyle opened the truck door and leaned inside,
grabbing the scarf from beneath the seat and shoving it into his
coat pocket. "Jaysus, lookie here." He pulled back with a silly grin
at his uncle and held up the keys. "Left them in the ignition.
Thought I had them under the seat."

"All good, my son. Go on, now. See your mother. She's in the
truck, sharp as a tack. Bonnie Gillard's in there with her. She got
all your mother's drugs and a nurse trained her about the other
stuff. Go on, now, you got nothing to worry about."

Kyle clapped his uncle's shoulder and was broadsided by his
Aunt Melita coming towards him and stumbling beneath a bundle
of coats and grocery bags in her arms.

"Swear be Jesus he lives by hisself," she said, and thumped her
bundle against Manny's chest. "Here, take something, quick,
before I drops it."

"Look at her, look at her stuff. Five minutes in the store and
she empties their shelves. Why don't you leave it in the car?"

"Because I'm not going straight home, you are. And half of
this goes in the fridge. Take it." She dumped the load in Manny's
arms, dimpled face ticking with annoyance, and then turned to

Kyle. "Come here, my love." She patted his cheeks with soft hands. "Don't you worry about your mother now. She's going to be fine. I knows because I've bargained me soul with the devil over this one."

"Thanks, Aunt Melita." He saw Kate talking intently with his father and looking past him towards his mother. "I better get going."

"You go on then. And I'll be back up tomorrow and make a batch of sweet bread. Hold on." She grasped his coat sleeve. "You make sure she don't get out of bed. Bonnie got her drugs and other things sorted out and so there's nothing for you worry about. Except feed her and keep her off her feet. You hear that?"

"I hears you, Aunt Melita. Thanks." He pecked her cheek and went over to Kate, who was now backing away from his father's truck.

"The police," she said, seeing him, "the police are coming," and she brushed past him, her hands to her mouth.

"What's with her?" he asked his father. "What's going on?"

"Get in the truck. Nothing you can do. Get in the back, we gets your mother home. Hurry up."

The police. He rammed his hand into the pocket with the bloodied scarf. He heard his mother's voice, talking to him from the cab. She sounded faint, weak.

"You stupid?" yelled his father. "Get in the gawd-damned truck, we gets your mother home."

He heard another vehicle coming down Bottom Hill. The police. The police were coming. He tightened his grip on the scarf with fright and leaped into the back of the truck. The dog trotted alongside as they drove, outstripping the truck as they pulled up to the wharf. Kyle jumped out of the back, his foot twisting beneath him. He cursed and limped on towards the shed in pain.

The truck door opened behind him, his mother's voice calling for him. He lurched into the dimly lit shed. Firewood stacked
two tiers thick lined the walls. A chopping block sat in the centre,
the axe resting against it. The car was motoring closer. His father
belted out his name and he bent near the low end of a wood tier
and crumpled the scarf beneath a junk of wood and went for the
door. Then he looped back inside the shed. The police. The
fucking police. First place they'd search would be the shed. He
grabbed the scarf again, balled it in his hand, and bolted outside
to the back of the shed. He looked up the wooded hillside and
started towards a grouping of rocks beneath a rotting black spruce.
The dog appeared sniffing and whining beside him and he spat in
rage. The dog, the gawd-damned dog would dig it out.

"Kyle!"

He turned back to the shed, dove inside. The car had driven
past and was parking on the other side of his father's truck. He
heard the doors opening and nearly cried with relief upon hearing
Sylvie singing out to their mother. And Ben, shouting something
about suitcases. Sylvanus shouted back, his voice drawing near the
shed. He stood there now, darkening the doorway. Kyle tucked
the scarf beneath his coat and backed away.

"Kyle!" Sylvanus's face was dark with worry, a strange light in
his eyes. "What're you doing?"

Kyle backed up against the wall.

"She didn't do it, Ky."

He nodded.

"What's going on? You hearing me? Your mother didn't do it."

He held out the bloodied scarf, unable to speak.

"What's that—my scarf? What're you doing?"

"She—" He ran a dry tongue over parched lips. "It's . . . it's
mine. She was wearing it. It's got his blood on it. Clar's blood."

His father snatched the scarf and looked more closely, seeing the blood. He threw it to the floor and landed his hands heavily on Kyle's shoulders.

"She didn't do it. Your mother didn't do it. It was Trapp."

Trapp.

"You hearing me? Trapp done it. I drove out fast as I could to tell you. Trapp done it."

Kyle shook his head. She did it. She did.

"What's you gone deaf? She didn't do it, b'y. Jesus, would I be telling you this if it wasn't true? She'll tell you all about it. I don't know about the scarf, and it don't matter. You hearing me, now?"

Kyle's hands were held out as though they still held the scarf. His father smacked them away.

"What's you gone foolish? Ky? Kyle! You hearing me?"

He leaned his head onto his father's shoulders and started to cry. He felt his father's arms tighten around him, heard his voice hushed like a prayer. "Sin. Sin. I led you to think it—gawd-damn sin."

Kyle pulled back, wiping at his face.

"You fine, now?"

Kyle kept wiping his face.

"Clar was after Bonnie. He was going to drown her. He had hold of her—had her bent over the wharf and your mother come out and caught him."

Kyle rubbed at his temples, trying to see it. His father hunched down on the chopping block, shaking his head in the way of the old-timers when a thought is too hard.

"You taking it in, Kylie?"

"It was *my* scarf. I gave it to her that morning she left for the hospital. She was cold—"

"Kylie, Kylie, it don't matter. He was going for Bonnie, is all. He needed an excuse. He seen the scarf on me—or thought he did, or some gawd-damn thing, and took it from her car. Blamed her for cheating and said he was showing it to your mother."

"What the fuck did he do that for?"

"To get Bonnie here. That's all he wanted. He knew she'd come to stop him saying things about me and your mother, dirty fucker. When I picked Bonnie up earlier that evening, that's where she was going, to his place. Stop him from coming here, but he was already gone when she got there."

"That's what she told you?"

"Just now at the hospital. I done what you was going to do— forced it from her and your mother, both."

"How come they kept it secret, then? Jesus Christ."

"That's another story. Your mother can tell you that one."

"What happened with Bonnie, then—after you dropped her off?"

"When she seen Clar was gone, she come here. That's what he wanted her to do, come here. Get her down by the water. Nobody around. He wanted to drown her."

"On our wharf. How'd he know we wouldn't be here?"

"I don't know, b'y. He took a chance. He would've liked it, drowning her on our wharf. He was sick like that. That's what Bonnie said. And she did come. She got here and the lights in the house were out and she was leaving again when she heard him coming along the beach. She hid right here, in the shed, thinking he'd go home if there was no lights on in the house. She stepped on the knife, she said. Figured it was God-given and took it. He sung out to your mother and that was it. Bonnie went after him. With the knife."

"She was going to kill him."

"I think she would've. She had that look when she told me about it. Guess only she knows that. Perhaps she don't know her-

self what she would've done. Didn't matter. Clar was too fast for
her. He shook the knife from her hand and he dragged her to the
lower end of the wharf. He had the scarf around her neck, that's
how he dragged her. Near choked her. She couldn't sing out, she
was clawing at the scarf, and he was dragging her, she couldn't get
on her feet. He had her over the wharf when your mother come
out. She heard the dog barking; it woke her up. And that's when
Trapp showed."

"Trapp. Where the fuck did he come from?"

"He was up at the fire. With Kate. He seen Bonnie coming
down the road and followed her. Luck. That's all it was. Perhaps
a bit more than luck—he got his stuff going on, too. When your
mother turned on the light over the door, first thing Trapp seen
was the knife. He seen what Clar was doing and ran for the knife.
Clar come after him, then."

"Jesus." Kyle sat down by the wood tier, wrapped his arms
around his knees, his legs shaking.

"Fierce," said his father. "Something fierce."

"Finish it."

"No more to it. They fought and—who knows. Trapp says
he didn't mean to—didn't know he got him till Clar let out that
screech. That's when he fell overboard. That's when I got there,
just as he was falling. I never seen Trapp. Only Clar falling. And
Bonnie running. And then your mother."

"What about the scarf? How did the blood get on it?"

"Don't know. Might be Clar's. He had it in his hands. Bonnie
said he hauled it from around her throat and went for Trapp. Perhaps he was going to choke him."

"Jesus, old man."

"Might be Trapp's—he got his own hand cut somehow.
Stabbed it himself, he thinks. Wicked stuff. Wicked." Sylvanus

hove out a pent-up breath. He dropped his head, rubbing the back of his neck with weariness.

"Take 'er easy, old man. Good thing you never got there, could've been a whole lot worse. No sense in blaming yourself for any of that."

Sylvanus gave him a sharp look. "Don't you worry now, cocky. I'm done with that, too. Taking on stuff. Like your mother says now, we're foolish mortals thinking we got all the power over everything. That young fellow out there, he got to figure that one out too. That's what your mother was doing by not telling—giving him time to figure it out. She owed him that, she said. She might be dead herself and Bonnie with her if he hadn't happened along."

"Trapp. He never *happened* along. He's been lurking about."

"That's it now, he got his stuff going on, like I said. You go on in the house, let your mother tell you that one."

"Where is he right now?"

"He's on the run. Go on in, your mother tells you."

"Tells me what? Go on and finish it, old man. This has been dragged out enough."

"Another minute won't hurt. Your mother knows the rest of it better than me." Sylvanus got up and bent by the wood tier, picking up a few sticks of wood. He looked down at Kyle. "You all right, Kylie?"

"Yeah, sure." He pulled himself to his feet and walked the length of the shed, hands clasped behind his head, staring at the rafters. "Fucking mess."

"Soon be over, now. I called the police before I left Corner Brook. We been through hell with this, but no more." Sylvanus stood up, clutching his armload of wood. "Go in, talk to your mother."

"Wait. He . . . Trapp was down by the bar a while ago."

"I told the police he was in Corner Brook. According to Kate."

"Kate? What the fuck do she got to do with this?"

"Your mother. Go see your mother."

Sylvanus vanished out through the door. Kyle bent down, legs still quivering, and picked up a few junks. Outside the shed he watched the darkening clouds descend like a pot cover over the western skyline. A flicker of yellow star lit Kate's cabin window. He went inside his house. It was lit up like Christmas—hallway lights on, living room lights, kitchen, bedrooms. His mother's voice was coming from the bedroom, intermingling with Sylvie's and his father's. Woodstove cracking like corn popping and sending warmth straight through the rafters. Full. His life felt full again.

Ben came from Addie's room, eyes stoked with sadness. He sat at the kitchen table, looking out the window at the darkling sea the way Sylvanus did when he was feeling something too deep to figure. Sylvie came in behind him. She looked from Kyle to Ben, dazed and unsure of which one to go to.

"My lord, Ky. You kept all this to yourself, then." She went to him, put her reedy arms around his waist and held on. Too thin, he thought. She's too thin. She's been through it. She pulled away and went and stood behind Ben, leaning herself against him, wrapping her arms around his neck and pressing her cheek against the curls of his bent head. "He's always done the best he could for Trapp," she said to Kyle. "You know it, don't you, Ben? You've always done the best for him. Despite all what happened."

Ben nuzzled his cheek against her hand.

"What all happened?" asked Kyle.

Ben wiped at his eyes, shook his head. "All history, now, b'y. For some of us, anyway. Trapp took a rap for me back in Alberta, few years ago. Drug deal went wrong. My drugs, my fault. He took the rap and done hard time. He was always a bit off, but that took a toll." He looked at Kyle with a sad smile. "Not one for Mother's ears."

"Thought we knew everything around here."

"There's the joke. He got worse after the accident. Few breakdowns. Sounds like he's having another one now. Fun stuff, hey? Christ. Calmer on the diamond fields of Sierra Leone."

"Trapp always made things harder," said Sylvie. She looked towards her father who was entering the room. "She all right, Dad?"

"Cup of tea, dolly. I'll make a pot." He looked at Kyle, raising his brows in a surly manner. "What's you keeping her waiting for? She wants to see you."

Kyle hauled off his coat, tossed it over the back of a chair, and went into his mother's room. She was lying back on a mound of pillows. Her face was peaked, her eyes feverish. More with excitement, thought Kyle, as she reached for him. Bonnie was hunched over the night table on the far side of the bed, a dozen pill bottles stretched in front of her, writing down information from their labels into a notebook.

He bent, kissed his mother's cheek.

"Time you shaved," she said, patting his stubbled chin, and then whispered, her words tight with remorse, "What I just put ye all through. I should've told your father."

"Should've told somebody. Christ, Mother." He gave a relieved laugh and sat in the chair pulled up by her bed. "Why didn't you? What's with the secrets?"

He looked at Bonnie accusingly and was instantly apologetic, feeling his past judgment of her.

But her eyes held no resentment. "Wouldn't be my doing," she replied firmly.

"She went along because I asked her," said Addie. "She's put up with something too, everybody thinking she did it. Her family phoning her, the police. I put all of you through it, didn't I?" Her face twisted with sudden pain.

"It's soon time to take your pills," said Bonnie. "Once the pain starts, it's no good." She turned to Kyle. "We have to keep timing her pills so's to head off the pain, else she'll be back in the hospital."

"She's being a tough nurse," said Addie through a weak smile. "You tell him, my dear. I saves my breath."

Bonnie looked at Kyle. "She didn't tell because she wanted to give Trapp time. He turned himself in to the hospital after—after he done it. The hospital knows him. He's been there a few times. He gets down. Breakdowns, you know. He told them he was going to kill himself, that's why they took him right away."

"Did they know what he done?"

"No. He never told them that."

"He's afraid," said Addie faintly. "He was in jail once and he's afraid of going back. He's not thinking straight right now. He's run off. Kylie, something you need to know. About your friend, Kate."

"What's she to do with all of this?" he asked, leaning closer.

"Bit of a shock for you. She's his mother. Trapp's mother."

"What? Jesus, what're you saying?"

"That's why we never told the police," said Bonnie. "Kate asked us not to. She wanted Trapp to get a handle on things. To turn himself in."

Kyle sat staring at them both in disbelief. "That's not possible. She's too young . . ." *I was fourteen when I had him . . .*

"Jesus Christ." He got up, coiled around his chair, sat back down, fixing his eyes on his mother with astonishment. "You—

we—none of us fucking knows who she is—Christ!" He sat back, shaking his head. The psych ward, Kate slumped against the wall: she'd been visiting Trapp. "Why did she keep it a fucking secret? And you, the both of you"—he looked at Bonnie—"involving yourself with her . . . *in something like this?* Oh, man!"

"He's estranged himself from her," said Addie. "She come here because *he* was always coming here. To see us. He feels he owes us for Chrissy. He just don't know what he owes us."

"But it was self-defence! He'd get off! What's with all the fucking around? Did he think they'd never catch him?"

"Ky, he's a sick boy. I was giving his mother a chance to bring him in."

"His *mother*! Jesus Christ. She been lying to us for months. Fucking lying! Jesus!"

"It's a hard one," said Bonnie.

"Hard. They've been putting us through hell."

"Because you didn't tell me what you and your father were thinking."

"Because *you* didn't tell *us* what you were *doing*!"

Addie sank back on her pillow. "I was asked not to," she said tiredly. "I didn't know it was going to turn into all this."

"He's all paranoid," said Bonnie. "Thinks everybody is after him. Kate asked for time to find him. She's afraid he'll hurt himself if the police find him first."

"Small thing to give, isn't it, a bit of time?" said Addie. "After what we've lost?"

He stood again, pacing the room with a growing agitation, then looked back at his mother. "When did Kate come to you?"

"That night. She had followed him."

"She was here, too? Jesus, half the fucking town was here?"

"Stop your swearing!"

He stopped pacing, surprised by the strength in his mother's voice. "Sorry," he mumbled, and sat, fidgeting with his fingers. Bonnie laid a calming hand on Addie's and looked at Kyle.

"Kate didn't see anything," she said. "Trapp fled just as she was getting here. We told her and she ran off, back to her cabin. She was hoping he'd go back there. She was taking it hard and she, well, she just wanted time." Bonnie shrugged. "Your mother said yes."

"And you, too."

"She said she'd explain later. She was pretty much begging us for time. And we gave it to her."

"She was so upset, Ky," said Addie. "If it were you, I would've asked for the same."

"She knows it's wrong not to turn him in," said Bonnie. "He wasn't so bad at first. She thought she could get around him. Get him to turn himself in. But he's after getting sicker. Your father phoned the police after your mother told him."

"I got to go," he said, and started from the room.

"Wait, Kyle."

"Fuck, no. Don't tell me no more."

"He needs our help," said Addie, her voice fading. He turned back, alarmed as she winced, pushing herself up on her pillows.

"Hold on now, my love." Bonnie was instantly leaning over her, her arm beneath her pillow, raising it a little. "How's that now? I'm getting your pills ready, we'll take them now."

"A minute, just a minute. Kyle, she's a good soul . . ."

"Mother, just—Jesus, just take your pills. And stop off worrying. You'll see to her?" he said to Bonnie and backed out of the room.

His father was pouring tea at the kitchen sink, Sylvia sitting at the table, talking in low tones to Ben.

"What the fuck," Kyle burst out. "Kate's his *mother*? Did you know that, Ben?"

Ben shook his head. "Not till your mother just said. He kept that one secret."

"That's it now," said Sylvanus. "Here, where you going?" Kyle was hauling on his coat and heading for the door. "Wait up there, brother."

"Waiting no longer, sir." He reached for the doorknob, pausing as rapid footsteps sounded from the outside.

"Don't open it, check first," said Sylvie, getting to her feet. Kyle was already turning the doorknob. He pulled the door open and Kate rushed inside, her wind-blown hair harnessed by her toque, her face flushed, her eyes more feverish than his mother's.

"He's going to hurt himself," she whispered, hands to her mouth in fear. "He's run off, he's going to hurt himself. I tried to follow him but he took to the woods."

Ben shoved back his chair. "Bottom Hill—or in the road?"

"Bottom Hill. He just showed up. I told him the police knew and he panicked and ran off again. He's scared."

"I knows where he is," said Kyle. "He's up at the old sawmill. I seen he was camping there."

"You," said Kate, going to Ben. "You're Ben? He always talks about you. He loves you. You're the only one he might listen to. He's . . . he's really paranoid, he's sick. I don't want him dragged away like an animal by the police. And he'll do something, I know he will. I've seen him like this before."

"We'll find him," said Sylvanus.

"No, no, just Ben should go."

"He won't know I'm there. Kyle, you wait here. Sylvie, close your mother's door, she don't need be hearing this."

"Suppose he's violent?" said Sylvie. "I've seen his temper, and if he's not in his right mind—"

"We owe him," said Kate sharply. "He took Clar down. He wasn't scared that night. He's scared now. And he needs our help." She looked at them all, her eyes skimmed with fear.

"We'll find him," said Ben. He strode out the door, Kate following him.

"Kyle, watch the house," said Sylvanus, following outside behind Kate and Ben. Kyle looked at Sylvie. "I'll just be outside," he said.

"No, you can't go too. Someone should be here, in case he comes back."

"I'll just be outside. Go sit with Mom." He flicked on the outside light in the rapidly falling darkness. His father and Ben were rustling through the bushes and vanishing up the path. Kate stood beside the gump, staring after them.

"I apologize for the secrecy," she said without turning. "I apologize deeply."

"You could've told me."

"No. I couldn't. Besides, who would've sold their cabin to a Trapp? You already burned us out of town, once."

"That the only reason you made yourself up?"

"I promised Vernon." She turned to him, an edge to her voice. "You know what it feels like to grieve a brother, Ky. Well, I'm grieving a son. Weigh that in your heart when you're judging mine. I'm all he's got. He's lost his sense of reality. That makes him the living dead and he's only got me to fight for him. And he don't know that because he's angry with me. Real angry, and he won't let me help."

"How come nobody recognized you?"

"I told you, I cut out—long before my family relocated to Jackson's Arm. And you might say I've aged somewhat. You want my sad song, Kyle? I've only ever sung it to myself."

He didn't want to hear. His anger was comforting. He wanted to walk away from her, just as he'd done to Sylvie all those times she needed to talk, and his mother.

"I understand if you don't."

He shrugged. "Pass the time, I suppose."

"Be mad, Ky. Don't matter, I did it for him. It's been three years now since I told him. My mother died a few months after your brother. I went home for her funeral. I seen what he was doing to himself about the accident. His guilt eating him alive. He's not loved many people, but he liked your brother. I breastfed him, Ky. In dark corners so's no one would see. Some part of him remembers those moments, his milky mouth suckling. We loved each other. And then I abandoned him. To my abusive father. I've had to live with that. Least I know where my pain comes from. He wasn't allowed that knowing. And so I told him. I thought— well, I thought he'd be open. That it . . . might bring him comfort. Or something like that. Sure as hell pegged that one wrong. He was disgusted. It felt incestuous to him. I thought he'd be relieved that his father wasn't his own, he hated him so much. Guess he's like Clar's dog, licking the cruel master's hand. Always sniffing for something that's not there."

"The only hand he had, I suppose."

She turned from him.

"Sorry. Look, you don't have to tell me this stuff."

"That's what I've never liked about you, Ky. You never look under rocks, scared something might bite you."

"I know where my pain comes from, Kate. It's not always a thinking thing."

"No. No, it isn't. But thinking is what brought me here. Knowing he needed to be around your family. Figuring if I put myself closer to you, he might come to me."

"Is that the only reason you struck up a friendship? Always felt you wanted something."

"Hey, it was you that kept coming to me. He did, too. Eventually. This is where I needed to be. Perhaps I might've told you if you'd asked. Not sure about that. Vernon made me promise not to tell who I was. That's his thing. Least I could give him—his privacy while he worked things out. Look, I didn't think it would take so long. He's a bit like you, there—don't like looking too deep. I mean that kindly, Ky. I found my son through you. And Clar Gillard."

He huffed with insolence. "Just how the Jesus do you mean that?"

"Your loneliness. Thinking your pain is something only you can see. I realized Vernon could see mine, too. I think that's what kept bringing him to me, here in my little cabin. He saw my loneliness. Felt it. Felt it like he felt his own. We were starting to make ground when, well, Clar Gillard happened."

"And just how does Clar fit in with your lovely little reunion?"

"He was a baby once. Where did his betrayal begin? What awful loneliness is that, killing the ones you love? They're the disheartened. And the abandoned. In the end, their loneliness is the only thing they're loyal to. Think of it, Ky. If we can't figure Clar Gillard, how does that look upon us? We're as blind he is." She looked over the darkening sea and towards the moon rising yellow over the hills. Then she looked back at him, wiped at her glasses, pushed them up on her nose as though to see him better. That old expectant look was back in her eyes. She didn't look like a stranger with that expression, she looked like Kate, searching for something.

"Another song coming, I suppose. The lonely life of the penitent?"

"Why not? Somebody should sing for the lonely. Else theirs would be an unmarked road, and how fair is that? I've never lied to you, Ky. Not in my heart. I hope you come to learn that." She stood before him, unapologetic in her manner, and for the second time that evening he felt the pang of his judgment.

A sound came to them from over by the cliff—a growl, followed by a sharp yap.

"I'd know that yap anywhere," said Kyle. "You hold on here," he said to Kate. "I'll go see." He let himself over the side of the wharf, boots scrunching through wet pebbles as he made his way across the beach towards the black mass of rock jutting into the sea. The tide was almost in; he'd have to scale around the cliff. He heard Kate's boots scrunching through the beach rocks behind him.

"The tide's in, you can't get around," he called back. He broke off, hearing the dog bark again. He grasped the rock wall, wet with groundwater leaking down its face from the sods crowning it above. He pulled himself along, the cliff cold, gritty to his hands. His foot slipped on cloven rock and he cursed as water soaked cold through both boots.

The house door opened, and Sylvie called his name. "Where are you? The police called. Ky? Are you there?"

He looked back. Saw her peering around the side of the house, a sweater hugging her shoulders.

"They said they're coming here. Ky?"

He wanted to shush her, to yell out and reassure her, but he was scared he'd frighten off Trapp, should he hear him. Kate was silent behind him. He looked down. The water was black, smelling of rotting kelp. Another sharp bark and he pressed harder against the rock, inching himself along. He tipped the corner of the cliff wall and stilled. A bit of moonlight filtered through scattering clouds and he saw the dog crouched just ahead of him, where he'd been the morning he stood guard over Clar's body. He was staring up at the back of the inlet, his fur glistening wet and quivering. The dog sensed his coming and was quiet now, except for a soft

mewling in his throat. Kyle looked up. Straight up the rock face.
He couldn't see anything, just black. He tried to get a footing on
higher rock, kept slipping back. Up to his ankles in water cold as
fuck. He looked up the cliff face again. The old sawmill was just
above and he strained to hear Ben's or his father's voice. The *whoop-
whoop* of a gull winging past. The clang of a buoy off from Hampden Wharf. A crab scuffling over rocks. Something else—a soft
sound—from up above. Something shifting, scratching against the
rock. The dog mewled and he hushed it. A flat voice, shivery with
cold, perhaps fear, drifted down from the rock face.

"He won't hurt you."

His eyes bugged out of his head, trying to see. "Yeah," he said.
"I know. He's just scared."

Silence.

"You have a dog?" asked Kyle.

A flat *Ha ha*. "Naw. No dog for Trappy."

"You can have this one. He got no home. Driving us nuts,"
he added as nothing more came from above. "You want him?"

A shaving of moonlight on the rock wall. Trapp was crouched
on a small ledge about forty, fifty feet straight up, roughly six feet
down from the top. Bony legs drawn up, bony arms hunched like
a stork readying to take flight. Slightest hint of a breeze and he'd
blow over.

"Be doing us a favour if you took him. Can't get rid of him."
Silence.

"What are you doing up there?"

"Ha ha. What're *you* doing down there?"

"Not much. Well. Looking for you, actually."

"Lots of people looking for Trappy."

"Sounds like it was an awful night."

"He wasn't scared."

"Who, Clar?"

"He never jumped. Everybody else jumped."

"Jumped where?"

"Before she blew— We heard the rumbling. Everybody jumped."
Kyle faltered.

"He never jumped."

"Yeah."

"Bad. That was bad."

"Yeah."

"Trappy don't like that one."

"Sylvie . . . she said it was awful loud. When it blew."
Silence.

"All them pipes blowing outta the ground."
Silence.

"Guess everybody was scared."

"Trappy still hears them."

"Sis. She says things happen, hey? That's what she says."

"Yeah."

"True, that. You should come down. Go for a beer?" He was
starting to shiver, as much from Trapp's words as from the iced
seawater numbing his feet. He lifted one of his boots, scaling the
cliff for a higher footing, but it slid back into the water.

"Who's there?"

"Just me. Slipped." He clung to the cliff, hearing movement
from above and not daring to inch farther. A minuscule draft of
wind might topple that scrawny-shouldered hulk readying for
flight. Then he thought of something.

"Hey, my knife. Did you drop it from up there or something?"

"Ha, ha."

"You dropped it? Were you hiding it up there?"

"Till I dropped it, ha ha."

"Why didn't you put it in the shed or someplace?"

"Too many coppers."

"It was self-defence, man. My father—he's already told the police. They knows it was self-defence. Come down, hey? We can talk about it if you want."

"He wasn't scared."

He forced his tongue to move. "Hey, b'y. Me, I'm scared all the fucking time."

"Feels bad about it."

"Yeah."

"Real bad."

"We moves on, hey?"

"Yeah. Trappy's moving on." He rose, hunched shoulders lifting into wings.

"Wait. Hey. Just . . . just a minute. I think I hears Ben. He come here, looking for you. You know that? Ben's here looking for you. He's—he's eager to see you, man. Came all the way from Corner Brook. Let's go find him, what do you say? Look, what do you say? We go find Ben, uh?" He stumbled for words, his fingers feeling like ice sticks clinging to the rock. He started quivering, water icing his legs. "You want to come down? Getting cold here. Like to go for a beer?"

A whisper from behind. Kate. "I'm going up there. Tell Ben where he is."

"Who's that?" Trapp's voice was tinged with alarm.

"The dog, man. Was talking to the dog. He's c-cold. Starting to shiver myself. Ha ha." He paused, a small wavelet brushing up past his shins. Be another ten minutes before the inlet filled with water and it still wouldn't cushion a jump. "I talked to the p-police. The sergeant, he's a f-fat old fellow, MacDuff. Wants a meal of squid. Thought we'd all go jigging next month, hey? Bring him a couple dozen. Me and Ben. You want to come? Take some squid to the old fellow?"

Nothing from above. Kyle strained to hold on. If he fell, he'd be stiffer than Clar within three minutes in that ice bucket. "What're you at, man? Let's g-go. Find Ben."

"Who's there?"

"Just me. The dog."

"Up there. There's somebody up there. Who's up there?"

"That's probably Ben."

"Ben?"

"Yeah. He's looking for you. I told you. Wants to have a beer."

"Shhh."

"It's just Ben," whispered Kyle.

Ben's voice, soft and easy and a bit jokey, floated down from above. "What the fuck you doing down there? Look at him, a fucking bird. What're you after smoking now?"

"Ha ha. Benji boy."

"Get up here, you silly fuck."

"Ha ha."

"What's so ha ha funny? Get the Jesus up here."

A mewl. Like that of the dog. He was crying.

"Move over, bud. I'm coming down."

"Not going to jail, Benji."

"Jail. They're planning parties for you, you silly nit. Aww, Christ, hold on, I can't get down there. You gotta come up, buddy."

"Ha ha."

"Come on, b'y."

"He was hurting her."

"You stopped it. Self-defence. No jail, I promise you this time. No jail."

"Not going back, Benji."

"That's what I just said, you silly fucker. What part you not getting? We just sign some papers, self-defence. You want me to yodel it to you?"

"Ha ha."

"Come on, man. Come on up, it's cold. Let's go get a beer. Come on, let's go get a beer."

"Katie? Is Katie there? I heard Katie."

"She's here. You want her?"

"Verny? It's . . . it's me."

"I'm scared, Katie."

"I'm not. I'm not scared. I'm staying with you this time. And the dog. We'll take him too, if you want. We can keep him at the cabin till we fix things."

"There you go, bud," said Ben. "You got yourself a dog. Come on, now. See my hand? Take it, buddy."

"Ha ha, Benji boy."

"Stop calling me fucking Benji, you sounds like Mother."

"Came out to see you, Benji."

"Well get up here, then. Let's go get a beer."

"Not going back, Benji."

"No, boy, I told you. You're not going to jail. We got it all covered, she's good, man. Come on up, now. Take my hand."

Kyle was staring hard. He could see Trapp's dark, hunched figure. He saw him move a bit to the right, away from Ben.

"Come on, buddy. Take my hand. Been too long, I miss you, buddy."

Soft mewls. He was crying again.

"Nothing's going to happen. You done a good thing, man, you did a good thing."

"Ben?"

"I'm right here, bud. See my hand? Take my hand."

"Not going to jail, Benji boy."

"Take my fucking hand, Trapp!"

"Not going."

"Vernon!" It was Sylvanus. His voice deep, strong. "Come on up now, my son. Been enough suffering. Come on up. It's all over now."

Kyle scarcely breathed, watching Trapp's shoulders rise, lean forward. He wanted to yell out, couldn't, held on to his father's voice unfurling like a strong rope down the cliff. "Come on, my son. You hearing me, Vernon? I'm making my way down. My young fellow up there, he don't want this. No rest for him till we're all resting here. No more suffering. I'll not take no more suffering over this. You see my hand? Take my hand, now."

The clouds scuttered; a blue light gleamed off black rock. Trapp stood with his head drawn back into his shoulders, his arms stretching out. Something moved to his left. He let out a sharp cry, a hand appearing out of the dark, reaching for him, reaching. "Take my hand, son. I can't stretch any farther. Take my hand. Take my hand, now. He wants you to take my hand." A cry from Trapp. A hurting cry and another, cut short. And he hung there, like a bird frozen in flight. The hand stretched farther, then farther, and Kyle sucked in his breath with fear that his father would tumble down the rock face. His fingers touched Trapp's, and then locked themselves around his wrist. "You're cold, my son. Let's go, now. We've got a fire going. Come on, now."

The breath left Kyle. He watched as Trapp's thin body, like a stickman shadow up there on the cliff, reached with his other hand onto his father's. He climbed slowly, his legs cramped no doubt, as were Kyle's, and frozen. Trapp's legs vanished out of sight, Sylvanus's voice fading, Ben's taking over.

"Christ almighty, skin and bones. What're you eating, putty from the windows? Not skinny, is he—see the sin on his soul.

Look, you're shivering, you're freezing, here b'y. Take my coat, take my coat, put it on." Ben's words faded, Kate's sounded over them, none of them audible, fading with the wind.

Kyle shivered uncontrollably. He turned, starting back around the cliff. His fingers too stiff to curl around the rock ledges. His feet frozen pods that kept tripping over cloven rock and sinking into the water. The dog had slipped into the ocean and was swimming alongside. They both reached around the other side of the cliff and Kyle saw the brown rental driving off from the wharf. He walked across the beach and climbed onto the wharf, his legs stiffer than two flagpoles. Sylvanus was standing near the house, watching the car vanishing up ahead.

"Where they taking him?" asked Kyle.

His father started. "Just about to come for you. To the hospital. They'll phone the police from there."

"No need," said Kyle. A police cruiser was coming down the road. He stood there with his father, waiting till it hauled up alongside and MacDuff painfully climbed out of the car, wiping his nose with a towel-sized handkerchief. Canning remained behind the wheel.

"Time I gave this up," said MacDuff, pocketing his handkerchief and tipping his hat to Kyle and Sylvanus. "We talked to your daughter," he said to Sylvanus. "She said Vernon Trapp was here."

"He was," said Sylvanus. "But he's gone now. He's at the hospital in Corner Brook. He's a sick boy, but . . . got a feeling he'll be all right."

"How did he get to the hospital?"

"His mother took him."

"Mother?"

"Kate Mackenzie," said Kyle. "He's in good form. He'll be cooperating from now on."

MacDuff looked at Kyle. He looked at Sylvanus. He looked at the dog, sitting by the door as though guarding it. "Nice work," he said, looking back at father and son again. "How long have they been gone?"

Sylvanus looked up at the stars. Kyle shook his head.

"Hard to say," said Sylvanus. "They'll phone you from the hospital. Sure thing."

MacDuff returned to the car, leaning in through the window and saying something to Canning, who immediately started talking into his radio phone.

"Found you some dried squid," said Kyle as MacDuff made his way back. "When things clear up, me and Verny will drop them off."

"Verny?"

"Alias Vernon Trapp."

"He's going to get off, right?" asked Sylvanus. "It was self-defence, that's pretty clear."

"I can't answer that, sir. I just sent a car to the hospital. There'll be an assessment by his doctors. See whether he can stand trial." MacDuff turned to Kyle. "Where did you find the knife?"

"Verny left it where he knew I'd find it."

"Why did you cement it in?"

Kyle looked at his father, shrugged. "Never know the mind of a squid."

"Hey?"

Sylvanus blew out a weighty breath. "Get to bed," he snarked at Kyle. "Else you'll be squirting like one. Will he need a lawyer?" he asked MacDuff.

"He killed a man, he'll need a lawyer. We'll let the courts decide if it was self-defence. We'll be going now." He turned back to his car, then paused. "How's Mrs. Now?"

"She'd be offering you tea if she knew you were here."

"Well, we won't put her through that. Some other time, per-haps, sir."

"Some other time, sir."

MacDuff tipped his hat again.

"A second," said Kyle. "The glove thing. Why were you wanting to know if we wore mitts that night? What the fuck was that all about?"

"Ah." MacDuff went over to the front of the house and bent, peering closely at the clapboard. Then he moved to the door. "It's gone now," he said. "The rain took it. But there were blots of blood on the clapboard, and then on the framing, here by the doorknob. No prints. Like someone had fallen, caught themselves with a mitted or gloved hand. I figured it out eventually." He looked at the dog, flopped down on all fours by the gump. "He must have had Mr. Gillard's blood on his paws. He must have leaped at the house at some point during that night, got some blood on it. Only thing I can figure."

Kyle looked at his hands, remembered the dream he'd had that night of the killing. About a dolphin and a dog barking, its nails scampering over his hand. Clar's blood. He hadn't drooled on his hand, it was Clar's blood.

"Did you know who done it?" he asked MacDuff.

"I knew it was squirrelled somewhere amongst you. Truth always comes out—just got to probe a bit, be a little patient. Good evening, then." He lowered himself slowly into his car, then looked up at Sylvanus. "I'm thinking of buying a cabin in on Faulkner's Flat, not far from Rushy Pond. What's the fish-ing like?"

"I knows a few spots."

"Roger that." MacDuff drew his legs in and hauled the door shut. Canning pulled the car around and Kyle stood there with his father, watching the cruiser drive off. Sylvie swung open the door.

"Somebody just called for you, Ky." She peered after the police car. "Is everything fixed up?"

"Yeah, it's fine. Who called?"

"A girl. Jewels? Whoa." Kyle was brushing past her. "She's not there now, I told her to call back."

"What the hell you tell her that for?"

"I could've said nothing, I suppose. Hung up on her."

"When did she call?"

"About ten minutes ago. She's at the bar."

The bar. He was inside the house now, looking at the clock. Ten past eight. He went into the washroom and skimmed off his wet clothes and scalded himself beneath the shower. He wrapped a towel around himself and went to his room, water streaming down his face from his soggy head. Bonnie was in there, hauling the blankets off his bed.

"What the fuck?"

"You're on the couch tonight," she said, stripping off his sheets. "And the rest of the week, most likely."

Jaysus. "Mind if I get some clothes?"

"As long as you changes in the washroom."

Jaysus. He bent, fumbling through his bottom drawer.

"Hey," she said.

"Hay's for horses." He stopped fumbling and looked at her. "Sorry."

She nodded, studied the sheets in her hands. "Something I want to say. If you don't mind."

"Sure."

"Why I kept going back. I know you wants to know that."

"No. Hey, that's fine."

"I thought if I loved him enough, it might catch hold of him. That he'd grow a heart. That's what I always thought."

"Right. Fine, then."

"Like the Tin Man. Remember him?" she said to his blank look. "From Oz."

"Right. You still thinking that?"

She shrugged. "Don't matter. Just thought I'd tell you."

"Hey, why not? Lion Man here, he's trying to grow himself some courage."

She smiled, small even teeth, first time he'd seen them. Nice smile, softened her face. He stood there, looking at her smile. She took it as though he were waiting for more from her. "I got tired, always giving," she said with a shrug. "Started giving to myself. That's why he tried to kill me, your mother says. Aside from his dog, I was the only thing loyal to him. Guess even he needed somebody." A shadow flickered across her face, the ghost of Clar Gillard. She chased it away with another smile that brightened her eyes and he saw her triumph. Whatever battles she'd fought with Clar Gillard, she'd defeated him before the knife found its mark.

He started feeling awkward standing there, his clothes bundled before him, and backed out the door. "Question," he said, pausing. "Why're you so taken with my mother?"

She was billowing a clean sheet over the mattress. "She don't see me as Jack Verge's daughter. Grab that end, will you?"

He stepped back to the bed, pulled the corner end of the sheet over the mattress, and backed out of the room for the second time. "Stay to the inside," he said, pointing to the bed. "Killer spring on the outside, here."

He went back to the washroom, dressed, and hurried down the hallway. Sylvie was talking with their mother in her room. He snuck past the door, not wanting any more delays, and booted it outside. Eight-thirty, eight-thirty, it was still early, she'd still be at the bar. He rounded the corner, wondering where his father was, and near tripped over him. Hove off by the side of the house, feet propped up on the gump, ruffling the ears of the dog splayed out beside him. His father was smiling. He was gazing up and smiling at the cloudy night. He looked like an old sailor who'd weathered a great storm and was now safely anchored to a pier of his own making.

"Turn on the light or something, old man. Near bloody tripped over you."

"Think now, I'm scared of the dark like you?"

"I could've been a bear for all you know."

"That's just it now, you're supposed to smell the bear before he smells you."

"That's just it now, and suppose your nose is plugged. You have a cheery evening now."

"Where you going?"

"Fishing."

He started up through the shortcut, pushing aside limbs and branches. Trail needed trimming. He took up whistling as he passed the old sawmill. It was quiet. The wind showered through the trees and something creaked from behind him. Jaysus. A shiver rode down his spine. He flailed the rest of his way up the path and out onto Bottom Hill. Widen that fucking path, tomorrow. The wind had picked up, clearing a star-pricked sky. Hampden windows lit yellow through the dark. The moon's broadening smile rose above the hills and glimmered amongst stars that were mostly dead and yet whose lights still shone through the eternal sky. He showed his fist to the proud evening star. "I'm taking her fishing," he yelled. "Screw you, buddy, barring me in the haunted house!" And then he near tripped, face aghast—it winked at him. Swear to Jesus, the star winked at him . . .